### The American and her secret:

It had been an accident, but in the end, that oily-faced man had died. Her heart hammered as his image flashed before her mind. Once again she'd had to run....

### The Brazilian cop and his secret:

He slogged through the teeming masses of feverish partiers, who spritzed the air with clouds of ether, bopping each other on the head with their plastic mallets filled with the intoxicating liquid. Ducking, he pressed on. Searching...always searching...

His son would have turned five this month.

**While the *macumbero* lures women...**

Also by Sue Star and Bill Beatty:

*Dancing for the General*

Also by Sue Star:

*Murder by Moose*
*Murder for a Cash Crop*
*Murder with Altitude*
*Murder in the Dojo*
*Trouble in a Politically Correct Town*
*Organized Death*

Also by Bill Beatty:

*Hell Down Under*
*Making Their Own Law*

# Burning Candles

# Sue Star and Bill Beatty

D. M. Kreg Publishing

DMKregPublishing.com

*For Al*

## Acknowledgments

Thanks to the many fine writers who helped with the various stages of this project: the Oregon Writers Network and the Inklings. Thanks to our tireless readers, who rearranged their schedules to accommodate ours. Special thanks go to the family, who is always there for us.

# Burning Candles

## Sue Star and Bill Beatty

# Chapter One

December 31, 1958

**She hadn't meant** to kill the man.

Standing now at the dark and open window of her bedroom in the Copacabana Palace, Linda Rose Armbrust stared into the night. There'd been a lot she hadn't meant to do.

In the distance beyond the hotel steps, the neon frenzy of this foreign city rushed along the avenue, a barrier of pavement beside the beach, curving away with the bay in the shape of a crescent moon. Directly beneath her window lay the calm darkness of sand. Moving shapes of midnight visitors spread across its shadows, carrying little dots of flickering lights— burning candles. Even from her window on the second floor, she could smell the sweet fragrance of flowers scattered about. Their dropped petals glittered, and tufts of sand glowed in the sparkles of candlelight. A tingling warmth stirred deep within her as she watched.

Free now.

But for how long?

It had been an accident, but in the end, that oily-faced man had died. Her heart hammered as his image flashed before her mind. Once again she'd had to run...

The memories were still too fresh. She pushed them away, gulping in the sweetly salty air. Pain knifed her bruised rib. She wasn't in the States anymore. This scene outside her window proved that. She focused on the pinpricks of light out there on the beach. Her pulse settled and a sense of calm washed over the swollen tenderness of her aches and bruises. Voices softly chanted, as if they were performing some sort of ritual ceremony, like a marriage to the sea. The hiss of lapping waves sounded like a chorus. Soothing, rhythmic murmurs vibrated the air and tugged at her as if a humming chord connected her to them. Somehow, she felt a part of them.

*Her* wedding hadn't been anything like this one.

She whirled around, swishing the silk of her brand-new negligee. A stranger lay naked and asleep atop the sheets of her bed. His face, soft. His olive-toned body, perfect. Their recent passion, delicious. Heat flared within her. Two fans droned on, but they only moved the hot, heavy air from one side of the bridal suite to the other.

There'd been no flowers, no candles, no guests at her wedding. All she'd wanted were the hastily signed documents. The passport with her new name. *Rosalinda da Costa.*

Because she would never be a victim again. Never.

Soft moans drifted chant-like from the beach, turning her attention back to the open window. Now some of the people out there were walking *into* the sea. Not swimming. They kept walking until the sea swallowed them. Moonlight sparkled on the froth of waves breaking gently over them. This wasn't a wedding after all. It looked as if those people meant to drown themselves.

Alarm shot through her, clenching her muscles into familiar knots of panic. It was impossible for her to rescue anyone because she couldn't reach them in time. It was already too late. Those who lingered on the beach would have to help, and now they started following the others into the sea, perhaps to do just that. Everything was okay, she told herself, until finally she believed it.

She was supposed to have drowned. That was the story he'd come up with.

And actually, in a way, it was true. Coming here, she felt as if she were drowning in the deceit of her new role. Everything had happened so fast. She'd thrown away all that had ever mattered, although without her little sister anymore, there wasn't much left to lose. What other choice had she had but to come here to this foreign place with Gilberto? She knew his name, but not much else. He was a Brazilian cop she'd only met a couple weeks ago, and now he was her husband. He had seemed a better alternative than a U.S. prison. Was it even real, this new life that she thought she was living?

Dazed, her jaw and face still throbbing, she leaned against the windowsill, half expecting to see the snowy mountain backdrop of Denver resolve through the blur of her mind. But it did not. The postcard image of sexy Rio de Janeiro, the famous beach and pillar mountains to either side, displayed as silhouettes against the glow of the city.

The view through the open window pulled at her like the tide. The damp, salt air caressed her flesh; the sweet smell of flowers intoxicated her lungs. There was magic in the air, and it was seducing her.

She turned away from the window and rummaged on the floor for the boxes of new clothes Gilberto had bought for her. With each crinkling, bumping sound, she turned back to look at him, sleeping like the dead. Amidst the cottons and silks, her fingers touched the strings of her new bikini. She carried it to the bathroom, where she slid out of the negligee, stepped into the strings, and wrapped a towel over her bruised body. Then softly, ever so softly, she padded across to the suite's door and slipped out into the hall. She ran all the way through the grand, pink, palatial hotel until her toes finally sank into sand, still warm from the day's heat.

Whatever magic had pulled at her through the window was tugging even harder now, out here on the beach. She kept running, past the lit candles, over flower petals and strewn seashells. She'd always been running, but she didn't have to anymore. That's what Gilberto had said. It was finished. Her past could never catch up to her here.

Her breath caught in shallow pants, and she winced from the sharp stabs to her rib. Lurching around women—where were the men?—she tried not to spray them with her kicked-up sand. They bowed and murmured prayers over their candles. She ran on to the water's edge and the tide sucking at her toes. More women lined the shore and threw flowers into the waves.

She had no flowers to offer to the sea. No candles, no seashells. All she had to offer was herself. And her own prayers. She was here, and here in Brazil was where she hoped to God she could finally stop running.

# Chapter Two

January 3, 1959

**Her flesh, bare above** the sundress, stuck to the vinyl chair where she sat, waiting, several mornings later, after her midnight swim. A breeze tunneled through this salon of the Copacabana Palace, sweeping over her and cooling the seaside air to a tolerable level. Linda had never felt so wilting hot in her life before, not even in Ohio in August, as she felt here in this place.

*Rosalinda*, that is.

Gilberto had left her here to wait for him while he dealt with the luggage, checking out, summoning a taxi. She watched him glide across the stone floor of the hotel's lobby with the sensuous grace of a cat, waving and chatting and smiling at everyone he passed. He must know half of the people here. Or maybe he just acted as if he did. She wouldn't know. She scarcely knew him. He was a friendly, forthright guy, cuddly and warm, with an infectious smile, something like a teddy bear's.

Not what she'd expected for a cop. At least, not in her experience. He was a Brazilian cop. Did that make a difference? She hoped so.

She'd met him in a pawnshop in Denver, where her money

15

ran out and her dreams of Hollywood had crashed. He'd called it fate—their instant attraction—and she'd called it chemistry, as in a drug. Whatever it was, it had made her a little nervous at first that he was a cop. But then, who else could she turn to after that oily-faced man forced his way into her apartment? She'd sure as hell needed someone's help. Gilberto was well out of his jurisdiction, and he seemed as interested in avoiding the local cops as she was.

His bedroom eyes suggested what he'd wanted in exchange for helping her. No surprise. It wasn't the first time. And later, when she'd asked what had happened to the body, he'd hushed her with kisses.

*Shhhh. It is done. We will never speak of it again.*

His plan included marriage, and that *did* surprise her. The wreckage of her broken dreams hadn't been her fault, so she'd snatched at the deal. It was the first time any of her men had ever suggested such a thing. She couldn't help feeling flattered. Besides, he had plenty of money, and she'd had plenty of nothing. Theirs was an arrangement—not love, for heaven's sake. Love was only something you found in the movies.

She felt now as if this world of crystal and gold, spinning around her, could not possibly be real. Maybe she was living a movie life, after all. That's what she'd wanted.

She could never make it to Hollywood now, not after running this far. So what? She didn't need those dreams anymore, now that she had Gilberto.

Her gaze, drawn to him like a magnet, followed his silky movements. She had to admit, he looked quite suave in his white linen suit and straw Panama hat. Each time he slid crisp bills to one of his attendants, a gemstone the size of a quail's egg sparkled from his ring finger. It made her remember that other ring, the one she'd been trying to pawn when she'd met him.

She caught her breath, and her sore rib pinched her. She would never have to worry about money again. What a dream! Could that possibly be real? She would have to make sure this arrangement worked. Let him think he was protecting her. He didn't have to know the full truth about her. Knowing all the sordid details wasn't part of their arrangement.

Her secrets were all she had left of herself. That's why her midnight swim with masses of women on New Year's Eve had felt so...exhilarating. She'd felt alive, then, as never before. Alive with a sense of sisterhood. It was a piece of herself that was all hers. When she'd slipped back into bed some time later, he'd still been asleep.

That she'd gone out and come back, all the while that he slept, never knowing, sent ripples of thrills through her. It gave her a sense of liberty that she'd never experienced before, had never known could exist. In an odd way, getting away with that which was forbidden filled an empty hole inside her. She didn't know what it all meant. Just that he didn't need to know.

"Are you rhhhready, my love?" Gilberto said, startling her. She hadn't seen him slip up to her side.

Nodding, she gathered up her shiny purse and spotless gloves and rose unsteadily onto her high heels. The accessories were all part of the costume she would need as Mrs. da Costa. She arranged her face into what she expected would look like a newlywed's adoring smile as he offered her a steady arm. She clung to his arm while she adjusted her gait, swinging her hips.

"We have a long drive today," he said, "to our new home." His voice was both a whisper and a purr, the way he spoke

English in his thick, Portuguese accent.

"We're driving? But..." She hadn't really thought about it. She knew he didn't live in Rio. He lived somewhere in the interior, somewhere she'd never heard of. It probably didn't even have an airport. Such a place was an ideal set-up for someone on the run.

He led her through the breezeway, their footsteps clicking, and hers wobbling just a little. Outside, the muggy air made her laboring rib feel as if she inhaled water.

"What do you think?" he said, beaming at a car.

It was just a car, lime green, with whitewall tires and fishtail fins. A bellboy held the passenger door open for her.

"It doesn't look like a taxi," she said, stuck in place. The two-inch spike of her right heel had sunk into the heat-softened goo between paving stones.

"It's not." A furrow wrinkled his brow where a curl of sandy brown hair slipped out from beneath his hat. "Is mine. A Ford Fairlane. I buy from a friend of my mother. American diplomat going home. A good deal for us, no?"

She couldn't help but smile at his enthusiasm. All for a silly car. Although, she wondered about the diplomat. What would it mean for her that her new husband had such friends?

She leaned on him to extricate her shoe while the bellboy pretended not to notice. The kid wasn't the only one watching her. They all were. Everyone that Gilberto had spoken to, and maybe more. She felt their eyes on her, and her skin prickled. Impatient, she kicked off both shoes, letting Gilberto help her once again. She darted barefoot the rest of the way to the car, while he followed, carrying her shoes. Her new luggage filled the trunk, and boxes of other purchases jammed together in the backseat. Dishes, and linens, and she didn't know what all. More would be shipped later.

Good God, how much more did a person need? Up until now, all that she'd ever owned had fit into half of a battered suitcase. And now, all this. With more to come. It must be true, that sensation she'd felt, swimming at midnight. She really *did* feel as if she were drowning.

She could get used to it, though.

Inside the treasured car, she settled comfortably against the bench seat while Gilberto climbed behind the wheel and pealed out of the hotel's driveway. With the car windows rolled down to catch the breeze, they raced through the blistering city, laid out in narrow strips between the sea and mountains. They crossed from one strip to the next, each one separated by sheer, mountainous rocks, dotted with shacks that looked like spitballs stuck to a wall. Finally, they came to the far edge of the city. The road turned inland, and they zigzagged up the sides of lush mountains, empty of any human life that she could see. When they reached the clouds, Gilberto stopped the car to let it cool down and to fill the radiator with water.

As the grayish white tufts of clouds misted and swirled around them, he told her about his family. His grandfathers had headed inland with the gold rush, eventually establishing gemstone mines that had stayed in the family for several generations. When his father died in the war only fifteen years ago, his mother kept things going, not only for the family but also for the mines. Very un-Brazilian-like, for a family not to be led by a man. But his mother had had no other choice. Linda could relate to that.

Damn, she was going to have to get used to her new name.

Rosalinda. It sounded so stuffy, and stuffiness didn't suit her.

There were seven da Costa siblings in all. The eighth one had died. Plus, there was a brother-in-law and four nieces and nephews. Not to mention all the aunts, the uncles, and the cousins. Gilberto hadn't told the family yet about their hasty marriage, but once he announced it, each and every one of them would be eager to meet her. She cringed at the thought. Couldn't it wait? She wasn't ready yet, to be the center of such attention. Especially while her bruises were still visible. The black eye was the worst, and she didn't want to have to explain it. Anyway, how would she ever keep all of his family straight? Her family had only consisted of one little sister, back in Ohio, and now Janie was gone. Linda didn't count their mother who'd ignored them and the stepfather who hadn't.

When the car cooled down, they drove on, leaving the clouds behind. The road rolled through gentle hills and a few dusty towns, where they stopped for gas. After that, it was all empty land. They drove for what seemed like hours and passed no one, all the while that he chattered on. She wasn't listening. Instead, she wondered if there was anything out here besides herds of scrawny cows with strange humps on the back of their necks. There were no fenced-off pastures to contain them, no farms with fields and farmhouses and barns where the cows had come from, not like what she knew in the States. This was wild land, with untamed thickets. It wasn't jungle, but rather a mess of creeping, green stuff. She wondered if there were people hiding somewhere in those pockets of greenery. Well, she'd wanted to be isolated, hadn't she? Now she wasn't so sure. Just where on earth was Gilberto taking her? To the end of the earth, it looked like.

"So, where's this city of yours," she asked, "where you said you're from?"

He laughed. "Is still many hours ahead on the highway."

"I have news for you, Gilberto, this is no highway."

"Of course it is. The BR-3. And it is paved, no? We stop soon for lunch. I know a place. You will see."

What she saw was that they'd forgotten to pack a lunch. The backseat was filled with boxes of necessities for their apartment—if, in fact, such a place did exist—but no food. She was accustomed to going without food, sometimes for days, but she wasn't sure Gilberto could make it.

And then a few buildings appeared next to the country road he considered a "highway." The assortment didn't look large enough to be a town, and it certainly didn't look like a restaurant. Here, they would have a *churrascaría*, Gilberto said.

It was a covered pavilion in the middle of nowhere, with a few surrounding shacks. But it was nice to stop and stretch her legs, even if she did have to put the heels back on. Delicious smells of grilling meat made her stomach rumble. A concrete pad held picnic tables overlooking a peaceful lake. She gazed at the water, remembering the silky feel of waves rippling over her body during her midnight swim at Copacabana.

"Do we have time to go for a swim?" she said, pointing at the lake.

The lively, coppery color of his face drained into mottled patches of pasty chalk. "You mus' never touch the water here."

She tipped her head sideways. No one ever told her that word: *never*. "Why on earth not? Come on, let's have some fun."

He shook his head and clamped his fingers around her arm.

21

"Because here there is schistosomiasis."

"Schisto...what? I've never heard of that." She twisted free of his grip and marched to the edge of the pavilion, gazing at the lake.

He must've thought she'd actually plunge down the hill, considering how fast he caught up to her, encircling her waist with his arms. She wasn't stupid, but she let him think he'd stopped her.

"I mean it," he said, and from the tightness of his arms, she thought he really did. "You don't understand about it."

He was right about that. She relaxed against his hard muscles, allowing the fire to rise within, sweeping through her as he kissed her neck and murmured in her ear.

Then he nudged her with a gentle shake, loosening his grip, and he steered her back to one of the tables. Her pulse still fluttering, she sat down where their places were set, and reached for a bottle.

"What's this?" she said, lifting it up. It looked like dark beer.

"Is *guaraná*," he said, sitting close beside her.

"Meaning what?" She took a cautious sip. It was soda, but it tasted like nothing she'd ever tasted before, pleasantly sweet, like drinking liquid candy. The heat of their briefly shared moment added an extra spice to the flavor.

His eyelashes curled and fluttered as he watched her. "It comes from a plant from the Amazon."

That made her stop and think and study the caramel brown of the bubbly drink. "No kidding?" There were so many unknowns here. "I hope there's nothing funny in it like that schisto-something stuff you mentioned about the water."

"No, no. In the lakes here, there is a..." He twirled his

fingers and squinted, as if searching his memory for the words. "A snail, that's how you say it. Snails live in the water here in my state of Minas Gerais. If you go into the water here, little..." He frowned again. "Little things from the snails get into your blood."

"Parasites?"

"Yes, that's it. Parasites. They make you very sick with schistosomiasis. Sometimes you don' know for many years you have the disease. We have no cure. They can kill you, many years later, those snails."

She shuddered and shrank away from him. What was she getting herself in for, coming here? And this was for forever.

"I don' mean to frighten you, but you must know. And you must never go near water."

That finished off any lingering heat she'd felt from his nearness only moments ago. She sat there watching the midday sun sparkle across the little lake. She imagined feeling the parasites squiggle through her bloodstream. She felt dizzy. Her vision blurred.

Had her midnight swim in the ocean done that, jumbling her thoughts and making her head spin? "What about the ocean? What unknown, frightening things are in that?"

"No wohrries, my love. The ocean is like a big bath. She cleans us every New Year's Eve at midnight on Copacabana. Is the festival to Iemanjá. Remember?"

"Iemanjá?"

"The *orixá* goddess of the sea."

"What are you talking about?"

"You were there."

"You were asleep." *How did he know?*

He winked at her, and then the waiter arrived with a skewer of grilled meat. As they dug into their food, she realized he must've followed her that night. The click of the door shutting had probably awakened him, and so he'd followed. Well, why not? He'd taken on the job of protecting her. She couldn't help it if she was curious about this new and foreign place. It was her new home.

"But why didn't you say anything?" she asked, and he grinned, and the waiter arrived with a second skewer of a different type of grilled meat.

His grin reminded her of what he'd said before. *It is done. We will not speak of it again.*

The midnight women she'd seen on the beach had skirted on the edge of danger, or so she'd thought. Perhaps that danger was what had drawn her to them. But now the entire episode felt less thrilling, knowing he'd been there, too, watching over her. He hadn't actually admitted it, but she could figure it out. Had he intentionally revealed this just now? She wondered why he hadn't simply approached her that night on the beach, instead of darting back to their room ahead of her and pretending to be asleep when she returned. But before she could ask, the waiter arrived with a third skewer of meat.

They finished their meal and headed back to the road again. Gilberto kept up his stream of talk, as if he just wanted to practice his English, but she cut him off, complaining of a building headache. She leaned her head against the vinyl interior of the car and vaguely watched the browning of the passing scenery of rolling, increasingly barren hills.

Did it matter that he'd followed her, like her private bodyguard? Not really. Not as long as she retained the freedom to come and go as she pleased.

She wouldn't have had such freedom, had she stayed in Denver. She probably would've ended up in jail, assuming she would've lived long enough to get there. Sure, it had been self-defense, but there was always the possibility a judge and jury wouldn't have seen it that way. Anyway, how long would an acquittal have taken? And which one of the dead man's pals would've awaited her once she'd gotten out?

The way she saw it, she didn't have any other choice but to come here. No one would find her here. Hell, she couldn't even find herself.

By sunset, with her head throbbing, he stopped the car on top of one of the hills they'd crested. A broad valley spread before them, cluttered with the rooflines of the city. In the distance, a few lights twinkled, and spears of skyscrapers rose from the haze. Belo Horizonte. Beautiful Horizon, it meant, on account of the surrounding mountains—hills, really. It was *his* city, Gilberto told her, Brazil's third largest. Almost a million, and no one had ever heard of it. Yes, there was an airport, but now they didn't need it because he had his own car.

They drove through the outskirts of the city to Barroca, one of Belo's up and coming neighborhoods, more down than up. Breezy, colorful houses encroached into wild patches of vacant land. Alongside one dirt road cut into a hillside, a blocky building sprawled. It was an ugly, rectangular block of chipped cement and faded orange paint.

Gilberto steered the fishtail fin car towards that building and into its underground parking garage, open at the bottom of the hill and secured with bars. He turned off the engine and grinned. "Here we are."

She blinked at the murky shadows in the far corner, where the garage dug into the side of the hill. Only a couple other cars parked here, along with a cart that held some rusty tools. This was it? She felt plastered to her seat. Finally, he came around to her side and helped her out of the car, pulling her by the hand toward a dim light in a stairwell. At the hillside street level, a central hall pierced the center of the apartment building. They climbed up to the next level, where he paused before one of the doors. He pulled a key ring from his pocket, rattled a key into the lock, and kicked the door open.

"Home," he said, sweeping her into his arms and lifting her off her feet. As he carried her over the threshold of the little apartment, she heard the creak of another door opening. Someone was watching. Someone knew she was here.

# Chapter Three

February 7, 1959

**It was hard to hide** with the neighbor spying on her, each time she came and went from the apartment. These last few weeks since leaving Rio, Linda had spent her time lying low.

Rosalinda, that is. Roz, for short, she'd decided. She'd been practicing her new name while her black eye faded and her bruised bones healed.

She hadn't wanted to meet his family yet, but he kept insisting. How much longer could she go on hiding, he'd argued? Besides, his mother already suspected something. He'd done his best to avoid his mother's questions, but he couldn't put her off anymore. Before Roz knew it, the summons arrived in a sealed envelope via the da Costa family chauffeur.

That should've given her a clue, but nothing could've prepared her for the marble pillars and gold leaf trim and gemstone studded floor of the palatial mansion where she sat now in the family dining room. It felt like a mausoleum. Or maybe a movie set, pretending to be a family home. His mother had thrown together this private, "little" dinner party at her estate so that the immediate members of the family could meet Roz.

God, it was hard to breathe. The thick and heavy air pulsed

with samba as a dozen overly curious da Costa faces, enough to be a seated jury, surrounded her around the dining table. They stared at her with a hang-jaw reflection of distressed fascination. Who was this American minx who'd stolen the attentions of their second eldest brother while he'd been away in the United States for just a few weeks? She couldn't tell them. Would do everything in her power to keep them from finding out. But then, she couldn't really blame them for their curiosity, now that the initial shock of Gilberto's news had settled over them.

As they inspected her, Roz felt mesmerized by the drumbeats of Carnival. Its bubbling and throbbing sounds carried ten miles out here from downtown and hammered at her as clearly as if the music were playing from the hifi set in the next room. She couldn't get it out of her head. The very air vibrated, echoing her racing heart, making her feel out of place. Everything was foreign to her. First, there'd been those midnight offerings to Iemanjá on Copacabana Beach, and now there was Carnival.

Gilberto was her only anchor in this strange, new place, and she scarcely knew him.

No, it was *she* who was the foreigner. And this was her new home. *Get used to it.*

She could expect regular gatherings of the family, Gilberto had told her. Tonight was special, a celebration to officially meet her new husband's entire family. In truth, she suspected, they wanted to inspect her. She felt like a specimen under a microscope.

The faces of his family peered at her over the length of the china-and-crystal cluttered dinner table. Pinned to the velvet cushion of her chair, she didn't know how to respond, or even how to act. She'd never been around so much wealth before.

Gilberto had tried his best to set her mind at ease in the car on the way out here, preparing her. It hadn't worked. When they'd arrived at the gates to the family estate, a moment of unbidden terror seized her. It was the sheer size of the place, and especially, the guards with rifles. Guards only reminded her of her desperate need to escape.

She'd suppressed that initial terror, having had plenty of practice with suppression, but then had to face the family, a brand-new experience. Throughout their inspection of her (she'd failed, what else?) the hum of music electrified the air and pulled at her. That wasn't all that tugged at her. Under the table, she felt the familiar brush of his fingers against her thigh.

She leaned into him, thankfully seated beside her, and felt the heat rise. "Later," she whispered into his ear.

The plain and simple truth was that they were in lust. There was no storybook romance for them. Maybe their passion was enough for now. Roz didn't know.

Gilberto's fingers inched across her primly pleated skirt and circled the outline of her garter belt's snap. "Prhomise?"

Smiling, she straightened up over her gold-rimmed place setting and caught his mother's gaze locked onto her. Daggers. The rising fire instantly chilled.

Anabela da Costa, the matriarch of the family, had a face shaped like a hawk's. Below the beak of her nose, there wasn't much—a small, tight line of crimson lipstick and the narrow point of a receding chin. But her eyes...they were everything. Her eyes were two nuggets that narrowed into simmering coals, missing nothing that moved in the room. Her eyes flared within the hard, angular lines of her stone-cold face.

One would've thought that Anabela would be happy that

Roz was making her son happy. He'd been alone too long.

But no.

Anabela spoke from her throne at the head of the table and all the while glowered at Roz. She knew that her mother-in-law wasn't talking *to* her because Anabela only spoke Portuguese, and Roz only spoke English. She'd learned a handful of Portuguese words by now, but not enough to count.

Words tumbled from Anabela's thin lips, and the red line of lipstick hardly moved at all. Crease lines crinkled the corners, tucks her plastic surgeon had missed. Being the head of the da Costa clan, as well as the family gemstone mine, Anabela hadn't aged well, despite all her props. The gemstones that she pinned into her artificially black hair and strung around her chin-lifted throat failed to give her any added sparkle.

While Anabela spoke, the rest of the family (already Roz had forgotten their names, just as she kept forgetting her own) sent surreptitious glances around the table. Their opinions registered clearly on their perplexed faces: why didn't the foreigner go back to where she belonged? Well, this wasn't the first time she hadn't felt accepted. The old Linda had had to grow a thick skin, not to let control queens like Anabela ever get to her. It had better be thick enough for the new Roz.

She wondered what Anabela was saying. It must be about her. What else? Gilberto's hand slipped off her thigh, reached up to his steak knife and carved his slab of beef. The blade glinted under candlelight as it slashed with meticulous intensity, reflecting his fury. She leaned away from him, but her gaze fixed on the knife. Whatever Anabela was saying was ticking him off.

Strange, how Portuguese could sound like distant waves

rolling around, echoing in a hidden cavern, when Gilberto spoke to her from the damp darkness of their bedroom. But when his mother spoke, the same language sounded like pigs fighting over the last cob of corn.

One of the sisters snickered. It was one of the twins, but she had no idea which one. They had a sassy air about them, and Roz thought she could've become friends with them in other circumstances. She'd never had a real friend before, aside from her little sister, and anyway, she couldn't even talk to the twins. One sister's cheeks flushed. Just what on earth was Anabela saying?

Roz might not know the words, but she could read body language, and she could tell that Anabela's words about her weren't kind.

Then she caught what sounded like "*Rio*" in the stream. Anabela was apparently quizzing Gilberto about their brief honeymoon.

No one else tried to speak while Anabela spoke.

She went on in her monotone, and finally Gilberto snapped back something that sounded like "*cayó*."

The twins giggled. The other sisters studied their dinner plates intently. The brother and the brother-in-law flushed. The children fidgeted.

Roz couldn't take it anymore. Five weeks of apprehension had simmered, boiling finally into these moments of panic, pressing against the back of her mind.

Her fork clattered to her plate. More faces stole glances at her. She wasn't accustomed to wasting good food, but she had to get out of here. Now. She scraped her chair backwards across the marble floor, sprang to her feet, and murmured to

Gilberto, "I can't do this."

The family gaped at her with astonished looks. Even Anabela lapsed into silence, apparently unaccustomed to any display that interrupted her.

Roz rushed out of the marble room, clicking across its stone floor in her new, Italian high heels, wobbling only a little. She fled under the crystal chandelier of the foyer to the front door, pulled open its heavy wood and let it fall with a thud, closed behind her. Outside, she gulped in the night air. Now what? She hadn't thought this through. She didn't even have her purse.

Pulling off the damned shoes, she flounced down the stone steps. She wasn't sure she liked her new image, with the fancy wardrobe, the heavy makeup to cover where the bruises had been, the bobbed haircut, and the bottle of ash blonde hair dye.

Where the steps emptied out onto a cobbled driveway, she paused to consider her options, breathing in the flower-scented air of the hillside garden. Nothing like those sweetly intoxicating smells to help calm her. Already her nerves had settled.

Dangling the shoes from her fingertips, she sat down on the bottom step. The cement edge of the step caught her silk nylons, sending runs tickling up her legs. A waste of good stockings, but Gilberto would buy her another pair. She waited for him to catch up to her, as she knew he would. He'd make up some excuse to the family, and eventually he'd escape his mother.

While she waited, the monotonous beat of Carnival music filled the air, never letting up. It surprised her the way it drifted out here, just beyond the edge of the city. The sound had traveled far, and yet sounded so near. Maybe there was a party going on nearby. Certainly not at Anabela's house.

Gilberto had told her about the family mansion, only that afternoon in the car on their way out here. It had been built almost forty years ago under the direction of his deceased father, Francisco the First. Back then, this had all been countryside, but now the growth of the city had almost caught up to the perimeter of the da Costa acreage. They'd had to erect walls surrounding the property. It was a half-mile or so to the gates from the house, which Anabela had ruled ever since Francisco's death in the war.

She wondered what Anabela had said about her back there at the dinner table. Not that it really mattered. What bothered her most of all was that she'd felt helpless because she hadn't understood.

She would never be helpless again, she'd sworn.

And then there was that spectacle she'd made of herself. Now she felt embarrassed about her sudden exit. Running like that didn't bode well for her new life here. She'd thought she was done with running.

How was she ever going to fit into a place like this, where they threw flowers into the sea for some goddess she'd never heard of, and they danced half-naked in the streets round the clock?

Not soon enough, the earth vibrated with the thud of his steps behind her. He sank down beside her on the step and grasped her arm, gently caressing her bare flesh. Each time he touched her, sparks of fire tingled through her, but now she shivered from the cool, damp cloth of the night air. It must be the altitude here in Belo, although it was only about half as high as mile-high Denver.

"You feel okay?" he said, stroking her arm.

She shook her head. "No. I just couldn't take it anymore. Maybe this whole plan of ours was a mistake."

"Is no mistake."

"They'll never buy it."

"Buy?" He wrinkled his brow.

"Why should they accept me, anyway?"

"They will, once they know you."

"I can't let them. If they knew me, they'd make me go back." And she couldn't go back. The reception committee at any U.S. airport would send her to jail first and ask questions later.

"I won' let you go." He hugged her tight and whisper-purred as if still groping her, the way he had back there, under the table.

"Is your mother always like that?"

"She only tries to help."

"Really?" That didn't sound like "help." Roz pulled away from him.

"She's an important woman, very efficient."

"You're defending her, but you didn't defend me back there. What was she saying about me, anyway?" Roz tried to convince herself that it didn't really matter. She was just curious.

He waved his wrist in the air, as if searching for the right words. "We must help you, now that you are part of the family."

*What a lie.* "Help me how? You can tell me the truth. What does she suspect? She said something about Rio, didn't she?"

"She has friends at the hotel."

"You said something back to her. What did you say?"

He paused, looking up to the starry sky. "Nothing."

"It wasn't nothing. It sounded like *cayó*."

He turned to her, and his shaggy eyebrows lifted. "You

heard that?"

"Yeah. What's it mean?"

"Fell. I told her you fell."

She stiffened, studying him in the dark while the steady thrum of samba washed over them. Her bruises had faded by now. There should've been no reason for any explanation. "But why did you tell her that?"

"She asked." He reached for her, drawing her close. His fingertips circled down her arm and started to work on her hand.

Anabela's friends at the hotel, Roz realized, must've reported about her bruises. Had they called her a bride or just the killer tramp that she really was, the woman sharing her son's bedroom? "What else does she know? Does she know why?"

"She knows nothing."

"Don't lie to me. She suspects something, I can tell. Look, all I want is to understand."

"What you want, Leen—"

"Don't call me that." Linda. He'd been about to call her *Linda*. She shook him off and lurched to her feet, wheeling around to face him. "We agreed."

"Sorhry." He rose, too, and dug his fists into the pockets of his white linen trousers. He glanced one way and then the other, into the darkness. No one else was here with them, or at least no one was visible. Armed guards patrolled the grounds. If one of them was near enough to hear anything, he wouldn't understand English. Would he know not to shoot? She hadn't thought of that, either, and another shiver coursed down her spine.

"What I want," she said, "is for everyone to know me as Rosalinda da Costa. *Senhora*. That's how it has to be if I'm going to stay here."

"Stay, *meu amor*."

It would be her choice, and no one else's, if she decided to stay. The way she saw it, she had no other choice. He didn't have to know that she felt cornered. Trapped. She turned her back on him and stared at the glow of downtown leaking above the horizon.

"I will talk to her," Gilberto said. "She will say no more."

"Great. But not now, not with everyone else listening in. Can you just take me home? Tell them I'm sick, or something." Because she couldn't face Anabela again, not yet. She needed some time to think things through. And space. Their little apartment in Barroca was not much to speak of, but it was all hers when Gilberto went away to work every day.

"Of course, *meu amor*. I will go tell them now that we are leaving." He hurried away, taking the steps two at a time.

In his absence, she assessed the dark around her. The drumbeats of samba echoed in the distance, never missing a stroke. Resolution as strong as their rhythm washed over her. She swore that woman was never going to do that to her again. Never manipulate her. Never leave her clueless. Never make Gilberto have to lie to her. Roz would never again not know what that woman had to say about her.

She hadn't realized at first, back in Denver when she'd suddenly had to flee, that she would have to learn Portuguese. Gilberto spoke English, sort of. Why didn't anyone else around here? She'd expected they would, but they didn't. Not even in cosmopolitan Rio had any of the waiters spoken English. She hadn't thought things through back in Denver, either. But now she knew what she had to do, just to keep that woman, her mother-in-law, from spreading lies about her. And getting away with it.

A whiff of tobacco drifted past her nose. The darkness of the open fields surrounding the driveway softened under starlight, and somewhere out there amongst scrubby grasses, the red embers of a cigarette flickered to life.

It was a guard, she told herself. No one else could've slipped onto the estate who didn't belong here. No one from her past. Still, her heart skipped a beat.

"Who's there?" she called out in her most forceful voice, trying not to sound like the prisoner she feared she'd become. No one answered, but then she hadn't expected an answer. The guards wouldn't understand her.

# Chapter Four

**Faceless, frenzied crowds** flowed through the night streets of Belo Horizonte like blood squeezing through veins. Bongos thrummed the relentless rhythm of samba, a broken record stuck on a single beat. *Carnaval* was a heartbeat gone wild, both steady and erratic, a mad race that knew no end. It was a time when no one slept, neither the giddy revelers nor the *Policía Civil* of Minas Gerais.

Especially not Detective Gilberto da Costa. He slogged through the teeming masses of feverish partiers, who spritzed the air with clouds of ether, bopping each other on the head with their plastic mallets filled with the intoxicating liquid. Ducking, he pressed on. Searching...always searching...

His son would've turned five this month.

These last few months he'd been closing in on the cult, which he swore was responsible for butchering his first wife and stealing his son. He wasn't going to quit that investigation just because the case was officially closed nor because new cases demanded his attention. One of them—another stolen son—was the Gonzaga baby kidnapping case, which had sent Gilberto to Denver. He hadn't found the baby, but he'd found a new lead on the murder of his first wife.

And he'd returned home with a new wife.

Roz was a living, breathing goddess of womanly curves, with eyes like aquamarine jewels and a husky voice that sent electric charges—

"Pay attention, lover boy," said Gilberto's partner, Ubaldo Ramos, as the two of them pushed through the crowds. Ubaldo surged ahead.

Gilberto swerved around a clown waving a plastic bonker. The crowds had already swallowed Ubaldo, but his partner was a head taller than most everyone else, keeping him conveniently in sight. Even though Gilberto had lost sight of their target, he knew that his partner, who had the eyes of a vulture and the nose of a bloodhound, hadn't. Gilberto pressed forward.

Tonight, he could almost taste the sweetness of justice. He and Ubaldo had been tailing a thief, an overgrown street kid, whose gangly limbs, thin facial hair, and sharp nose suggested he was more adult than adolescent. He went by the nickname of Picapau—woodpecker. An apt nickname for someone who killed birds. He was the only link Gilberto had to the dark, forbidden cult that was involved in his first wife's murder.

Finding the kid again tonight had been a lucky break. He'd ducked out of the *favela* while Gilberto and Ubaldo were keeping that shantytown under surveillance for the Gonzaga kidnappers. The way Picapau kept dodging them only confirmed in Gilberto's mind that he was guilty.

This street kid played the innocent, being a victim of poverty, but he was also a crafty survivor of the street. Gilberto could swear that Picapau knew the cops were on his ass. He'd played with them, leading them here to the city center. This was where he had a chance of escape, blending into the general confusion downtown.

The masses on the streets danced as if possessed, along with the parade of samba trucks, little more than rolling platforms that carried the ever-drumming drummers and gyrating, scantily-clad dancers. It was a writhing party, caught in a mindless trance as it snaked its way through the avenues, flowing across Picapau's path.

*Não.*

The possibility of losing the kid again filled Gilberto with loathing. He scanned the crowd, searching.

If anyone could keep that kid in sight, though, it would be his partner, knifing through the masses of bodies. No one could elude Ubaldo. Gilberto felt lucky to have a partner like him, someone who'd been born into a family of police officers. Someone who knew his way around the criminal underworld.

"You see him?" Gilberto said, catching up.

Ubaldo chuckled and exhaled cigarette smoke, drifting in Gilberto's face. "You don't?"

"Where is he?"

"You're just anxious to be done here and get home to the North American," Ubaldo said. "Go on, then. Get out of here."

Gilberto scowled. "Her name is Roz." His new wife. "She has nothing to do with this," he said. "Let's call in backup and get this asshole now."

"Don't need any help." Ubaldo dipped his head to one side. "Over there."

Gilberto looked in the direction where his partner nodded. A samba truck drove slowly along the tree-lined avenue, farting diesel fumes into the sultry air.

"Not the truck, stupid," Ubaldo whispered. "The alley on the other side of the street."

Gilberto squinted, masqueing the irritation of his partner's unnecessary insult. It took all of his social graces to ignore the constant slights, the price he paid for having a partner as skilled as Ubaldo. Besides, squinting helped reduce the glare. A necklace of bare lightbulbs draped across the truck, streaming light out into the dark of night, blinding him to the dark.

"I don't see anything." Uneasiness gnawed his gut. Maybe Ubaldo thought the two of them could take Picapau without any help, but street kids were scrappy, strong as ribar, fast and ferocious as piranhas.

Ubaldo grunted. "The asshole is dealing to a couple chicks." He tossed the stub of his cigarette to the pavement and ground it out with the sole of his leather shoe. "I'll cross in front of the truck. You cross behind. Once we're on the other side of the street, we'll take him in the middle. Cut off the kid's escape. Got that?"

Gilberto nodded uncertainly.

His partner was already gone, leaving Gilberto with little more than faith in Ubaldo's skill. And Gilberto *did* trust him. Ubaldo never missed anything.

Gilberto slipped into the swarm of dancers and one by one dodged their sweating bodies and their upturned arms. Steeling himself, he resisted their offer to sweep him along in their rapture, and he swam upstream, against the current of music. Samba throbbed in his head and resonated through every cell of his body, down to his toes, like an infection invading his body. He pressed on.

Yes. *Carnaval* was an infection. Spreading fever through

the body of his country. *O Brasil!* That's why he would never bring Roz here to the samba streets. Where the contagion could so easily carry her away. He didn't want to lose her, too. As he'd lost his first wife.

And his son.

The reminder of that loss—five years ago, but still fresh in his mind—shot a pulse of adrenaline through him. He surged onward, into the diesel cloud behind the truck.

When he finally spilled onto the opposite side of the street, he drank in the night air with a shudder of relief, as if he'd clawed his way onto a sandy beach after battling riptide. He spied Ubaldo in the distance. Even from afar, Gilberto could read the scowling look on his partner's face, which said, *About fucking time you showed up.*

Gilberto flinched from the implied message. He clenched his mind, closing off the weakness of his failures to the women in his life.

He wouldn't fail Roz.

It was darker on this side of the avenue. The trees were healthier over here, and the skyscrapers were tighter. Third-rate offices by day. The ground-level businesses shuttered by night. Although the avenue was a major artery of the city, dead pockets like this one existed. Not forgotten, but avoided. Pockets of dark became the domain of lowlifes.

Where street kids prowled.

At a signal from his partner, Gilberto moved swiftly down the street, a mirror reflection of Ubaldo's movement. They marched as if on a collision course, timed to meet at their center—the mouth of the alley.

He wondered how Ubaldo had managed to spot the deal

from all the way across the street. Through samba traffic. Not that he questioned his partner. God, no. Ubaldo was the best. Ubaldo came from a long line of cops, unlike Gilberto, the disappointing son of a mining family empire. He was damned lucky to team up with such a legend like Ubaldo. And Ubaldo never let him forget it.

Gilberto slowed his step as he approached the corner, where the alley met the avenue. Samba thrummed half a degree softer behind him. Ubaldo waved him to a halt. The plan had changed.

Gilberto ducked behind a bushing poinsettia, its springy branches wrapping around him, while Ubaldo disappeared into the dark throat of the alley. Alert. Ready. He waited.

But he couldn't let Ubaldo walk alone into a situation where the plan had gone wrong. Gilberto edged forward. He strained to listen over the beat of samba that numbed his head. He drew his Glock and slid out of the bush and around the corner like a shadow.

Ubaldo's back faced him in the alley. No one else here. Either the dealing street kid had melted away into the air or Ubaldo had been wrong.

That couldn't be right.

Gilberto crept forward. Ubaldo stood, staring down at a bundled lump at his feet. Trash on the hard packed dirt.

A flicker of light from a passing samba truck in the avenue behind them trickled across the alley, giving just enough light to see. A pair of women's legs folded beneath the lump of her body, lying in a pool of blood.

# Chapter Five

**Two days after the** spectacle she'd made, running out of her new mother-in-law's dinner party, Roz found the rain-slickened gray building, rising up like a watchtower on the edge of downtown Belo. Carnival drums were still hammering, although God knew where the source of the sound was. They'd never lost the beat, all these hours later, not even during off-and-on downpours. Wet strands of air vibrated around her.

Her head throbbed, a residue of yesterday's migraine, and she took a deep breath. It was like breathing water. She climbed the steps, half a story high, leading up to the double doors of the entrance, where she grasped one of the brass handles and yanked. Inside, a gloomy hallway stretched away before her. She paused to let her eyes adjust, and maybe to harden her heart, just a little bit.

The last time Roz had seen the inside of a school building, she'd been Linda then. Seventeen and pregnant. Nine years ago. A third of her life had passed since then.

Shaking off raindrops, she dug into her shoulder bag, a leather prop that Gilberto had bought her to go along with her new image. He'd rescued it from his mother's house before any of her new in-laws could paw through its contents. They wouldn't have found anything. She was careful about things like that.

Now she pulled out the business card Gilberto had brought home to her the night before, clicked across the stone floor to a steel receptionist's desk, and handed it over to the young woman sitting there. Her sun-kissed flesh screamed Brazilian, unlike Roz's Midwestern USA pallor.

The Brazilian smiled, dazzling white teeth against her bronze. Then she glanced down at the card, which she should've recognized right off. The little logo of helping hands entwined around a blue globe indicated this very language institute in whose hallowed halls Roz now stood. Next to the logo on the card was a name: Teresinha Prado. A distant cousin of the da Costas, several times removed.

The receptionist's fingers stumbled over each other in her haste to pick up the clunky receiver of the black phone on her desk. She whispered unintelligible words into the mouthpiece, as if lowering her voice might prevent Roz from understanding. No problem about that. Didn't this woman realize that's why she was here?

Roz hadn't picked up much Portuguese yet, but she understood the receptionist's meaning clear as day.

*Não.* No.

"So, she's not here?" Roz said in English, struggling to keep frustration from creeping into her tone of voice.

She'd expected that the receptionist in a language school would understand another language, hopefully English. But this place was the middle of nowhere. Belo Horizonte was one of the cities that guidebooks advised tourists to skip.

The receptionist shook her head. A flush ruddied the high bones of her cheeks, and she avoided her gaze. She was lying.

Roz reached for the card on the desk and turned it over. "She told me to come today. See?"

Teresinha had scrawled a note on the back side, stating the day and time of the private language class she'd set up for Roz. Gilberto had come home with the card last night, just one day after their blow-up (and make up) following that so-called welcome party at Anabela's house. A perfect solution, he'd said. Cousin Teresinha happened to be an English teacher, so she must know how to teach Portuguese.

The receptionist shook her head and mumbled more incoherent words.

This had to be the right place where Teresinha worked. The address matched. Apparently, Roz was going to have to find the cousin without any help. Well, fine. A burning sensation gnawed at her insides, but she swallowed her rising alarm and gave the receptionist a thin smile. She snatched the card back, and then darted around the desk, plunging down the hall, leading to what she supposed were classrooms.

The receptionist jabbered scolding words at her, but words had never stopped Roz before. Resistance always triggered her own resistance. Did she have a choice? Not that she could see.

"She must be here somewhere," Roz said, poking into one empty room after another. Where was everyone?

Nine years later and half a world away, and classrooms still looked the same as they always had.

Her rain-dampened shoes squeaked as she hurried down the hall. High heels weren't very practical, but if Roz didn't dress her new part, Gilberto's mother would ask too many questions.

They couldn't have Anabela upset, God no.

But why not?

Roz didn't know. She knew one thing. She had to learn her new husband's language if she was ever to survive in this bottom-of-the-world place no one had ever heard of.

"May I offer assistance?" someone—a male someone—said from behind her in a formally clipped British-twanging voice.

Relief swept through her. Someone actually spoke English! Stumbling, she whirled around. "Yes, I'm looking for Teresinha Prado. You know where she is?"

"Hmmm." He was a hunk, on beach party break. The hunk drummed his chin with sensuous fingers, tapping out a bongo rhythm.

"You wouldn't, by chance," he said slowly, thoughtfully, "be the young woman referred by Dona Anabela da Costa, would you?"

Roz came to attention. "Anabela's my mother-in-law, but she didn't refer me."

"Ah. Perhaps I made a mistake."

"What did she say about me?"

"So you are the one? The North American?"

"No! I mean, yes, I guess." She was losing control, and she couldn't have that.

Gaining control was why she'd come to the language school in the first place. She hated it when people talked about her. In a language she didn't understand. Especially when she wasn't present for the conversation. She could never hope to have any sort of control without language.

"I see." His gaze swept her up and down, evaluating. If he was looking for her bruises, he wouldn't find them. "You have an arrangement, is that right?"

"I have an appointment," she said, stiffening. A throbbing pain knifed through her left temple. Anabela must suspect something about the arrangement with Gilberto.

"I'm Lin— Uh, Rosalinda." Thanks to the way he'd unnerved her, she'd almost slipped and said *Linda*.

"Rosalinda da Costa," she said. "That's who I am." Not Linda Armbrust, her birth name.

Bongo fingers clasped her hand in both of his. "Please accept my warmest congratulations."

"Thanks. But what about Teresinha? She told my husband that I should come here today for Portuguese lessons."

"Ah, madam, I regret that is not possible." He took her arm and squeeze-tugged, as if he meant to steer her towards the front door.

"But why not?" She twisted her elbow loose from his grip.

"Senhorinha Prado no longer works here."

"No... That can't be right. It was just yesterday... She gave her card to Gilberto..." Red flags popped in Roz's mind. Now who was lying? Roz hadn't come this far in the world without learning when to back off. When to change the plans. She'd had to be flexible, quick in the mind, to get where she'd got.

She shrugged. "I must've made a mistake."

From somewhere in the dim grayness of the damp hallway came the soft, whispering sounds of hushed voices. Then a door snicked shut.

This man who was trying to get rid of her glanced over his shoulder, and Roz took that opportunity to turn sharply on her heels. "Thanks for your help."

And she meant it. He'd helped her see the way things were going to be, unless Roz did something about it. She marched back the way she'd come, pounding the hallway with the staccato echoes of her footsteps. At the receptionist's desk, she said, "Do you have a phone directory?"

The bronze woman babbled something at her, reminding Roz of her resolution to learn the language. She would *not* let Anabela ever foil her plans again. She would *not* let her new mother-in-law spread who-knew-what kind of gossip about her. They were lies. No matter that there might be a little truth in them.

"Never mind." Roz spied a newspaper folded on an end table next to some vinyl benches in what she supposed was a waiting area. More like a holding cell. She snatched up the paper and shoved through the double doors, outside.

The rain had stopped, but muggy air weighed on her like a lead blanket. She clattered down the steps of Teresinha's former workplace. On the sidewalk, she leaned against a stone wall and thumbed through the newspaper, searching the ads.

There. *Inglês.*

She hailed a cab and showed the driver the address from the paper. The driver nodded, said something, and motioned her into the backseat.

As the taxi wound through nearby city blocks, she wondered what had happened to Teresinha. The cousin had given Gilberto one of her cards. Only yesterday. That didn't sound to Roz as if she'd had any plans to leave her job. At least not willingly. Maybe she'd called in sick today, but the man had been clear. *No longer works here*, he'd said.

Teresinha hadn't just stood Roz up. Someone hadn't wanted her to instruct Roz. Perhaps had even fired her. Because of *Roz*, the cousin had lost her job. Roz didn't want to think she was responsible for that.

But someone was.

The all-mighty Anabela? She'd referred Roz to the school, that man had claimed, but in truth, it had been Gilberto who'd set things up. Anabela had had nothing to do with Roz's coming here today.

If Anabela had the kind of power to meddle in her son's affairs and furthermore, to get a language teacher fired, then she probably also had the resources to find out about Linda Armbrust.

Not if Roz could help it.

# Chapter Six

February 9, 1959

**That very day, Roz hired** Luis Andrade as her new Portuguese teacher. A short, wiry man, he moonlighted as a private tutor when he wasn't working at the language school Roz had found listed in the newspaper's ad. His rates were reasonable, and that meant she could pay for her lessons from her allowance without too many sacrifices. Best of all, Luis claimed never to have heard of the da Costas.

Probably a lie, but as long as he wouldn't report back to Anabela, Roz didn't care if he lied or not.

She stewed the rest of the day about her new mother-in-law. Anabela had to expect that Roz would eventually learn Portuguese. How could she not, if she were to stay here? But the truth was that Anabela didn't want Roz to stay. No one wanted her here. She should go away and leave the darling boy alone. *That* must've been the true meaning behind the hateful words about her at the family dinner table, words that had angered Gilberto, despite what he'd claimed she'd said about wanting to "help" her. In truth, the only help Anabela wanted was how to sabotage Roz and force her to get the hell out.

Teresinha had been the first casualty of Anabela's sabotage.

It was hard to believe that her mother-in-law's spite went that deep. If Anabela had been responsible for removing

Teresinha from her job, just to prevent her from teaching Roz, then she could've also been the mastermind behind that little scene of humiliation back at the school. Maybe she'd even lain in wait, watching, snickering. Roz wondered what either she or Teresinha had ever done to deserve such treatment.

She'd dared to marry Anabela's son, that's what.

If that woman was going to be that way, then fine. Roz could play her game. And then some.

"Poor Teresinha," Roz said to Gilberto later that night over a supper of scrambled eggs, her specialty. She'd added some crusty bread and a salty, white cheese from a small grocery she'd happened across downtown, shortly after hiring Luis.

"Mmmm," Gilberto said between mouthfuls as he shoveled in his food. "Delicious."

"It's just eggs." She didn't know much about cooking, never having had an excessive amount of food lying around. Now she couldn't even read a cookbook. The one he'd bought for her was written in Portuguese.

He wiped his mouth with a cloth napkin—something else from the boxes of purchases from Rio—and kissed his fingertips. "I am a lucky man. You are very clever."

"Quit avoiding my questions," she said. "You haven't told me yet what happened to Teresinha."

He shrugged. "Maybe someone will know at *O Clube*. Are you going with the family this week?"

"And let them talk more about me in front of my face?" She snorted.

"They will expect you there. The family reserves a private area by the pool every week. Everyone is supposed to go."

"Are you going?"

"I have to work."

She laughed, but not happily. "There is this little problem of communication, see? Your cousin was supposed to help me fix that. Why didn't she keep her appointment with me?"

He pushed his plate away and scraped his chair back from the small, square table that separated the kitchen from the living room of their apartment. Folding his arms across his chest, he said, "She is getting married soon."

"And so, she plans to quit her job? Just because of that?"

"She will not need to work."

Roz sprang out of her chair and grabbed the plates. "She only gave you her card yesterday!" She dumped the plastic dishes into the sink and whirled around to face him. "Yesterday, she thought she needed to work. Why'd she make that appointment with me if she meant to quit teaching?"

He didn't answer.

Roz placed her hands on her hips and glared at him. "She *did* make that appointment, didn't she? Or did someone else make it for her?"

The ends of his mouth turned down, a gesture she was beginning to recognize that meant he didn't like the conversation. "I guess she changed her mind," he said.

Roz didn't like the conversation, either. "Then why didn't she let me know?"

"She probably tried to. She would've called Dona Silvia, our neighbor. She's the only one in our building with a telephone, but you know how the dona is. Maybe she forgot to give you the message."

He was changing the subject, trying to steer Roz's focus away from Teresinha and onto their nosy neighbor who liked to spy on everyone, the new, foreign bride in particular. Roz wouldn't be steered. "I'll bet Teresinha had some help changing her mind."

Anabela.

Although why, she had no idea.

Gilberto turned his back on her and strode across to the open window of the living room. He stood there several silent minutes, peering out at the ruts in the hillside that someone called a street. Darkness was falling, and finally he slid the louvered shutters closed. Since there seemed to be no screens in this entire country, shutters kept the largest beetles out.

"Well?" Roz said. "Was it your mother?"

He glanced over his shoulder, giving her a woeful, teddy bear look of guilt and maybe some pain. "*Mãe*?"

She sighed, hating herself for nagging, but she couldn't help herself, either. Her future was at stake. She spoke slowly, enunciating clearly. "Did your mother set up that whole fiasco?"

"Fi-as-co? What is that?"

He was deliberately annoying her. Pent-up frustration erupted, and she blew out her breath through gritted teeth. "You think it was easy for me to find that address in the first place? And then Teresinha wasn't there. Even though she'd said she would be there. Because someone canceled the appointment, except they didn't bother to tell me. You know how easy that is when you can't communicate? That's what 'fiasco' means."

She hugged herself, trying to keep the sobs from slipping out, but her arms shook. Trembles convulsed through her.

He rushed to her side and wrapped his arms around her. "Shhh," he whispered, covering her with kisses.

It must be true. Because he'd never denied it.

Anabela had subverted her. And furthermore, Gilberto had known all about it, Roz could swear.

"Why'd she do that?" Roz said. "What does she suspect?"

"Is nothing, *meu amor.*"

But Gilberto had helped the subversion, whether willingly or not, Roz didn't know. He wouldn't tell her.

What else wasn't he telling her? If they were to have a war of keeping secrets, Roz would win. She had no doubts about that. Lessons with Luis would just be one more in a long string of her secrets. That one, at least, should be easy to keep.

\* \* \* \* \*

Roz let Gilberto pamper her, thinking she was helpless.

Because she'd never killed a man before. Not that she hadn't wanted to, a time or two. Faces flashed to mind. The snake-eyed man back in Ohio who took the angel of her little sister. And later, the oily face of the man in Denver.

But that had been self-defense, for heaven's sake. She'd had to fight back—she sure as hell wasn't going to hand over her hard-earned money. She hadn't been sure anyone else, like a jury, would see it her way, especially considering where the money had come from, washing dishes at a strip joint, sure. But Gilberto did. And then, when she found out who the dead man was—the worthless son of some Rocky Mountain crime boss—she let Gilberto rescue her. That had only been the first time she'd let him think she was helpless.

He did something with the body, she didn't know what. He'd said it was better for her not to know. They were in this together, and whatever he'd done, it kept the two of them a step ahead of the Denver cops and also Daddy's boys.

Back there in Denver, while she was still on her cot in some clinic Gilberto had found, he promised to take care of her, if only she would marry him. She didn't know where such an offer had come from out of the blue like that, nor what marriage meant—her own mother had never actually married the creep who called himself "stepfather"—and yet she'd agreed. It was a way out.

When the clinic doc was done patching her up, she and Gilberto had slipped out. He used his family money to take her to Mexico and arrange for the judge who married them. She didn't know if it was legal or not, but it didn't matter, because in the end she acquired the documents to accompany her new name. Using them, they flew to Rio, where his efforts and five days on the beach saw her through the worst purple blooms of her bruises.

Sure, maybe in retrospect it had been too hasty, but she couldn't afford to stick around much longer, not back there in Denver. She wasn't sure why he'd done what he'd done, all for her. Why he'd offered her the way out. Lust, she guessed. Lust was more likely than love. He'd been a cop for seven years and had spent too many off-duty hours alone. Already now, he knew more about her than anyone else had ever known. He knew what she'd done back there in Denver.

It was why she couldn't ever go back. Why she couldn't let Anabela kick her out. Why she had to make this language learning a success.

\* \* \* \* \*

The next day, while Gilberto was away at work, Roz flipped through the pages of her new cookbook, scanning the gobbledygook arrangement of letters and symbols. There weren't even any pictures. She sighed. Most of these words weren't in the little dictionary Gilberto had bought for her in Rio. She would have to find a more comprehensive dictionary if they were ever to have anything more complicated than scrambled eggs.

Sounds coming from the hall outside her apartment distracted her. Footsteps hammered and voices snapped, echoing off the hall's sterile cement and plaster. By now, Roz recognized most of the sounds in her apartment building— the bouncing step of the teenagers from the floor above, their animated voices, and the creak of Silvia's door across the hall as her nosy neighbor kept an eye on everyone.

Whoever was out there now was a newcomer. Those sounds didn't belong. Roz listened, alert.

There were only three apartments on her floor. Hers and Gilberto's was the most spacious, taking up the entire width of the building, about the same width as two double-wide trailers. Across the hall were two smaller units, separated by stairs. Silvia's apartment was one of them, facing the hillside "street," while the third apartment overlooked the back. Out there was where an empty piece of land lay, and a ravine cut through the middle of it. As far as Roz knew, that back apartment was vacant.

The voices cut off, and the footsteps stopped. Silvia's door creaked, and then a fist pounded on Roz's front door. Her apartment had a back door, too, only a few feet away from the front door. Whoever was knocking was apparently not a delivery person.

A pair of visitors stood in the hall, and at first, Roz didn't recognize them. The woman wore white gloves and a hat with a veil pulled down to her red lips. The man who stood behind her wore a uniform and cap. Roz remembered him. He was the da Costa chauffeur, who'd hand delivered the dinner invitation from Anabela.

The veiled woman was Anabela herself. She swept across the threshold, uninvited into the apartment, and shoved the door closed behind her. The chauffeur remained alone in the hall, left to deal with Silvia's scrutiny. Anabela lifted the veil and hooked it to the top of her pillbox hat. Her hawk-like face peered at Roz as words slipped out of the unmoving, red line of her thin lips.

"*Bom día*," Roz said, randomly inserting the greeting in the midst of Anabela's monologue.

Apparently it was a mistake, as Anabela launched into a tighter-sounding stream of commands. Her tone never rose to indicate a question.

"If you're looking for Gilberto," Roz said, "he's not here. He's at work."

At the mention of that name, Anabela fell silent for a couple of heartbeats. She gazed around the room, assessing the spare place—the couch and coffee table were the only pieces of furniture in the living area. Her glance lowered to the floor, where Roz had dropped her purse and shoes. Damn, there was a dead beetle lying upturned on the shell of its back. Then Anabela's gaze lifted toward the kitchen table, where the cookbook had flipped closed on account of its stiff spine.

Anabela grunted something and stalked across the room

toward the kitchen.

"You want something to drink?" Roz said, wondering what, besides the bottle of mineral water she could offer. She hadn't boiled water from the tap yet, not as she was supposed to.

Anabela eyed the dirty dishes soaking in the sudsy sink, sniffed, and marched on. The little room off the kitchen was supposed to be the maid's quarters, but Roz didn't have a maid. She used the space instead as a storeroom for all the boxes they had not yet unpacked. Whatever Anabela was looking for, it wasn't there, and she wheeled around, retracing her steps to the living room.

"Did Gilberto know you were planning to come over?" Roz asked. "Too bad he didn't let me know."

Anabela paused again, apparently listening to the mention of her son's name. Her eyes glittered as she scanned the place, taking it all in, and then she plunged down the little hall that led to the bedroom and bathroom.

Roz trailed along behind. "I was just now getting ready to clean up the place."

Gilberto's male smells hung in the air of the room with the rumpled bed coverings and soiled laundry. Did his mother notice? Probably, the way her back stiffened and words snapped out of her. She stalked across the room to the chifferobe, yanked open its door, and surveyed the wardrobe Gilberto had bought for her.

"Are you looking for something?" Roz said.

Anabela snorted out more words and reached inside the wardrobe, riffling through the cottons, linens, and silks. She turned with a scathing glance and marched on, to the bathroom. Roz's pill bottles and makeup bottles crowded together haphazardly on the sink, the windowsill, the top of the commode, the edges of the bathtub. There were no shelves. Anabela picked up a tin of aspirin. Roz ate them during her migraines. The tin dropped, sliding behind the toilet. Anabela shook a gloved finger at Roz and stalked back through the apartment.

She said something that sounded like "police see ya," and then stormed out, slamming the front door of the apartment behind her.

"Nice to see you, too," Roz said to the closed door. She folded her arms across her chest, pinching herself until her knuckles ached.

How dare that woman come through here like that! Gilberto would hear about this, and he would deal with his mother. He would tell his mother that such behavior was not acceptable, never. Roz didn't care who Anabela da Costa was.

Maybe it was payback for the way Roz had run out of her dinner party. No longer the gracious hostess, her mother-in-law was now the hawk in full hunting mode. Had this hawk spotted the charade of her son's marriage? She would likely expose Roz, and then what?

Police-see-ya.

# Chapter Seven

**The smell of death** and chemicals vented through the tunnel-like hall of the morgue. For a moment, Gilberto thought he glimpsed the famous white light shining at the end of the corridor. Then he realized it wasn't God who awaited him down there but merely light spilling out into the hall from an office. It was the office of his sister Carlota's husband, Dr. Benjamin Brandão.

Ben was the next closest thing to God, according to Gilberto and Carlota's mother. Ben had followed in *his* father's footsteps, *Mãe* always liked to point out with a lift of one delicate line of her penciled-in eyebrows—her trademark gesture meaning "unlike you." Never mind that the footsteps were those of a physician and not of a gemstone miner, as Gilberto's father had been. It was the principle that mattered, and the endurance of family tradition, passed down through more than a century of pure blood from Portugal.

Maybe so, but there was nothing anyone could do, not even *Mãe*, to turn back time, to unmake history.

In spite of the impossibility of measuring up to the family expectations, Gilberto had long ago conceded a grudging respect for Ben. His brother-in-law worked up to his elbows in death, chasing the same cause. Justice.

Eager to call it a day, Gilberto strode swiftly through the basement hall. His heels tapped against the stone floor and echoed throughout the emptiness of the palatial building surrounding him. Everyone else had already gone home by now. The sound of his footsteps matched the ache in his head, feeling like nails pounding into his skull. This, brought on after too many hours sifting through the odd bits and pieces of his caseload that he kept locked away in his desk drawer at the station, and more hours tracking leads that only led to deadends. They were cases that refused to be tracked, and there were too many of them for one sane person to manage, not even with Ubaldo's irregular assistance.

He wouldn't have his workload any other way.

Because such days of hard work as today invited delicious evenings. He was on his way home now, by way of the morgue. And soon, Linda's—ah, *Roz's* magic—would unpluck each tormenting nail driving into his mind, one by one with her sensuous fingers. Something to look forward to at the end of shift. She never failed to enchant him, not even after their arguments, which came far too often. Was this normal? His first wife had never fought him this hard.

He never knew if a simple act of tenderness on his part or a gesture of friendship from someone else, like the family, would yield a meltdown on the part of his new wife. It was as if inner demons drove her, holding her at a distance from him. Something kept her from trusting fully in him. There were things she didn't need to know, things that had nothing to do with her.

But that unknown thing which troubled her...he hoped it

wasn't connected to the files he kept locked in his drawer back at the station.

He stepped into the pool of light spilling out from Ben's office.

"You're late," Ben said.

*So are you.* But Gilberto kept the thought to himself, waiting while Ben's gaze remained fixed on the scattered papers cluttering his desk. Despite his brother-in-law's long hours, not a hair was misplaced from his perfect crown of tight waves, mostly black with a dignified touch of gray. Unlike Gilberto's wayward curls, a dirty color of sand. He combed them off his forehead with his fingers while Ben motioned him to a metal folding chair propped against a bare wall.

"Traffic was a beast." Gilberto approached Ben's desk. He preferred to stand, towering over the steel surface, waiting until Ben looked up. "Thanks for staying late for me."

"It's not for *you*, brother. I have too many goddamned reports to file. Give me another minute while I finish this."

"Still, I owe you one."

Ben grunted and scribbled notes on the papers before him. "More than one."

"Convey my apologies to Carlota when you get home to your cold supper."

"She's used to it by now." Ben paused his pen and looked up with a smirk. "You, on the other hand, go home to a warm bed and..." The color drained from his face, along with his voice, and he quickly lowered his gaze. His pen slipped from his fingers.

"Rosalinda." Gilberto had to remind himself of her new name as well as reminding Ben.

"Of course." Ben watched his pen roll away, as if unsure what to do. "Forgive me. It's just that...the way you...I don't know. These days, you lift your chin, you square your shoulders, and there's a spring to your step. It reminds me of...happier times. My congratulations to your new bride."

"But she likes to be called 'Roz'," Gilberto said, avoiding the unspoken reference to those days of sorrow for his first wife.

"Roz." Nodding, Ben reached for his pen.

Gilberto waited, watching his brother-in-law scrawl hastily across one paper after another. He glanced at his wristwatch, at the papers littering the desk, and at the credenza behind Ben where framed photographs of Carlota and all four children lined up like trophies. He looked at his watch again and sighed.

Ben chuckled while he wrote. "You missed Carlota's reception last night after Mass."

Shit, he'd forgotten. "I had to work." Gilberto's work had pushed the existence of the family to the back of his mind. It happened every time when a case consumed him. Like this one. The asshole who'd killed the woman last week during *Carnaval* wouldn't get away.

"That's what your wife is for," Ben said, "to remind you. But yours is North American and doesn't know these things. Fortunately, Carlota will help you train your new bride."

Gilberto spun on his heels and paced the office. "It's not her job. It's up to me to remember."

Ben looked up from his papers. "Anabela was disappointed."

Gilberto shrugged. His mother was always disappointed, especially in him.

Ben exhaled long and slow as he laid his pen and papers down and pulled a file folder out from under one of the stacks.

"Too many goddamned reports, if you ask me."

Gilberto nodded. Too many assholes, that's what he meant.

"Your victim was only in her teens," Ben said, flipping open the folder.

"Have you i.d.'ed her?"

Ben shook his head and thumbed through the various papers inside the folder. "That's up to you and your detective buddies. But here's something that might help you." He opened a small envelope and lifted out a silver necklace. "She was wearing this."

Gilberto held out his hand, and Ben dropped the thin chain and charm into his palm. Raising the charm toward the fluorescent ceiling lights, he squinted at its silvery nugget shape, only about half the size of his thumbnail. Its delicate lines carved it into a *figa*—a miniature fist, where the thumb inserted between the index and middle fingers. It was a good luck charm. Supposedly the good luck only worked when the *figa* had been a gift. Considering the girl's outcome, this had apparently not been a gift.

This *figa* wasn't cheap, he could tell from the intricate details of the design. One of the family jewelers might recognize its workmanship. While Ben looked down at his folder, Gilberto dropped the necklace and charm into his shirt pocket. "What about the rest of what she was wearing?"

"Lab's not done with it yet. You'll want this file, too, yes?"

"Of course. What else can you tell me?"

Ben leaned back in his chair. "I have a hunch," he said, and then paused, as if waiting for Gilberto to urge him on. He didn't, and Ben continued. "She came here from a small town, given the length of her hair."

"Her *hair*?"

"Believe what you will, but the way her hair appeared never to have been cut in her life, and the way it was braided and wound into a coil is not the style of our fashionable city girls these days."

Gilberto glared at him. "What else have you got, something besides your hunch?"

"Not all our reports are in from the labs yet. I can only tell you why she died."

"So? You going to tell me?"

"You won't like it."

"I already don't like it."

Ben looked up, studying Gilberto. Compassion shone from his coffee-brown eyes. "All right. Shortly before her death, she'd had an abortion. It had obviously not been the work of a real doctor. We found abrasions, like what you'd find as the result of clumsy work from common kitchen tools. She lost too much blood. That's what killed her."

Gilberto curled his fingers into a fist. Abortions were illegal, but that didn't make them uncommon. "You saying it was the abortion itself or the asshole who performed it?"

Ben sighed. "Same difference."

Gilberto held his breath as the image of his first wife's face flashed through his mind. "Could you tell...how far along the fetus had been?"

Ben shook his head. "I'm sorry. It was gone."

Of course. Gilberto knew that. Flushed down the toilet in the backstreet clinic where the girl had gone. "I just meant... What did you learn from the tissue samples?"

"Look, our drawers are full of corpses. The labs are backed up."

"You don't have to offer any excuses," Gilberto said, pacing the room.

How far had the girl wandered from her clinic, before collapsing in that alley during the middle of Brazil's biggest party? The crime team had not spotted a trail of blood that would trace the girl's route. And Picapau had an alibi. All that time he'd spent leading the cops on a long chase, eventually leading them to the girl, meant that he hadn't killed her. But if he'd deliberately meant to distract them with that chase, then it could mean he was guilty of something else. Perhaps he'd had something to do with setting up the abortion and, consequently, the girl's death.

When Ben didn't volunteer more, Gilberto went on. "She bled out in the alley, then?"

Frowning, Ben steepled his neatly manicured fingers together. "It looks that way."

But Ben was still holding back, Gilberto could tell, and he'd had enough. "What aren't you telling me?"

"It's not so simple."

"I just hoped you could tell me something from the condition of her uterus."

"Steady, pal." Ben's voice dropped to a shade above a growl. "You'd better sit down."

Gilberto stopped pacing and waited, standing.

"Her uterus had ruptured," Ben said. "And there were traces of an acid chemical in her vagina."

Gilberto let out his breath through clenched teeth. He leaned against the doorframe to stop the room from spinning around him.

It wasn't just a question of being illegal. This was the work of a butcher, someone who was more interested in his victim's money than her welfare. Possibly, he was even the same butcher who'd killed his first wife. Whoever he was, Gilberto intended to find him. But how many more women would have to die before then?

# Chapter Eight

February, 1959

**As the days of February** rolled by, Roz patrolled the streets of downtown Belo Horizonte. Her classroom had always been the streets. Now, she was in a hurry to learn, thanks to her urgent need to cement the change of her identity. Gilberto must've talked to his mother, because Anabela hadn't barged into the apartment again. Nor had the police been to "see" Roz and kick her out of the country. It was only a matter of time, Roz thought, before Anabela's next attempt at sabotage. In the meanwhile, Roz felt pressured to work on gaining her own control through language. That way, her new mother-in-law couldn't rule her life.

One of the first things she learned was that there were two seasons in Brazil: Carnival season, and not Carnival season. Just because the week-long frenzy had ended with Ash Wednesday and the start of Lent nearly two weeks ago, it didn't mean that the bongo drums had silenced. It didn't stop children from setting off firecrackers randomly along the streets.

Such knowledge came compliments of Luis Andrade, her new Portuguese teacher. Luis had agreed to meet with Roz three times per week, and for the record, she hadn't flirted once. She was a married woman now, and just not interested in those games, at least not at the moment. Maybe never again. She wasn't going to leave herself vulnerable to anyone, not even to her new husband.

He would never know how much it tore her apart to think of that helpless, little aborted baby—no, fetus—who would've been a nine-year-old kid by now.

If Roz had let her live.

Who in hell had Roz thought she was, God? To decide if someone would be allowed to grow. Or not.

It hadn't been a "her." It had been a fetus. Not a real someone.

She took her mind off questions like that, unanswerable questions that twisted her heart inside out, by diving into what had to be done. Like learning Portuguese.

The lessons always took place away from Luis's school, because she insisted. Schools were a dead place for her. Usually they met for an afternoon *cafezinho*, and sometimes they met for lunch, but always in a different place. What mattered was that Anabela didn't own Luis the way she'd owned—and stifled— Teresinha Prado.

She listened to the music of Luis's voice, to the rhythm of the language, to the breaking waves. It surprised her that she had a skill at mimicking his accent. But why not, considering the dreams she'd once entertained of Hollywood? As her vocabulary grew, she learned things about verbs she'd had no idea they could do. She learned parts of speech and grammar rules she'd never even known existed.

The days she didn't meet Luis, she wandered the streets alone, under the trees trimmed like giant hedges along the main avenue, through the clash of smells of spices and herbs and who knew what else at the outdoor market, into shops where only the clerks handled merchandise behind glass-topped counters. She frequented the movies, trying to read Portuguese subtitles, and she thumbed through magazines at corner newsstands. She eavesdropped on conversations everywhere, all the way from arguing neighbors in her apartment building in Barroca to the buses that took her downtown. In the city park she practiced her growing language skills on vendors. Coconut ice cream became her weakness; squabbling parrots at the market, her favorite show.

As the mysteries of language unlocked, pieces of meaning started to take hold in her mind. Clarity slowly tumbled out from the swishing sounds, and she began to distinguish one word from another. Then entire phrases.

At home, she practiced her growing collection of phrases on Gilberto and swore him to secrecy—about her progress, not Luis. She didn't tell him about Luis. She let him believe she was picking up the language on her own, maybe chatting with neighbors. The truth was, there wasn't a neighbor in their apartment building that she wanted to meet.

Until one day she glimpsed a young woman, who appeared to be in her early twenties, carrying a box into the third apartment across the hall from hers. A new neighbor? Roz watched for her again, until Silvia caught her snooping, and then she reminded herself that she wouldn't know what to do with a potential friend, anyway. She already had a confidante in Gilberto, although that didn't mean he had to know the entire truth about her. She preferred *not* to let people know her. Because she didn't always like herself very much, either.

She turned back to her dictionary and her lessons with Luis.

She wasn't sure why she hadn't told Gilberto about Luis. Maybe a little part of her feared that he'd report to his mother. Well, so what?

What it boiled down to was that he didn't *need* to know about Luis, because Luis was a detail that didn't matter. It was the outcome that mattered, not the means of achieving it. Besides, she was good at secrets, too, just like Gilberto was, being a cop. She didn't mind his secrets, really, but if he was going to keep his, then so would she keep hers. She'd learned the hard way never to reveal too much, and yet... His seductions almost tempted her to forget what was best forgotten. As for her past, she knew that he would do whatever it took to protect her. That was partly what made him so...sweet. A word she'd never been able to use before to describe any of her men (but this one was).

Such as, the little gift he brought home to her one day as a surprise: a transistor radio. She listened to it regularly. She read her dictionary every day and wrote out lists of new words. Each day she mastered some of them, understanding a little more. Still, she couldn't capture the words on her own tongue and speak them back.

But it was too soon. She'd only been doing the formal lessons for a couple of weeks, and she was here for the long term. She didn't have to speak. Not yet.

Because in the meanwhile, she was managing to avoid Gilberto's family.

First of all, she declined further invitations to return to the mansion for more family gatherings. Two more dinners had elapsed since that ill-fated one that she'd run out of. Indisposed, Gilberto claimed on her behalf, or at least, that's what he told her he'd said.

But that wasn't all. Family members were expected to attend weekly mass. That was easy to avoid, as she wasn't Catholic.

And then there were poolside get-togethers at their private cabana at *O Clube*, unless a prestigious social engagement pre-empted. Roz had no engagements, and the family knew it. She was expected there, along with other invitations from the siblings, and good lord, there were a lot of them. The da Costas were Catholics, capital C.

Gilberto played interference for her each time, telling them a pack of lies. Sometimes it was a migraine, and sometimes he attended family events alone, whenever his work allowed. He reported back how they "understood" that she hadn't been able to make it. More lies. The newlyweds needed a little time. He wouldn't be able to hold them off much longer, he said, but Roz wasn't ready to join them yet. She had her secrets to tend to. Let Anabela think she'd won for now. After all, wasn't Roz's absence exactly what her mother-in-law wanted? Let her think that the little American must be depressed, holing up until she could wing her way north forever. And by the way, good riddance.

But Roz could never go home again, not even if she wanted to. Not that she did. So this was going to work out. She would make it work.

* * * * *

Mostly, Roz was on her own, as Gilberto rarely had a day off. And then one day, he did.

His day off coincided with a dry day at the end of February, and he said *no more of this*. It was a beautiful late summer day, too beautiful to stay cooped up inside with her radio, her exercise books, and magazines (he thought they came from the corner grocery next to the garage entrance of their apartment building). Rainy season would soon let up. If she didn't want to go to the pool with the rest of the family, then the two of them would go to the park. It was about time that she, as *Senhora da Costa*, learned her way around her new city, and he would show her.

She almost snorted with laughter. She already knew the layout of the city in its wheel configuration. The major avenues were spokes of the wheel. She already knew every bus route to the perimeter of downtown. Where to switch to the *ônibus*, an electric bus that took her deeper into the center. She knew all the taxi stands. Since her husband never offered her the use of his fancy car, perhaps because she had no driver's license, how did he think she could ever explore?

He didn't know. And that's exactly the way she wanted to keep it. Luckily, telephones were rare here, and they didn't have one in the apartment for him to be able to check up on her. Nosy Silvia was the only resident in the building who had a telephone, and that's where he had to call if he ever wanted to reach her.

So it wasn't hard to keep him in the dark.

But she could understand his need to assert himself. After meeting his mother at the family mansion, where Anabela had played queen, and after the way his mother had inspected the little apartment as if she owned the place, Roz couldn't blame Gilberto for wanting to control his own small kingdom. It was a Brazilian thing, she learned from Luis, that men ruled the family.

Something else to find another way around.

It must aggravate Gilberto that his mother, instead of him or one of his brothers, had taken his father's place, wearing the pants in the family, after Francisco Senior died. Perhaps that was why Gilberto took other, smaller pleasures, such as the car he'd bought from his mother's friend, the American diplomat. It made Roz a little uneasy that this slight connection existed to a Real Somebody from the States, tenuous as that connection was. She supposed that the family's prominent social position—or maybe being a cop—had given Gilberto access to an information network, perhaps one that included visiting diplomats. She didn't know what he could dig up about her history if he ever decided to ask his network for help.

Why would he ever? He'd helped her escape. He wouldn't betray her now.

Lingering paranoia consumed her, that's all this was. Eventually, she figured, it would have to let up. Nearly two months here in Belo still felt too soon for her to feel at ease. It would take a little time for the foreignness of the place to go away. Already, it seemed slightly less foreign, just through her wanderings and acquiring a tiny fraction of the language. Like everything else she was learning, she would have to learn how to relax.

It wasn't easy.

The park on a sunny day could be just the right place to learn. Under the sun, she almost felt the weight of her paranoia drain away. Her step lightened, and the chill surrounding her heart slowly thawed. She supposed it was the altitude here in this mountainous highland of Minas Gerais that produced an occasional shiver, unlike the coast. Coming here, she hoped she'd run far enough.

Gilberto was prattling on and on to her in his whispery, purring voice, pointing out tropical bushes and flowers in city park. The birds and the butterflies. Butterflies large enough to be birds and as colorful as the flowers. She balked when they got to the lake, remembering what he'd told her about schistosomiasis, but he held her hand protectively and led her along the path circling the lake. She felt herself relax at his side, and when he pointed out the ducks and laughed, she laughed, too. He told her about coming here as a child, and about the family dog he'd had while growing up, a Labrador. His father had driven him to Rio for the pick of the litter, and they named him Inho (which, she now knew, thanks to Luis, was the diminutive form of a word). She laughed at the story and said, "Ironic, since he must not have stayed little very long."

"*Sim*." He slowed his step. "How fast you learn, *meu amor*."

Before he could quiz her further about her progress, she spied a colorful umbrella ahead on the path, flagging an ice cream vendor. He noticed her noticing, and when he offered to buy her one, the tension of her doubts instantly snapped back into place. Was this the same vendor, with whom she usually chatted, practicing her stumbling phrases?

What did it matter, she told herself, even if he was. And he was. His round face, brown as a walnut, crinkled into a smile as he greeted her with the silly expression he saved for her, "*Dona Gringa!*"

She nodded and looked down at the winding walkway as he quoted the prices and flavors, enunciating clearly. He added some other phrases that she didn't understand, took Gilberto's cruzeiros, and handed them their wrapped, frozen bars.

They walked away in silence, savoring their iced coconut. Roz held her back stiff, feeling the vendor's gaze on her.

"You know him?" Gilberto finally said, looking sideways at her.

She shook her head, said "*Não*," and forced herself to laugh.

"But I think you do," he said, grabbing her arm. "He knows you are not from here. Why don't you tell me about it?"

"There's nothing to tell."

"Nothing?"

"That's right." She yanked her arm from his grip. "Just like you always tell me 'nothing' when I ask you questions."

A flush spread up the side of his neck as he fell silent.

She went on. "Like that dinner party at your mother's house, and you wouldn't tell me what she was saying. It was about me, and it wasn't nice, is that why you won't say?"

He hesitated, then sighed, and then finally spoke. "*Mãe* was angry at me for not telling her sooner about you and me. Her friends at Copacabana told her first, that a beautiful woman was staying there with me. And she asked about your black eye, because they told her about that, too. Did you want me to tell her the truth, instead?"

A shiver swept through Roz. Gilberto had promised to protect her. She was willing to bet that he hadn't counted on having to protect her from his very own mother, whom he clearly respected. Roz had always envied the idea of having a mother one could respect, and now she was only making it harder for her husband by keeping information from him. It wasn't information that mattered, but he deserved better than her lies.

"The ice cream vendor lets me practice my Portuguese

lessons," she said, and then added impulsively, "because, you see, I've hired a tutor. His name is Luis Andrade."

Gilberto smiled. "I know."

She smiled, too, amused by the irony of trying to keep a secret from a real detective. She'd failed.

So she changed the subject. "Tell me more about your dog."

Sometimes he and the family brought Inho here to the park to play fetch, he told her, and he would buy the dog an ice cream, too. Perhaps one day when he and Roz had their own place—a real home, instead of the hastily acquired apartment in Barroca—they could get a dog, another Inho, would she like that? She didn't know. She'd never been around dogs much and certainly had never owned one before. It had been hard enough for her mother to feed just the three of them. Hard enough to care for herself.

They finished their ice cream in companionable silence as they continued along the lake, strolling in the shade cast by clusters of regally tall palms. Ahead, a flood of sunlight bathed an open area of grass. The wide, thick blades were clearly not Kentucky bluegrass. A couple of children kicked a ball around, and Gilberto pulled her to a stop to watch. She felt a quiver run through his arm as she leaned against him.

A woman's voice sounded from behind, calling to the children, something about the lake. It was a small victory for Roz to pick out that much—*lago*—although she couldn't understand the rest. Beside her, she felt Gilberto's muscled arm tighten. He stiffened his shoulders, holding himself erect, as the woman closed the distance fast behind them. Roz realized it wasn't the children the newcomer was speaking to, but to them. Her husband's cheeks flamed, and he pulled away, letting loose of her hand as he turned around.

She turned, too.

The woman looked familiar.

"*Bom día*," Gilberto said, greeting her. He followed this with more words that Roz didn't understand. She recognized their sharp edges, their short snappiness, in what she considered his policeman's voice.

Now she placed the vaguely familiar woman as one of Gilberto's sisters. They'd met at that dinner party at the family mansion. She was the eldest, perhaps. She certainly looked older, the way she carried an invisible, tired weight upon her shoulders.

Roz couldn't remember her name.

She didn't know, but she thought that what Gilberto said to his sister was more than just a casual hello. He was speaking deliberately faster than Roz's ability to understand, but she managed to pick up a few snatches, anyway.

"Mom says," the sister said in Portuguese, and "I have..." But Roz didn't know what she had nor what their mother had said.

Gilberto cut off his sister before she could say anymore, as if he wasn't sure about the limits of Roz's grasp of the language. Apparently, he didn't *want* her to understand their exchange.

When his sister spoke, her mouth twitched open, exposing sharply pointed teeth as she fired phrases at Gilberto. He fired back. Mixed in with the unintelligible mess, the sister's gaze fluttered across Roz, and her arm waved at the children playing ball.

Gilberto pulled Roz close to him. "Remember my sister, Carlota?" His purr turned to a growl.

Carlota, a stick-thin, surgically unenhanced version of Anabela, fell silent during his brief switch to English. She had the same nugget eyes as her mother, although hers were a lower grade of simmering coal. This sister had the same tight lips as her mother, painted crimson, although tiny, permanent lines radiated out from them. She squinted in the sun and stretched her thin lips into a smile aimed at Roz.

Such a tiny smile with half-hearted life, but it filled Roz with a shred of hope. "Yes, of course," she said, still in English. It was too soon to reveal that she could probably handle a simple greeting in Portuguese. She played the part of dutiful wife, smiling as she transferred her empty popsicle stick to her left hand and took her sister-in-law's hand in her right. "What a pleasant surprise to see you here." *A surprise, yes, but pleasant?* Her heart pattered, and she shifted on her feet, twisting the leather of her sandals.

Carlota's tiny smile faded, along with her limp handshake. Tipping her head to one side, she apparently hadn't understood, not even that small amount of English.

"Two of my nephews," Gilberto said, pointing at the children with their ball. "I'm going to tell them hello, while you two talk. Carlota studied English in school."

He trotted away, leaving her here alone with Carlota. *Oh joy.*

She wondered if he'd known that his sister would be here today. Was that why he'd insisted on coming here, instead of somewhere else? Or had Carlota known she and Gilberto would be here, stealing some private time to build a bond just between the two of them? They really hadn't had much chance to get to know each other, beyond bedroom talk. When they weren't arguing.

However it had happened, Roz felt hijacked. A dark storm cloud had moved across the sun, spoiling her day. Carlota's appearance wasn't by chance, Roz could swear to that. She didn't believe in coincidences.

"You think..." Carlota said in English, struggling to smile between her words, "...*apartamento*...is good place for you?"

Roz smiled back and spoke at a normal rate. "You should ask your mother. She checked it out. She should know if it passes muster."

A puzzled frown creased Carlota's face. "My mother she say...no good, but Isabela no know better."

Roz had no idea what Carlota was suggesting, nor why Isabela—now she remembered that name as that of another sister—had anything to do with Roz's daily life in her new apartment. She doubted that Carlota had sought her out in the park to inquire about her accommodations. There had to be another purpose she was *here*, and not somewhere else with the family.

"Isabela? That's one of your sisters? Is she here in the park, too? I thought the family was supposed to be at *O Clube* today?"

"*O Clube*, yes! Is very, very good." Then Carlota sighed, a small sound of pleasure, as if proud to have spoken that much in English.

"But why aren't you there with them? I thought it was sort of expected for everyone to go." Roz couldn't imagine what it would be like to have a family, let alone one that did everything together.

"Go? *Mãe* say my English is more good. That's why I go here today."

*Mãe*, Roz had learned, meant mom. So. Anabela had put Carlota up to this, whatever Carlota was up to. It didn't surprise her. "Your English is very good," Roz lied.

"No very good." Carlota stretched her thin lips into an exaggerated frown.

"Did you go to the States to learn it, too, like your brother?"

Carlota held up three fingers and said, "Three brothers."

Gilberto had already told her about his two brothers. The older one was a priest, who'd remained silently remote that night of the disastrous family dinner. The younger one had something wrong with him, a brain injury, or something that kept him isolated from the rest of the family with his private nurse. He hadn't joined them for dinner.

Roz didn't know how she was supposed to respond about Carlota's brothers. She shrugged and glanced around for a trash can.

"You have many brothers?" Carlota asked.

"Nope. No brothers." She pushed the memory of her little sister Janie to the hidden depths of her mind. "Gilberto says there are seven of you." Eight, including the sister who'd died. "I can't imagine having so many sisters and brothers."

Carlota nodded, as if she understood. She paused and then took a deep breath. "Everyone has big house where you are from, yes?"

Red flags flared in Roz's mind, and she held her breath. She wondered what Gilberto had already told his family about her, if anything. Whatever it was, it hadn't been enough, and the family must be dying of curiosity for more. Apparently, they'd sent Carlota as spokesperson, and she would report back.

Roz clenched her popsicle stick and shook her head. Her

mother's trailer on the wrong side of the tracks in Parma, Ohio could've fit inside the living room of the apartment she now shared with Gilberto. Not that she was complaining. At least she and Janie had had their own bed back then. When she was a kid, she couldn't wait to get out of her mother's trailer. She just hadn't expected it to happen the way it had, first losing Janie. And then, the creep who'd raped her. She'd had to go in search of a clinic in Columbus where she could get her back-room abortion. Her chest squeezed.

Wanting to change the subject, she pointed at Gilberto, kicking the ball around with the children. Give some Brazilians a ball, and they turned it into soccer. "They're good at that, aren't they?"

"*Filhos*, very, very good."

Children. But that's not what Roz had said.

Carlota's face pinched into sharp lines. "My brother he need *filhos*. You give him many *filhos*?"

Roz stumbled, feeling as if she'd been punched. "We, uh, haven't talked about it."

Carlota's frown deepened. "How you know my brother?"

In other words, was Roz good enough for him? Of course she wasn't. They'd met in a pawnshop in Denver, except she was selling and he was buying. They'd practically come from different planets. Even if she could tell her new sister-in-law about it, she wouldn't. "We met at a party," she said with a shrug.

Carlota's face brightened. She must know that word. "Elvira *e* Olivia," she said. "*O Clube, sábado.*"

Elvira and Olivia were the twin sisters, and something was happening on Saturday. The twins seemed fun, and Roz wouldn't mind getting to know them better. Besides, she could use a little excitement. "Are they having a party?"

"*Mãe* say you go."

That settled it. Roz no longer felt semi-amused by Carlota's stumbling attempts to converse. She wasn't going to agree to go anywhere her mother-in-law commanded, not until she gained better control of Portuguese. She didn't want to depend on Gilberto to translate for her. She couldn't be sure that he wouldn't censor it for her. Until she learned the language, she'd never know.

She shrugged noncommittally. "It depends on Gilberto and his work."

"My brother," Carlota said cautiously, "he work very, very hard."

Roz laughed, but not with enthusiasm. Carlota didn't have to convince her of that. "Look at him play now." She wished she could end this one-sided conversation. She wished Carlota would go away, now that she'd done her duty and relayed Anabela's order to attend the twins' party.

"You make good for my brother. He very, very...how you say? *Triste.*"

Sad. She knew that word, too. But she couldn't let on that she knew, and besides, she didn't think the way his passion filled their bedroom each night meant that he was terribly sad, so she said instead, "He's awfully good to me."

Carlota grinned, lighting up her face, as if she'd understood. "Is awful. No baby."

Roz's heart lurched inside her chest. How did Carlota know? Or, maybe Gilberto was longing for a child of his own, and that's what his sister meant. A baby wasn't part of their deal. But now... Maybe a child would be the answer to everything, to growing a family and settling her nerves. She wondered if a child would help her fit in better here. If that ever happened, then no one from home could find her. A child would complete her change of identity.

Or maybe it was a mistake, asking for another disaster, another broken dream.

# Chapter Nine

February 27, 1959

**Roz listened silently** to Gilberto's reassurances all the way home from the park: he'd had nothing to do with staging that encounter with Carlota. She wanted to believe him, and so she did. Because she'd come out in the open about her lessons with Luis, she felt as if only the truth existed between them anymore. Not the entire truth, but it was more than what she'd ever shared with anyone before. She'd never really come clean before, not even with Janie, and certainly not with her roommate in Denver. She had to admit now that this new sense of trust, although awkward and hesitant, felt kind of good.

Good, but it didn't overcome deeper matters that still troubled her.

"Why doesn't your mother like me?" Roz said as Gilberto parked the fishtail fin car in the underground garage below their apartment building.

"She doesn't know you yet." He locked the car, and they crossed to the stairs into their building.

He hadn't automatically disagreed, which meant he agreed. So it was true. Roz hadn't imagined his mother's dislike of her.

Anabela had clearly been the mastermind behind that scene in the park. And then there was that day Anabela had burst into

89

the apartment unannounced and inspected everything. If that was her mother-in-law's effort to get to know her, then it made Roz wonder. How well did Gilberto know her?

Better than anyone else ever had before.

And somehow, that pleased her. Glowing inside, she couldn't wait to get upstairs and celebrate the remainder of the hours of his night off. Never mind about her mother-in-law. Her husband was on her side.

Before he could insert his key into the front door of their apartment, Silvia, the nosy neighbor with the only telephone in the building, pulled open her door across the hall. "*Oye*," she called, the equivalent of *hey*, to get their attention. There was a phone call for Gilberto.

Roz's spirits dampened as she sulked alone into their apartment and closed the door behind her. She sank down onto the empty couch. The call was surely someone from the station, summoning him to work for an emergency. But when Gilberto returned several minutes later from Silvia's telephone, he announced a surprise for her. Special friends had invited them for dinner, all last minute. She felt a little miffed that he would choose someone else over her private company to pass the evening with, but his enthusiasm for going out was too strong to resist. Besides, their relationship had moved to a new level of trust. She felt ten pounds lighter than she'd ever felt in her life.

That evening, he picked out the green silk for her, because it matched her eyes, and she agreed because she liked the way the skirts swirled when she swung her hips. It matched her lighthearted mood. He reminded her not to forget the stone martin fur stole, now that autumn was cooling the nights.

This was cool?

Cool-*er*, perhaps, than when they'd first arrived in Belo. It *was* cool here, compared to blistering Rio during their brief honeymoon. She checked herself before laughing in his face. She'd wondered why he'd added the fur to her wardrobe, but she couldn't resist its border of tails, and how they...swung.

But now when she slid her dresses aside in the chifferobe where she thought she'd hung the stole, she couldn't find it.

Had she actually unpacked it? The last of the boxes that he'd had shipped from Rio stacked in the empty maid's quarters behind the kitchen. She remembered gasping when she'd seen the stole in the box. She was sure she'd unpacked it, but maybe she'd left it in the box, unsure what to do with it, thinking there'd been some sort of mistake. This was the tropics, after all.

She crossed through the apartment to open the boxes one by one, searching. Gilberto helped, grumbling all the while.

They couldn't find it.

Finally, he shrugged it off, saying it didn't matter. It would turn up, and it wasn't winter yet. Odd, she thought, because she knew that it *did* matter to him. That's why he'd included it in her wardrobe. He went on to explain that they couldn't delay any longer, searching. They were already late, which would be a terrible affront to his friends, who were North American.

She sensed his anxiety, and that only made her hesitation all the stronger. She didn't want to go, but it was one of the things she had to do, if she was ever to fit into her new life here.

His friends lived in a high-rise apartment building across town, where the streets were paved and a doorman had to let them in. Roz was glad the little apartment she shared with Gilberto in Barroca fell far short of this grandeur. She liked being able to come and go anonymously every day, without leaving behind a trail of her movements and a witness, other than nosy Silvia, to record it all.

Helen and Sam Clinton lived on the eighth floor. Sam, who was almost as wide as he was short, held the door open for them. A handle-bar mustache curled across the lower third of his face, and his shoes squeaked as he whisked them inside. Lamplight glowed throughout the spacious living room, highlighting the newly in vogue style of carpeting that spread from one wall to its opposite. It made the room look even larger, but the real blessing, said his wife Helen, who was a head taller than Sam and straight as a stick, was that the carpet muted their voices. Thankfully, the baby was already down for the night.

Aromatic smells wafted out through a kitchen door as Helen disappeared through it. She'd excused herself while Sam mixed cocktails. Rattling ice, he explained that he and Helen were from Virginia, but before Brazil, they'd been in Guatemala. And before that, Honduras. Or maybe Honduras had been before Nicaragua? As he filled martini glasses, Helen returned with a tray of canapés. Sam passed around the glasses, and before Roz could refuse, he lifted his in a toast to the new couple.

Although she remained zealously on guard against too much alcohol, refusing ever to become like her mother, she felt obliged to take just one sip in response to such warm congratulations. Her sip was like swallowing a bolt of lightning, and the liquid fire made her sway on her feet. Her mother had staggered much more than this, most of the time. How on earth had she survived so long? Roz spied an end table where she could casually abandon her glass under one of the lamps.

Helen invited them to sit and relax, leading the way to the

grouping of sleek furniture. The couch felt too stiff for very much comfort.

"Gilberto says you're from Colorado," Sam said, fixing his gaze on Roz over the rim of his glass.

"A lovely place," Helen added from her armchair opposite.

Roz glanced at Gilberto, beside her on the couch. Was that the official story of Rosalinda's origin? What else had he said about her? He shrugged, and so did she. "Um, that's right."

"What were you doing back there?" Sam wouldn't let it alone.

"Oh, Sammy." Helen shook her finger at her husband. "You left the office behind hours ago." Her laughter tinkled, and then she turned to Roz. "He can't help himself. It's what he does—interviews, you know."

Understanding lanced through Roz, stiffening her spine. "Interviews," a polite term for interrogation. Police work. Her husband's job must have brought him together with this friend from Virginia. Sam must be an American cop.

Leaning forward, she felt poised to jump up and run away before he could probe too deeply, but Gilberto shifted closer. He touched her arm with a light caress, a reminder of his presence. His strength. His promises of protection. He stroked her arm, tracing tiny circles with the tips of his fingers, and slowly, the tightness in her core started to evaporate. She couldn't leave, not this time, and certainly not without Gilberto at her side. With a soft sigh, she folded herself into the crook of his arm.

Helen laughed again. "What do you think of Brazil so far? You've only been here...what? A few weeks? We wanted to have you over right away, to welcome you, but this was the soonest we could persuade your husband to bring you."

"Dear," Sam said, "they're newlyweds. Leave them alone."

"I like it here," Roz said. It was a little remote, compared to before, but that was exactly the way she wanted it.

Gilberto winked at Roz. "Too bad it's been so busy at work."

"When isn't it?" Helen said. "Work, work, work. Let someone else do some of it for a change. You and Sam stay far too busy as it is, if you ask me."

"These are interesting times," Sam said. "With the construction of the new capital. Brasilia. Doctor Kubitschek wants to make sure that it gets done before he leaves office at the end of the year."

"Kubitschek?" Roz said. "Isn't that the president? I didn't realize he's also a doctor."

Sam laughed. "He isn't. Just because someone has the title doesn't mean he's a real doctor. Everyone's a doctor here who has a college degree."

"Or runs a scam," Gilberto said.

"See what I mean?" Helen said to Roz. "You'll have a lot to learn here. I just wanted to have this little party and let you know that we're here to help, in case you have any questions."

Roz murmured her thanks.

"Dear," Sam said with a scoff, "aren't you forgetting she has Gilberto for that? He knows this place far better than we do."

Helen flicked her wrist. "I'm talking about the American community, silly. There are only a couple dozen or so of us here in Belo, not counting the missionaries. Nor the Canadians."

"Canadians aren't Americans," Sam said.

Gilberto scoffed. "But of course they are. We all are. They are North Americans, as you are. There are also South Americans. And then there are Brazilians. But all of us together, we are Pan

America."

Roz startled from the passion flowing through Gilberto's silky voice. "There are missionaries here? In a catholic country?"

"Exactly," Sam said with a wink, then took a long swallow of his drink.

"They do tireless work with the poor," Helen said. "And they help with teaching duties in our school."

Sam's gaze never left Roz's face. "You weren't always in Denver, were you? Didn't you do some sort of social work with children that took you to various places? Maybe I misunderstood."

Roz's heart fluttered. What did he know about what she did or didn't do? Or was he only voicing his suspicions? And what about Gilberto? What did this man, her husband, *really* know? When she spoke, it was barely above a whisper. "Yes, I'm sure you did. Misunderstand, that is."

Gilberto took her hand in his and held on tight, almost as if he expected she might jump up and run away, as she'd done before, during Anabela's dinner party. It was as if he sensed the urgency of her desire to flee. "Actually, she worked in retail."

The pawnshop, he meant. So that was their cover story. She'd been there, pawning her ring for cash, when she met Gilberto, a customer. He'd taken quite an interest in the ring. Now she understood that it was probably because of the similar, blue stones his mother liked to wear. Back then in Denver, after that first night in the pawnshop, Roz had told him the ring had belonged to her grandmother.

*A lie.*

She wondered if she should also clear the air about that ring, but it was behind them now. It was too late, and it didn't matter anymore. She'd spied the blue stone, sparkling from a clump of weeds next to a park bench where someone must've dropped it. She'd taped a notice to the bench, listing her roommate's phone number for contact about a lost personal item, being intentionally vague. After two days, the note disappeared, but her roommate never received any call. Two more days, and Linda had headed to the pawnshop. There were bills that couldn't be put off any longer. She'd tried to find the owner, although maybe not hard enough.

"And is that how the two of you met?" Helen said brightly. "While shopping?"

Roz murmured in agreement. "Something like that."

"How interesting." Helen turned to Sam. "Dear, you and I would never have met at all if you'd had to go shopping." Then she turned to Roz. "They don't have stores here, like the wonderful, brand-new malls we have back home, but you must come shopping with me one day soon. I'll show you where to go. We have to rely on the local shops, because the nearest PX is in Rio, but even if it were nearer, it's basically worthless. Although, that doesn't really matter, because you can find almost anything you want here. We don't have all the comforts of home, of course, but—"

"Dear," Sam said, interrupting Helen's monologue, "she doesn't have PX privileges."

Helen's lower lip puffed out in an exaggerated pout. "I suppose she could send her maid out for things she might not otherwise know where to find."

"We don't have a maid," Gilberto said.

Sam waggled his eyebrows and laughed. "The lovebirds would lose too much privacy."

Helen's face flushed as she sipped her drink. Roz slipped her hand out from under Gilberto's and nibbled one of the canapés, a triangular shaped pastry tasting overwhelmingly of salty fish.

Helen set her drink down and giggled. "I believe you might be able to get someone daily who actually doesn't *want* to live in. I'll ask at the next Women's Club get-together. You must come, too, of course. Maybe one of the ladies will know someone for you. If I were you, I would worry about living out there where you are, on the edge of town. It's also at the edge of a gully, you know, where there's a..." She lowered her voice and lifted her brows. "*Favela.*"

"*Favela?*"

Helen patted her chest. "It's a squatter's camp, where people live in cardboard boxes tucked into the side of those gullies."

Roz glanced at her husband. "And the police allows this to happen?"

He shrugged. "The rains wash them away, but they keep coming back."

Roz tried to digest this. At least her mother's trailer hadn't washed away. She turned back to Helen. "And what does having a maid have to do with this *favela?*"

"It doesn't," Sam said with a laugh. "Don't pay any attention to my wife."

"Now, dear," Helen said. "Of course it's very important, especially for a newcomer. A maid who knows her way around can tell her things not to do, things that would get her in trouble if she didn't know not to do them."

Roz's attention pricked. "Like what things?"

"Oh, for instance, you never want to approach a house that

displays burning candles in the window."

"Why not?"

"Just don't. Trust me."

Roz wasn't inclined to trust anyone other than Gilberto, and that was only partially. She turned to him now. "What do you know about this?"

He turned away, visibly flinching from her gaze, as if it had pierced him. "She's right. You shouldn't go to those neighborhoods."

He might as well have doused a fire with oil. As soon as she could, she would ask Luis, her Portuguese teacher, where she could find a house with burning candles in the window. She turned back to Helen. "What's it mean?"

Helen caught her husband's glance, and she rose from her armchair. "I'd better go check on dinner. See how Marta's coming along with it. She doesn't always follow my instructions."

"Perhaps I can help," Roz said, jumping up from the couch and following Helen around a corner and into the steamy kitchen. She didn't know much about cooking, but she wasn't done yet with her questions. She wanted an answer.

A young woman with coffee-colored skin stood before a stove, one hand planted on her wide hips as she stirred a skillet of frying onions, bits of tomato, and rice. Helen spoke haltingly in Portuguese and lifted the lid of a pot on the stove while Marta nodded.

Helen turned to Roz with a happy smile. "We're almost ready." She darted across to a counter where a platter of puffballs sat. "Would you take the *pão de queijo* out to the table? Marta wanted to make them for you. Hers are the best ones you'll ever taste anywhere."

Cheese bread. Roz already knew about the little rolls, thanks to Luis and their afternoon lessons in coffee shops. "Sure," she said, "but first I want to know what you meant back there about burning candles in windows?"

Helen patted her chest and laughed. "Oh dear, Sam is right. Don't listen to me."

"But you seem to think it matters."

Helen lowered her voice and turned her back on Marta. "I'm sure I've exaggerated. We just don't understand, that's all, about some of their beliefs. We don't have anything like it in the States."

"Like what?"

"Well, maybe we do in some areas. It's sort of like voodoo."

"Voodoo?"

"They can make bad things happen to people they don't like. But don't worry, they're just superstitions. It's all so very different from our ways." Helen frowned and bit her lower lip as she lifted the platter and thrust it into Roz's arms. "Whatever you do, don't get mixed up with any of those cults. It could be dangerous."

Roz held her breath. "What kind of bad things?"

"If you had your own maid, she could tell you. Not all of the cults are alike, and she'd know the difference. You wouldn't need to worry about it."

Roz wasn't worried. She felt an electric interest spark through her.

# Chapter Ten

March 5, 1959

**For a city, Belo Horizonte** was young, having been founded only three years before the birth of Gilberto's mother. He'd always thought of both of them as timeless. They were his rock. But sitting now in the surveillance vehicle with Ubaldo, he realized he was wrong about that sense of permanence. From their vantagepoint on a hilltop overlooking the central plateau, the city almost looked alive, the way it sprawled in the distance, spreading and changing as it crept ever closer to the ring of treasure-bearing hills that surrounded Belo.

And threatened the da Costa family's livelihood.

Gilberto's attention drifted back to the threat that was closer at hand—the blocky, pink stucco house. The muddy road leading up here into these foothills at the edge of mining property wasn't much wider than a cow path. The house, huddled atop one of the ridges, was a house of cultists. Gilberto knew this because of the burned-down stub of a candle that displayed on the windowsill.

He felt both sick to his stomach and tantalized by the promise of justice. He scrunched low, creaking the vinyl passenger seat of the unmarked Jeep. His partner, the driver, had parked about twenty meters away from the house, wedging the Jeep between a broken-down samba truck and an ox cart, idle and unhitched. Chickens squawked as they roamed freely around the tires, in and out from under the vehicles. The Jeep and its occasional bursts of static from the radio made a conspicuous addition to the otherwise openness of this terrain.

Scrub brush surrounded the house, which sat mostly alone on this cow path road. Farther along, three more blocky houses squatted amongst the bushes, all on the side of the track that overlooked the city.

Not too far from here, downhill in the bushes below, the body of Gilberto's first wife had been found.

Resisting those ugly memories, he focused on the square chunkiness of the pink house. Its size made it look as if it contained no more than a couple of modest rooms, but the laundry that spread out across the bushes of the vacant land to either side of the house suggested many occupants—all women.

His pulse raced. He felt more certain than ever that this house was the connection to the butcher of pregnant women. The street kid nicknamed Picapau had finally slipped up today. He must not have noticed the cops on his tail because he'd led them here, all the way from the *favela*. Gilberto didn't think it was a coincidence, which made him wonder if the woman they'd found dead from a botched abortion during *Carnaval* had been one of the women whose underwear now dried in the bushes.

His gut told him she'd lived here. And it looked as if there were several more women who frequented this house. God willing, they wouldn't also become targets of death. But where were they?

All appeared quiet. No one, not even children ventured outside. Perhaps the women were hiding inside. At least Picapau was in there. Gilberto knew, because he'd watched the kid disappear through the wooden door next to the window. He could be up to no good in the company of the women who must occupy this house.

Gilberto had first spotted the kid last winter, bent over the gruesome task of killing a large bird. Maybe a vulture. But he'd slipped away then, before Gilberto could intervene with his questions.

A dead vulture had been left on his doorstep the day his first wife had disappeared.

They were different incidents with dead birds, but the act of sacrifice was the same. It suggested that a cult might have been responsible. Gilberto had been looking for the kid ever since.

He'd almost found him, only last December, when the kid had been caught with stolen jewelry. But since that was his first offense—at least what the police knew about—and since the jails were overly crowded, his colleagues had let the kid go. At least they'd learned his name—Picapau—and had thought to take a photo, which was clear enough for Gilberto to recognize him. The kid's premature release was an example of the incompetence they constantly worked against, Ubaldo had said, but never mind. They would catch him again.

Today could be that day.

"We have wasted enough time here," said Ubaldo from behind the sunglasses he liked to wear while on surveillance. He struck a match, bringing to life the tip of his cigarillo. It glowed like a thing alive, a pulsing heart, a beacon to alert the hiding occupants of the pink house that the *Policía Civil* was onto them. Ubaldo smoked openly, as if flaunting his presence, as if teasing the criminals, calling to them, *See me on your ass? I'm coming for you, but not until I'm good and ready.*

Ubaldo made the game of hunt and chase harder than necessary to get the job done. Ubaldo, the hunter, reveled in the hunt.

Was that what it meant to be a cop?

Gilberto hated the hunt. He just wanted to get the job done. "It's only a waste if he sees us watching him," Gilberto said, "and runs away from us again, before we can learn anything from him."

"So what? This kid is just a petty thief."

"He's going to lead us to the *Carnaval* butcher. Maybe he already has."

Ubaldo snorted. "Instead of chasing Picapau, we should be looking for the kidnappers who arranged the sale of the Gonzaga kid up north. Or better yet, we should go arrest some rabble-rouser who spouts bullshit against Kubitschek. Then we'd have someone to practice on, using your friend's interview techniques. That way, the captain will forget about any other failures."

"Don't be so sure of yourself."

"Why are you so sure? Is it because of the *gringa?*"

"Her name is Roz." It was true that she was foreign, and consequently unfathomable at times, but that had nothing to do with Gilberto's discomfort now.

"You going to let a woman tell you what to do, man?"

"When you get married, you will have to think of someone else besides yourself for a change."

Ubaldo laughed. "You were supposed to bring back the Gonzaga kid from Denver, and instead you brought home a wife. Now you're an expert on women, because you're on your second wife already."

Gilberto balled his fist. He considered a range of retorts, or maybe he should just punch this asshole. Nobody—not even the fine Ubaldo—could speak lightly of that dead subject about his first wife.

In the end, he let it pass. He sighed, guessing that Ubaldo must feel as frustrated as he was. They'd made no progress on that kidnapping case. And that wasn't all. Maybe he *should've* listened to his mother, as his partner thought he always did. He didn't. Maybe he should've taken over the family gemstone mine after Papi died, instead of becoming a cop.

But the war had swayed Gilberto off the family business career track. Brazil had welcomed a flood of immigrants after the war, and among them were Nazis—the very enemy who had killed Papi. Gilberto had joined the police force to keep such evil villains from ever regrouping. He wanted to make certain the criminals stayed out of business forever. To clean up the filth of the world.

Filth had taken his first wife. And his missing son.

Gilberto's presence on the force hadn't made any difference yet. But all that would change soon. "Let's go get him and bring him in to the station."

Ubaldo chuckled, spurting puffs of smoke into the stuffy air of the Jeep. "On what charge?"

"Murder."

"He's a thief. He didn't cut her open."

"You don't know that."

"Hell," Ubaldo said, "we don't even know if he knew the girl."

Picapau *did* know her, Gilberto was sure about that. Furthermore, the kid had met the girl *here*. And there'd been others, too. His first wife, he was certain.

Gilberto had been gathering documents over the course of his investigation about the cult—photographs, mostly, and some filed reports. He'd locked them all away in his desk drawer back at the station. He'd had to lock them away because of his colleagues' fears about investigating illegal cults. Black magic could kill an enemy, and no one would be the wiser.

Gilberto knew by now that the cult was drawing young, impressionable women from small surrounding towns here to the city. And he would bet that this house of the cult was the specific place in the city where they were coming. He didn't think his first wife had come here willingly, but he couldn't be equally certain that Roz never would, especially considering her unrelenting interest in Helen's unfortunate slip of the tongue last week.

Lucky for Roz, he didn't think she could ever find her way here on her own. For one thing, this was the opposite side of town from their apartment. And for another, the buses didn't run this far out, since the dirt roads became impassable with ruts from rainy season. It had been hard enough for Gilberto and his partner today. He'd followed the street kid here on foot between passing rain showers, and then he'd called Ubaldo on the walkie talkie with directions. Two sinuous tire tracks had allowed the Jeep to crawl carefully up the slick hill.

But Gilberto did worry that Roz would find someone who would bring her to forbidden places such as this one. He'd known that she was going out for language lessons, even before she admitted it that day in the park. Dona Silvia, the neighbor with the telephone in their apartment building, volunteered the information, and more. But he didn't understand why Roz remained vague about the rest of her daily adventures. He couldn't help but wonder what else she kept secret. He knew so little about her, other than the fact that she was his destiny.

Somehow, she'd acquired his first wife's aquamarine ring.

He didn't know how the ring had ended up in Denver, but he *would* find out. Meanwhile, he'd never expected to fall under Roz's spell during his initial inquiries into that matter. Her magic kept him blind to everything else about her besides the fire she ignited in him, just at the titillating sound of her husky voice. Away from the source of the spell, he felt as if tiny holes riddled his heart, and those holes filled with countless questions and—

"Are you sure Picapau didn't slip out the back?" Ubaldo said, interrupting Gilberto's wandering attention.

Gilberto fidgeted in his bucket seat. No, actually he didn't know that. With the brushy vegetation surrounding the pink house, and the back side invisible from this angle... It could be possible that he'd missed the kid. "If he's gone, the dona of the house will know where he hides."

Ubaldo snorted. "She won't tell you. She's probably just the kid's mother, and he's brought her some money that he stole. She won't turn him in to us."

"This has to be the place we've been looking for. Look at their laundry."

"Laundry will never convince a judge," Ubaldo said with a laugh.

"When we take him in, at least one more delinquent will be off the street."

"And the cutter goes free."

"The dona will tell us who he is. She would know to send

the girls there if they needed his services. We'll make her talk."

"Go talk to her, then."

"Okay." Gilberto climbed out of the Jeep, shut the door softly, and waited. When his partner didn't follow, he leaned through his open window. "You coming?"

Ubaldo straightened over the wheel. "I'll wait here. In case dispatch calls."

Gilberto hesitated only a minute. Surely the fine Ubaldo had no fear of a house of the cult? Then he turned away, hurrying past the samba truck. Whoever owned the truck would already be saving their cruzeiros for costumes for next year's *Carnaval*. The snuffed out candle in the window didn't necessarily indicate that the dona of the pink house was involved with any of those preparations—although the truck's presence suggested there could be a connection. A favor, perhaps. Instead, the candle signaled that this was a house where cult believers who'd been wronged for whatever reason could feel welcome. In this house they could ask the medium to speak to the spirits who would set their wrongs right, by whatever means available. Sometimes that meant a sacrifice.

Gilberto called it murder.

A low hum of voices wavered from inside the pink house and floated out the open window where the burned down candle sat, stuck to its sill. He paused in front of the door with his fist poised in midair and tried to listen to the words, catching only a bit about lost love. His heart twisted with memory, and he pushed those unwanted memories aside with new visions of Roz. He'd been ready to fall hard under her spell, ready to replace the bad memories with good, new ones. His knuckles lowered against the splinters of the warped door, and as he knocked, the voices inside broke off. He waited, heard nothing, and knocked again.

Wood creaked with rushing movement. Bumping thuds sounded from the square interior of the house.

"Who is it?" finally a woman's voice said from behind the closed door.

Gilberto turned, looking back at the Jeep where Ubaldo's cigarillo glowed over the top of the steering wheel. He turned back to the closed door and said, "a friend, that's all. I'm looking for...a lost friend."

The door creaked open, no wider than the narrow width of a young woman's face. She had wide, round eyes that peered up at him. The chocolate color of her skin almost made her disappear, blending into the shadows.

"I believe she came here," Gilberto said, looking past her shoulder into the shadows of a bare room. A rectangle of light outlined a door to the back room.

"There is no one else here with me," the girl said, and then instantly bit her puffy, lower lip. "I mean...no lost girl, that is."

She looked as innocent as a baby bird, clearly not the lady in charge of a house, let alone this house of the cult. Budding into womanhood, she appeared to be around fifteen or sixteen, scarcely older than his niece, Carlota's daughter. A shudder rolled through him at the thought of his niece caught in a house like this, working, doing who knew what in exchange for the privilege of an audience with the medium to spirits.

"Perhaps I could speak to the dona?" Gilberto said. The lady of the house was not necessarily the medium, but she would know how to contact the one connected to this candle.

"Dona Mariana cannot be disturbed at the moment." The girl lifted her voice and called over her shoulder. "The *dom* will tell you, if you don't believe me. Edgar!"

Gilberto had overheard the girl talking to someone, to Picapau, the street kid, he suspected, because the kid was in there. Gilberto had seen him with his own eyes. Either someone else was here, too, or Edgar was Picapau's real name.

No one stirred from the light of the back room, or wherever he was hiding. Ubaldo's guess had probably been correct, and the kid had ducked out the back. "So, Edgar is the man of this house?"

The woman-child spoke in a small, breathless voice that hinted at her anxiety. "You'll have to come back later."

Later would be too late. Gilberto glanced at his wristwatch, making sure that the girl noticed its gold trim. He reached into his trouser pocket for the folded cruzeiros he kept there, handy for buying whatever information he sought. "It's very important. What's your name?"

The young woman's breath caught as she eyed the money, but avoided his questions. "No one speaks to the dona before it is time. When it's time, she will light the candle. That way, you'll know."

He didn't want to frighten this girl by pointing out the dangers of cult fanaticism, especially for innocent, impressionable young women such as herself. He needed information now, before another woman died. Another death wouldn't happen if Gilberto had anything to do with the matter.

"Maybe you could help me?" he said. "My friend is a young woman about your age and height, with long dark hair in a braid. She's a lot like you, I think."

He feared.

Her gaze flitted from the folded bills in his hand to something in the room behind her, someone or something outside his range of vision. He took that opportunity to edge forward, carefully jamming one foot across the threshold.

"Please, *senhor*," she said with a cry as she turned back to him, leaning heavily against the door standing half-open between them. "I don't want trouble."

He dug into his shirt pocket for the *figa* and dangled the necklace of the miniature fist before her. "She was wearing this when she disappeared."

The girl in the door gasped and took a step backwards. "My friend wore one just like that!"

"What's your friend's name?"

But the girl said nothing as she fixed her gaze on the necklace.

"Perhaps her name is Fatima?"

She looked up and sputtered. "How...how did you know?"

He shrugged, not confessing that he'd guessed. A missing person's report had come in to the station about a seventeen-year-old girl named Fatima Souza from Sete Lagoas, a small town not too far away, where girls let their hair grow into unfashionably long braids, according to his brother-in-law. He was betting the reason Fatima was missing was because she'd become the unidentified victim from *Carnaval*. The missing girl's uncle was on his way now to the morgue to view the body. Soon, they could finally have an identification. In the meanwhile, Gilberto had to rely on his gut.

"Do you know where Fatima is?" he asked.

"No, *senhor*, I haven't seen her for several weeks." She grasped at the collar of her blouse, as if searching for a *figa* of her own that wasn't there.

"Where did she go?" He thrust a worn, soft bill into her hand, folding her fingers around it and lowered his voice to a level that couldn't be heard, in case someone listened from the shadows. He didn't think Picapau or anyone else was there anymore. No one had answered this girl's calls to Edgar.

"I don't know!" Her head bobbed, a cross between a shake and a nod. She clutched the money tightly and sobbed, pushing against the door. It wouldn't close with his foot in the way.

"You are Fatima's friend," he said. "She was from Sete Lagoas, and so are you, yes?" Actually, he didn't know that. He was making it up, but he thought it a reasonable guess.

"Was?" the girl in the door said, bursting into tears.

"I'm sorry." He waited while she trembled with cries.

"You have her *figa*," she said with a shriek. "Something happened to her! Tell me what it is."

"I'm sorry," he said again. "The *figa* did not bring her good luck, as it should have."

"But how did you get her *figa*? And who are you? You said you're her friend."

"I am. You can trust me."

She shouldn't, though. He was a stranger to her, but if he showed her his badge, it would only make her more wary. The police had an unfortunate reputation for corruption, which was part of the filth Gilberto wanted to clean up. She really could trust him, but of course she wouldn't know that she could, even if she knew who he was. Especially if she knew.

"You didn't tell me your name," he said, sliding another bill to the tips of his fingers.

"Irmã."

He waited for her to give him her last name, but her jaw

clamped shut as she snatched the money away.

"What would you say, Irmã, if I knew of a place where you could earn more of that each day, just for yourself, for cleaning house and cooking for a *gringa*, and nothing more? Nothing expected of you in exchange?"

Irmã gave a weak laugh. "There are no jobs like that, not for someone like me, a girl with no skills, not here, not anywhere."

A distant noise squawked from behind Gilberto, sounding like the radio in the Jeep, but he ignored the probable summons from dispatch. "It would be better for you away from here."

"You don't know what is better for me."

"I could take you to your new job right now, if you like."

She hesitated, the whites of her eyes shining in the dim light. "For a *gringa*, you said?"

He nodded as unease rolled through him, anticipating the blow-up with Roz. But that was better than letting this girl fall under the influence of Picapau and later finding her body, bloodied in an alley. For all he knew, she could already be pregnant.

Besides, Irmã could be useful to him if only he could gain her trust.

"Wait for me," Irmã whispered, "while I get my things." She shoved the door harder against his foot, sending a sharp pain snapping through his ankle, a small set-back compared to his sense of victory.

The Jeep's door squeaked just then, and he turned to see Ubaldo waving at him to come. He looked anxious, as if he needed to take a piss fast, and Gilberto responded only with a hand gesture to wait another moment. Shaking his head, Ubaldo flung his cigarette stub to the ground and strode across the distance between them. His partner could move fast when he wanted to, and seeing his urgency now filled Gilberto with dread.

"Let's go," Ubaldo said. "There's been another one."

# Chapter Eleven

March 5, 1959

**Throughout the** twenty-six years of Roz's short life, she had always been drawn to the forbidden, like the moth to a flame—the flame of a burning candle. During the week since the Clintons' dinner party, she'd dodged Helen's shopping invitations, using the excuse of a migraine. It was true, but even if it weren't, she'd have come up with another reason. She stayed far too busy for casual shopping, since three times per week she had to take the bus downtown for her language lessons with Luis. During the other days, when Gilberto was away at work, she explored her own neighborhood, Barroca.

But she never found a house with a burning candle. And Luis wouldn't tell her what it meant.

There was plenty to learn in her own neighborhood, even if she couldn't find a burning candle. Barroca was a hilly area, being on the outskirts of the city, although not so far away that it merged into the larger hills. Out there was where the family estate lodged behind walls, under protection of armed guards. Gilberto had explained to her about the need for security in these dangerous times. Poverty drove the danger, and a wealthy estate such as the family's was always a target for thieves. While thieves roamed the streets anywhere and considered widely spaced bars on windows as an invitation to squeeze through and help themselves to anything that might provide for their families, she was not to worry in Barroca. It was a safe neighborhood, although she couldn't help but wonder if a thief had scaled the bars outside and slipped in through a window to steal the stone martin stole. It hadn't turned up anywhere.

But Gilberto still insisted that the neighborhood was safe, as long as she stayed on public streets and didn't stray into the *favela* or any vacant stretches of land. And especially, he reminded her, the nights he was away on duty, she needed to stay inside.

Roz suspected that at night was when she was more likely to find the burning candles, but at least for now, she would respect his wishes. By day, she prowled the streets of Barroca, up one hill and down to the other side, along cobbled streets and dirt roads, past ugly concrete apartment buildings like hers and newer homes of stucco walls, tile roofs, glass sliding doors, and decorative stones, like the ones across the street from her building. Giant, flaming poinsettias spilled over the walls surrounding those houses. They were larger and more modern than any of the houses she'd ever known in Ohio, including the ranches and split levels of boomtown that had sprung up after the war.

But it wasn't just the style of houses that made the streets look different here. In Barroca, vultures ruled the sky. The monster birds soared everywhere. They didn't discriminate, as they circled silently over fancier houses as well as the more modest homes in blocky apartment buildings or one-room houses. No matter where she walked, whether around her neighborhood or to the street where she could flag the bus to stop, vultures circled overhead. They were patrolling their feeding grounds, which she supposed must be quite rich.

She couldn't remember ever seeing more than one or two vultures in Ohio, and so the novelty of their existence here always pulled her attention upward to the sky.

As it did today. She'd left the apartment shortly after the young woman who was her new neighbor across the hall had gone out, carrying a briefcase. Roz felt glad that she wasn't tied to a job, that she had the freedom to explore, without having any particular destination in mind. She watched the vultures' sweeping trails, as usual, except this time a sensation of vertigo overcame her. Goosebumps crawled along the back of her neck, and her knees went weak. It was the same feeling as what she'd experienced in Denver, when that oily-faced man had stalked her before breaking in to her apartment.

Was someone following her now?

But that stalker was dead, and his body disposed. Only Gilberto knew where. They wouldn't speak of it again.

Catching herself before she fell, she leaned against the nearest wall, which enclosed one of the nicer houses, a creamy two-story, one street over from her apartment building. She glanced over her shoulder. There was no one there. Paranoia had trained her body never to forget, starting early back in Ohio when her mother's boyfriend had tormented her. All these years later, paranoia still controlled her, even here. That's what was happening now, she told herself. No matter how hard she tried to adapt, she couldn't shake free of the ghostly feel of fingers round her throat.

No one followed her anymore, she reminded herself. She'd changed her identity.

Still, her breath came in short gasps, and she felt dizzy. It had happened before, and it could happen again.

She couldn't stay this way, clinging to the cream-colored wall, but she couldn't lead a possible stalker to her apartment, either. Pushing away from the stucco, she hurried her step, trying not to trip over her stumbling movement.

Randomly, she followed the direction of the soaring vultures and headed downhill. At the bottom of the hill was a large, vacant area, only a couple of blocks from her apartment building and one hillside away from one of the *favelas* of town. It was a dead area, carved with gullies and covered with scrubby patches of weeds, and it smelled of dead animal and orange peels that had been left in the sun too long. It was one of the places she'd promised Gilberto that she wouldn't explore.

She stood there at the edge, looking in, feeling as if someone watched her.

Larger than just a vacant lot, it was a blank area that the city skirted around, including the *favela*. A ravine slashed a gap through the middle. Not even the shantytown spread here, as if there was something poisonous about this place. Large pieces of cardboard tossed among the weeds, flattened as discarded boxes. She couldn't imagine living in a box, as Helen had said some people did. She didn't see anyone near the cardboard, but what if someone *did* live here? Did the vultures fight them for food? They roosted here in massive gaggles...or whatever it was that they clustered together in. They watched her now through the extra folds around their eyes, eyeing her as a potential food source. At any moment they would flap their great wings, lift up into the air, and swoop down on her, devouring her for lunch.

It was more about the vultures, and less about her promise

to Gilberto, that made her turn away from the vacant, dead area of the ravine.

She wondered if it was the vultures that had made her feel as if she was being watched. She wanted to believe that, but she didn't rule out the possibility that it was someone real. She couldn't risk returning home yet, showing a stalker where she lived. Or did he already know? The tickling sensation of ghost fingers on the back of her neck wouldn't go away.

She wandered the long way around to where she could catch the bus. Along the way, she only saw a child, a young boy of eight or nine and little more than skin and bones. He wore no shoes, and he skittered along a parallel course as if also heading for the street where the bus ran. Once there, he dawdled nearby but avoided her gaze.

She pulled out her wallet and offered him bus money. His entire face, thin as it was, beamed with a smile as he bowed his head and mumbled a prayer of thanks while taking the money. But when the bus showed up, he didn't get on with her. All the way downtown, Roz kept thinking of the boy. She should've given him more money, so that he could buy shoes. Would he, though?

She switched to the electric bus to the center of downtown, where she ducked in and out of stores. And finally, while worrying about the boy, she realized that she'd lost the tickling sensation of someone watching her. Whoever had been following her was gone now, she felt certain. She was also sure that she hadn't imagined it. Determined not to let anyone hold her prisoner in her new home, she caught a cab home. She was a da Costa, after all.

She only hoped that her goosebumps hadn't been brought

on by the thing she feared the most—that someone loyal to the crime boss father of the dead man back in Denver had found her.

# Chapter Twelve

March 5, 1959

**Belo Horizonte was** growing faster than Gilberto could learn all of its new streets, but his partner knew them. Ubaldo's jaw twitched all the way across town, to one of those new streets. The address where dispatch had sent them was near the industrial sector.

Gilberto didn't like the situation any better than his partner, but he'd already offered the girl, Irmã, a lift to her new job. Bringing her along on their way to this assignment was better than dropping her off at the station first, telling her to wait there for him. His colleagues wouldn't have been able to hold Irmã. She would've told them lies and then she'd have disappeared, and Gilberto would've lost his opportunity to draw the information he needed out of her. He preferred to do it his own way, biding his time.

The house at the address was small, subdivided into one-room apartments. Ubaldo told Irmã to wait for them in the backseat of the Jeep as he parked behind two other police vehicles. Gilberto suspected that his caution was all for nothing, and she would be gone by the time they handled their business. Neither of them told her what the business was, but they didn't have to, considering the police presence and gathering crowd of curious onlookers.

Gilberto climbed out of the Jeep with a weary sigh, following his partner. He was already thinking ahead, to when he would have to look for Irmã, as well as Picapau the street kid, who might also be known as dom Edgar. All this, while searching for Fatima's killer. Gilberto always seemed to cycle back to the beginning, but that was his life as a detective.

And now there was a new victim.

The woman who'd reported the body was waiting for them. Short, plump, and middle-aged, she wore no makeup, and her clothes sagged. She frowned and bit her fingernails as she explained that one of the victim's children had cried for help, forcing her to go by bus to the police station, and then return with the first pair of responding officers. Ubaldo nodded at her story, and then swept past her, leaving Gilberto to deal with her.

A ripple of irritation tightened his muscles as his partner joined the buzz of activity that already invaded the little cube of a house. They'd arrived late. He glanced over his shoulder at the Jeep, where Irmã watched through the window with an anxious frown.

Pulling a notepad from his pocket, Gilberto turned back to the woman. "Your name?"

"Joana Morango."

He jotted down the name and then watched Ubaldo, who was just visible through the front door, talking to the police officer inside the house. His partner would be getting the details of the victim's death.

Gilberto stayed with Joana Morango. "Do you know the victim, *Senhora*?"

"Not very well," Joana said, spitting a fingernail from her

teeth. "She was a young mother who moved in here with her kids a few months ago. She took the room across the hall from me."

"And her name?"

"Angela. I never knew her last name. But that's what she was, for sure, an angel flying home. There was never a more faithful daughter of God. She never missed Mass or confession."

"You liked her?"

"She was gone most of the time, working, but when I saw her, she was always nice."

"You know where she worked?"

"One of the pubs downtown. I'm not sure which one, but I remember that she changed jobs several times, so maybe more than one place? She worked mostly at night, and when she was gone, I could always hear her kids fighting and crying."

"She left the children alone?"

"The oldest one is eight or nine, and she looks after the rest. Besides, they were supposed to come to me if there was a serious problem. I said that was okay, since I felt sorry for Angela. I know how hard it is to make ends meet."

"And they came to you today?"

"They were huddled in the hall, crying, when I came home from work. It took a while to calm them down enough to find out what was wrong, but they finally told me. When they'd come home from school, at first they thought their mother was asleep in bed. But then she didn't wake up, and they noticed blood dripping out from under the sheets."

Gilberto winced as his pencil poised over his notepad. He didn't know yet how the woman had died, but dispatch had called it suspicious. "Could they see any wounds on the body, where the blood was coming from?"

"No, thank God. The sheet covered her. But I can guess—"

"Before you guess, you must tell me if you, or the children, saw anyone else around. Anyone coming or going from this place?" He scanned the people gathering in the street, curious, no doubt about the police presence, but perhaps one of them had been responsible for murder.

Joana shook her head. "I was at work. I saw no one. Only the children."

"And did they tell you if they saw an intruder? Or anything else suspicious that might've contributed to their mother's death? Maybe something lying around that was used as a weapon?"

Tears slid down Joana's cheeks. "There was no intruder, and there is no weapon. It is all a terrible mistake. Angela only meant to stop being pregnant."

"Ah." It was as he'd feared from the first mention of bloody sheets. Another botched abortion.

"She already had enough children, poor things." Joana sniffled.

Gilberto felt as if a ball of lead had lodged in his gut. "Where are the children now?"

"They went with me to the police station, and someone was supposed to come get them, a friend, I think."

"Did Angela have many friends?"

"She had one girlfriend that I saw a few times." Joana curled her fingers and touched their tips to the side of her neck. "She had a goiter."

That narrowed it down, Gilberto thought with a sarcastic scoff. "Anything else? Do you know the girlfriend's name?"

Joana shook her head. "I'm sorry. But I think she's from a

small town, not from here. She always wore skirts that were a little too long, and she's young, probably in her twenties."

Gilberto frowned. "What about the boyfriend?"

Joana spit another nail onto the ground. "There wasn't one."

"Someone made her pregnant."

"Not a real boyfriend. No one ever came around to help with anything. Poor little children didn't even have enough beans and rice. I had to feed them some days. What else could Angela have done? How could she possibly have provided for another child?"

"I don't know, *Senhora*," Gilberto said, gazing at the bystanders, wondering if the boyfriend was out there now, watching. "But there *was* someone. Did she ever mention someone she'd met?"

Joana shrugged. "She met plenty of men where she worked. She said nothing about anyone in particular. Why should she? She was too young."

"Did she ever come to you for advice? Maybe she asked you where she could go for help?"

Her eyes opened wide, two saucers of fear. "She would've been arrested."

"Not if she'd gone somewhere quiet that the police don't know about."

"*You* are police."

"It is my job to find the person who did this to her, and I won't stop until he's off the streets. Will you help me?"

Joana swallowed long and hard. "You could ask at the markets where they sell herbs and poisons."

He nodded. He'd already been to the *feira*, but he hadn't found a vendor yet with useful information that would lead him to the abortionist. "Thank you, *Senhora*, for all your help. We may have to contact you again later, but you are free to go now."

He waited until Joana drifted away toward the crowd milling at the side of the street before he returned to the Jeep. Irmã still sat in the backseat, her gaze fixed on the spot where Joana had merged into the group. He muttered a prayer of thanks under his breath that Irmã was still with him.

"Are you okay?" he asked. "It will only be a few more minutes."

"What's going on?" she asked, her eyes round.

"I'm sorry to have to tell you, but there's been an unfortunate accident."

"Is this where the *gringa* I am to work for lives?" Her voice rose with a waver of anxiety, and her hand fumbled for the Jeep's doorknob.

"No, not here. We will go there next, in just a few more minutes." He rested his hand on the door of the Jeep, as if he could prevent her from fleeing.

"But why did we stop here?"

He looked away for inspiration but found none in the gray sky. Clouds were building for the next downpour. He'd wanted to give Irmã plenty of time to adjust to her new, safe conditions, working in his home, before revealing exactly who he was. He'd wanted to prove to the girl that he was a good cop, and yes, good cops did exist. Because it would be necessary to gain her trust before he ever attempted to question her further.

"You see," he said with a weak smile, "my partner and I are detectives. With the police."

She leaned away from the open window, fading deeper into the interior of the Jeep, and clutched the collar of her blouse.

She remained silent.

"My wife is North American," he said, "and you will be working for her, not for me. I am away from home most of the time, because my job is to catch bad guys."

He had no other choice but to tell her now, sooner than he'd planned. He would never force her to stay against her will.

"Only a few more minutes, I promise." He pulled open the front door and reached for the camera bag on the floor. "I have to take a few photos, and then I'll be right back."

He only hoped she would still be here when he returned.

* * * * *

As soon as the taxi pulled up at the base of the hill, as near to her orange apartment building in Barroca as the ruts would allow, Roz knew something was wrong. A Jeep parked on the hillside road, angled astride a rut next to the front door of the building. Roz had to step carefully through the mud, walking around the Jeep to reach the door to her building. She felt the piercing gaze of the Jeep's driver watching her, even though his face hid behind sunglasses.

Sunglasses in the rain?

She yanked open the door to the building, wiped the mud from her shoes, and ran up the flight of stairs. Her slapping footsteps echoed back at her, off the cement walls. When she reached the landing and paused to fish in her bag for her key, her neighbor's door squeaked behind her. Silvia said something Roz didn't understand. Before Roz could jiggle her key into the lock, her apartment door opened on its own. Roz jerked back.

Gilberto stood there in the doorway, grinning at her.

Relief flooded through her. "What are you doing home this time of day?" She tried to push her way past him, but he blocked her entrance.

"I have a surprise for you."

In her experience, surprises weren't always a good thing. The way he shielded his surprise from her now made her shrink back another step.

He grabbed her by the wrist and pulled her into the living room. Someone else stood there, a young woman, hugging herself. "Come in and meet your new maid."

Roz twisted out of his grip. "What do you mean? We didn't agree to this. Was this Helen's idea?"

He pushed the door shut behind her, cutting off anything else that Silvia might learn from their exchange. "It was a good idea, though, don't you think?"

Roz folded her arms across her chest, refusing to answer him. How dare he bring a stranger into their midst? How could Roz hide, living her lie, if someone watched her day and night? Perhaps this woman wasn't a stranger to Gilberto. If Roz tried to ask for simple information, her questions would come out as a demand, and then that ugly side of herself that she didn't much like would emerge. She couldn't create such a scene in front of this person who seemed mysteriously important to Gilberto. *Just look at her.* She was a tiny thing, a very young woman who was scarcely more than a child, no older than a teenager. Sixteen at the most.

"Don't worry," Gilberto said, as if reading her. "You can say what you think. She doesn't speak English."

If that was true—and why not? Gilberto had no reason to lie to her—did he?—then this childlike woman wouldn't be a very effective spy.

"You'll like her," he said. "Her name is Irmã." The way he pronounced her name was impossible to repeat. The sound seemed to disappear somewhere into his nose.

"Irmaong?" Roz said, trying to imitate the sound.

The girl looked up, blinking with round eyes, dark as night. They were like windows into a fear even greater than what had been driving Roz's flight. The panic on Irmã's breathless face made her look even more like a child, as if she could burst into tears at any moment.

Roz gasped. Her shoulder bag slipped, dropping with a thunk to the floor.

This girl's frightened look was the same one that had haunted Janie her last year of life. In fact, Irmã could be a brown version of Roz's little sister, the way her delicate features reminded her of a doll's face.

Roz had failed her little sister.

This could an opportunity for Roz to make up for her failures, a second chance. She hardly deserved it. "Okay," she said, softening her voice. She held out her hand.

Irmã took her hand and gave her a shy smile in return. With her brief squeeze, the warmth of her flesh sent a warm link tingling through Roz.

"Where did you find her?" she said to Gilberto as Irmã slipped free of her hand. The new maid ticked her tongue as she picked up Roz's bag and set it on the bench beside the door.

"It doesn't matter. She knows her duties."

"But why us? Why does she want to work for us?"

"It's not up to her. Sometimes things are meant to be."

Roz didn't know what he meant, but despite her suspicions,

she felt sorry for this budding young woman, the same way she'd felt sorry for the barefoot boy at the bus stop. Perhaps in this new home of hers, Roz could actually find a purpose for being rather than simply hiding away.

It didn't take long after Gilberto left again for work, that she saw how deeply shy Irmã was. Almost as if she, too, was in hiding. They were sisters in spirit. An unspoken alliance formed between them.

* * * * *

Roz confessed to an initial horror at the invasion of someone unknown to her, but as the weeks passed, she changed her mind. Gilberto's stubborn determination to avoid answering her questions suggested that there was a lot more to the situation than he was willing to share. No matter how hard Roz tried to get information from him, he wouldn't tell her. Perhaps he didn't really know, but clearly, there was more to Irmã's story. And if Roz was ever to get it, she would have to learn patience.

Something else to learn.

Roz had to admit that it wasn't so bad having someone else around who did the daily chores, simplifying life in her confusing world. She could get used to being waited on. Irmã's first task that day she'd arrived was to help Roz unpack the rest of the boxes in the little room off the kitchen. The fur stole never did show up. Irmã moved her single, battered suitcase into the maid's quarters, making the room hers.

Roz had to remind herself more than once that Irmã was not really Janie. She was a maid, and she liberated Roz from household jobs, giving her the gift of extra time. In addition, she turned out to be useful in many other ways. None of them, no doubt, in the way Helen had intended with her advice. Irmã didn't speak one word of English, giving Roz plenty of practice with her growing skills in Portuguese. And to top it off, every night after cleaning up the kitchen after dinner, the maid hid in her room and never bothered the dom and dona. *Dona Rosalinda!* Roz thought she might get used to this lifestyle of leisure.

But then there was Anabela.

# Chapter Thirteen

March 28, 1959

**It was the sunny** end to rainy season when Roz decided it was finally time to face the family and test her rapidly improving language skills. Besides, there was her new image to uphold—decadence. She was getting good at it, thanks to having a maid, whose live-in presence was more of a convenience than an intrusion. Irmã didn't seem to mind doing the boring, daily tasks. More than anything, Roz wanted to fit in, to belong here, if only her mother-in-law would give her a chance.

It had been over a month since Anabela had burst into the apartment, inspecting everything. That was the last time Roz had seen her. The apartment would probably pass inspection now that Irmã had taken over its management. Roz had other things to occupy her mind. Her big, growing secret these last few weeks continued to be acquiring language. It was the means of completing the change of her identity. Such a plan should be harmless to Anabela, and any day now, the bubble of Roz's secret would have to burst. Anabela was a smart woman, and she had to guess that Roz was learning Portuguese. Language surrounded her day and night. What Roz was counting on was that Anabela wouldn't realize the extent of Roz's drive, nor the depth and speed of her learning.

Gilberto seemed pleased when Roz told him that he wouldn't have to come up with an excuse this week for her absence from *O Clube*, that she would finally join the family there. Naturally, he couldn't go. He had to work. He arranged for one of his sisters, the one who was in charge of sales of the gems from the family mine, to pick her up and drive her.

When Isabela—Isa for short—showed up at the apartment's front door, she stood half a head shorter than Roz and a few pounds curvier. Her wide, grinning face radiated a tenderness that made her look more like Gilberto than any of the rest of the da Costas, and this warmed Roz to her right away. Isa had soft features, mostly smiling mouth and unruly curls. Freckles sprinkled across her face like spilled cinnamon, and her eyes looked like warm chocolate, rather than the simmering coals that fueled her mother.

After exchanging basic greetings in Portuguese, Isa kept babbling, oblivious that anyone else might not know her language. She laughed about how happy Roz had made the family by spending the afternoon with them. It was the right thing to do. And furthermore, Roz had given Isa the privilege of taking her there. She apologized for her lack of English and regretted the absence of her brother as translator. But Carlota would be at *O Clube* today, and her older sister was eager to translate for all of them.

Isa's effervescence made Roz smile. She ached from loneliness. Language separated her from most everyone. She couldn't confide in her husband's sister, while at the same time deceive the family. She didn't like deceiving them, but she didn't see that she had much choice. At least for now.

Roz pinched her fingers together in the gesture meaning

she'd only understood a little of Isa's ramblings. In truth, she'd followed about half of it, but she wasn't ready yet to reveal her growing language ability—not until after she'd figured out how well she could trust the da Costas, if at all.

Her sister-in-law kept chattering the entire way across town in her Mercedes, breaking the otherwise awkward silence for two people who did not share the same language. Isa didn't seem to expect any response from Roz, which suited her fine. She understood enough to realize that Isa was gossiping about the twins' scandalous behavior at their recent birthday party. When Isa laughed about Anabela's horrified reaction, Roz laughed along, liking this sister-in-law even more. Her brothers were wise to stay out of it all, Isa opined, but she worried about what Carlota's children were picking up. It was a changing world, no? Every once in a while, Roz inserted the simple question *quem é* at the mention of various names, asking who they were. Isa listed her sisters and brothers, nieces and nephews, and even a few cousins. Roz smiled until her face hurt.

When they finally pulled into the parking lot at *O Clube*, the lushness of the place contrasted with sterile city. It reminded Roz of a hidden oasis. Isa led her into the grounds, and Roz felt a sense of calm surround her. There was an old, settled feel here that she'd not noticed elsewhere in the city. A row of palm trees separated the tennis courts from the pool area. The rhythmic, soft thunks of tennis balls pierced the air.

By the pool, the silky tones of a bossa nova played from hidden speakers. Sun sparkles glittered across turquoise water, where a couple of children thumped a beach ball back and forth. The pool's Olympic size dwarfed their bobbing heads. Roz scanned the sun-bathed stone slabs of the terrace surrounding the pool for an attending adult, but no one hovered close. The only other people here, about a half dozen in total, lounged in puddles of shade cast by the white tents of cabanas. Isa waved, shouted a greeting, and hurried to join them.

Roz felt a lump rise in her throat, but she swallowed it away. Sooner or later, she was going to have to face the family. Alone. Without Gilberto's strength at her side. The time had finally come.

Anabela, wearing a skirted bathing suit and a towel draped over her legs, lounged in a central position in the shade, with a daughter flanking each side. Isa bent down to greet her mother with a kiss, and then Anabela tilted her cheek expectantly toward Roz. Hesitating, mostly with surprise, Roz followed Isa's example and planted a kiss on Anabela's cheek. Her skin stretched tightly across her cheekbones and smelled of lavender. Anabela spoke a civil greeting to her in Portuguese, inquiring about her health, but Roz pretended not to understand anything beyond *bom día*. She felt breathless, not having expected such politeness after the scathing way Anabela had inspected the apartment.

Whatever Gilberto had said to her must've worked.

Roz was sure she hadn't misread her mother-in-law that time or the first time, either, when she'd met her at the dinner party. Maybe time healed everything, or maybe Roz had earned some respect by giving herself time and space away from Anabela's commanding presence. Whatever was the reason, Roz felt a spot of warmth blossom inside. This was going to work out. The family was finally going to accept her.

The others followed Anabela's lead, and kisses were exchanged all around. Roz remembered Carlota from the park, the eldest daughter, whose marriage to the doctor had left her with a sour face and a dubious hesitance toward Roz. And who could forget the spoiled twins, Olivia and Elvira? But there were a couple of men that she'd never met before. Carlota introduced them in her halting English.

Jacinto Silveira was a cousin who worked at the family's mine, although his exact position was not clear to Roz. He seemed younger, given the way his thin build and the sparse amount of chest hair gave him an underdeveloped look. Baby fat jiggled on his cheeks as he dipped his chin, avoiding her direct gaze. He shook her hand and murmured "at your service."

The other man, Klaus Hoffman, was older than Jacinto and related to the family somehow. Carlota couldn't make herself exactly clear about the connection.

"Never mind, I speak English," he said with a heavy accent, bypassing Carlota's introduction when she stumbled with the words. "I can tell you. I am father-in-law."

"Pleased to meet you, Mr. Hoffman," Roz said, shaking his hand.

"He is doctor," Carlota said, "no mister."

*Just like his son, Carlota's husband*, Roz thought, piecing together the family connections.

His slick face gleamed under the sun. "Tonio is my very special patient," Dr. Hoffman said. "Twelve years now, ever since after the war. But please, you call me 'Klaus'."

Tonio, the disabled brother who never attended these family gatherings, had nearly drowned as a child, Gilberto had explained to Roz, and was left seriously brain-damaged. "How convenient," Roz said, sliding her hand from Klaus's tight grip, "that someone in the family can also treat him."

"Yes. Convenient." His chest swelled, raising thick gray hairs and the belly spilling over his swim trunks. His gold jewelry and neatly Brylcreamed black hair added to his air of accomplishment. She wondered if the presence of this man reeking of self-importance explained Anabela's show of politeness today. She had an audience.

Isa embraced the doctor, calling him Uncle Klaus. She spoke rapidly to him, something about how glad she was that he was here today, especially since Roz didn't speak much Portuguese yet, and Carlota's knowledge of English only went so far. The young cousin Jacinto looked quickly away from the hug, wearing a scowl on his face. He was jealous, Roz thought, jealous of the attention Klaus was giving Isa.

"Please," Carlota said to Roz in English, waving at an empty lounge chair, "sit."

"I think I'll swim first." Roz had to show the family that she wouldn't necessarily do whatever one of them wished. She dumped her bag, pulled off her terry cover-up, and dipped her toe into the ice-cold water. She'd learned to swim a modified dog paddle in warm, mud-silkened lake water back in Ohio and had never touched anything like this before. But now, with her toe in the water, she was committed. She could feel the family's scrutiny on her back, almost hear them hold their breath. Goosebumps prickled her. Even the children already in the water paused their splashing and watched as she jumped in, feet first.

She thought her heart must've stopped from the shock of a liquid ice cube encasing her body. As she bounced furiously up and down against the numbness, voices resumed their chatter. She picked up bits and pieces between the splashes.

"Ah, so she's the one he chose," Klaus said in Portuguese.

Isa giggled, and said something about Denver.

"What does he see in *her*?" Klaus said. "There must be a reason. What do you know about her?"

"Oh, uncle, don't be mean." Isa went on, her voice bubbling about Roz's story.

Amidst splashing sounds, Roz only caught parts of it, something about a fairytale romance, and then there was mention of finding a vacant apartment. Roz couldn't hear most of it. She paddled toward the beach ball that had gone over the head of one of the children, recovered it, and threw it back. The children squealed with laughter and included her in their game.

They hammer-fisted the ball back and forth while the family went on talking, their voices rising freely and carrying on the breeze. Occasionally, when the beachball game shifted Roz's position closer to the edge of the pool, she caught more bits of the conversation. They'd drifted from the subject of her and now were talking about the mine and the family business.

"Jacinto," Anabela said, "what can you tell me about Larry's problem?"

Larry? Roz wondered if he was yet another cousin, although the name didn't sound very Brazilian.

The ball smacked her in the face.

"There is no problem," Jacinto said, "now that I'm home from Africa. We don't need Larry anymore, that's all."

Roz pounded the ball back to the little girl in the pool.

"We can't let him go," Anabela said. "The cost is too high. Remember that he found that new...(Roz didn't know what Larry had found, because she didn't understand the words)... while you were away."

Roz wondered what Larry had found, and if Jacinto was taking a job away from Larry, but she couldn't very well ask. They thought she didn't understand their language at all. It was too late to correct them now. For one thing, it would ruin her cover, and for another, they'd think she was spying on them.

Well, she was.

Having been on the run more than half of her life, she'd learned the potential usefulness of gaining information acquired without the knowledge of the informants. As long as the family thought she couldn't understand them, they would speak more honestly and truthfully in front of her, as they had been doing today at *O Clube*. Her window of opportunity wouldn't last long before they realized she could understand, but in the meanwhile, she never turned down an opportunity. For now, she mentally filed away the tidbit about Jacinto versus the unknown Larry and whatever it was that Larry had found. She would ask Gilberto about it later.

Water splashed in her face, and Carlota called the children out of the pool. Roz had had more than enough, too. The children gave Roz a shy smile as they climbed out and wrapped in towels. Roz followed, tingling all over. She lathered up with baby oil, and a waiter brought her an icy cold glass of *guaraná*. She'd acquired a taste for the nectar sweet Brazilian soda ever since Gilberto had introduced it to her. Things were starting to look up.

Settling onto her lounge chair, she listened to the family's chatter and followed the gist of what they were saying.

Roz had carefully thought to bring along a paperback in English as her prop to hide behind. She pretended to read (true crime was her favorite—God, her troubles could be worse) while listening to the family gossip freely around her. The secret about her growing language skill gave her a sense of power in her otherwise helpless situation.

She didn't like helplessness.

Isa changed the topic of conversation from the problem of Larry to gossip about other members of the family. Roz wasn't the only one who had missed these occasions at *O Clube*, although she was the only one without a proper excuse. Gilberto rarely came, on account of his job, which didn't count in Anabela's eyes as a real excuse.

Anabela launched into the faults of her son.

"He doesn't even know," she said in Portuguese with a laugh, "that they can't keep a..." (*something, something*—Roz didn't understand the words) "...in a box. It was a good thing I was able to save it for them. I told my son I will keep it safe for them at the house. If he wants it so badly, he can come get it. But he's forgotten. He forgets everything these days."

Carlota tittered, listening to her mother's tale. Isa fidgeted, flitting from one chair to another. The twins sipped their caipirinhas, the rum drink that apparently had caused the trouble at their birthday party. Klaus snapped open a newspaper, and Jacinto dove into the pool.

Roz gripped her paperback until her knuckles ached. Something in a box... Her mother-in-law had rescued it, and Gilberto knew all about it. The only thing that Roz knew about that had come in a box and was no longer in its box was the stone martin fur stole that Gilberto had bought for her. Was *that* what Anabela referred to? But then... That meant... Anabela would've entered the apartment while Roz had been out. Had she actually done that? Roz wouldn't put it past her, but she had no idea why Anabela would've taken the fur stole. Even worse... if this was true, then Gilberto *knew* his mother had done it. And yet he hadn't said anything.

Before Roz's racing pulse could calm down, Anabela went on. "It's this foolish job of his, you see. That's what makes him forget about the rest of us."

"Don't you think," said Carlota, "that it's his new wife who makes him forget?"

The pages of Klaus's newspaper crinkled.

"God help us," Anabela said. "She's not even Catholic. She's a sinner, and she's trying to take him away from us. That's what encourages him to keep that job. Her opposition only makes my tasks harder. But I will help him see the truth of his mistake. God willing, he will quit, and the sooner the better. He is the only one who can take over the family business before I die."

Roz lifted her paperback higher, as the others assured Anabela she wasn't going to die. Roz had always thought that having a cop for a husband was probably the best kind of protection she could ever ask for, and now she was being blamed for his love for his work. And what about Isa? Isa handled sales for the mine—what must she be thinking to hear her mother speak like that? Why couldn't Isa take over the family business?

Carlota changed the subject. "I think she's fatter than she was when I talked to her in the park."

*Who, me?*

Roz stared holes through her paperback, forcing her attention on the page and not on the hurtful words that surely referred to her. She flipped a page so hard that it tore. Fat, was she?

Then it occurred to her that they might be goading her,

trying to find out if she understood them.

"Careful," said Isa, who apparently had the same thought. "Our new sister already understands a little, and before you know it, she will pick up the rest. Knowing our brother, I'll bet she's already enrolled somewhere in language classes."

"She's not," said Anabela.

"How do you know that?" Carlota said.

"I have my methods."

"What she means," one of the twins said, "is that half of Belo works for her."

"Maybe one of her spies will tell us if she's pregnant," said the other twin. "That could explain the extra roll around her waist."

"God help us," Anabela said, "if she becomes pregnant, like Catarina. He's never gotten over her."

The paperback slipped from Roz's grip and fell with a thunk to the stone surface of the terrace.

*Catarina?*

# Chapter Fourteen

March 28, 1959

**At the ninth pub** they visited, an employee finally recognized Angela from the photo Gilberto had taken of the body.

"Yes, she worked here," the man said, wiping up a spill from the highly polished counter, "but not for long."

Gilberto glanced at Ubaldo with a smug grin that said *I told you we'd find her*. Ubaldo looked away and shrugged.

"Angela Cardaso was a good kid," the barkeep said. "Sure am sorry she had to die. You know how it happened?"

Ubaldo snorted. "She got involved where she shouldn't have."

"Our investigation isn't complete yet," Gilberto said. "Can you tell us anything that might help us find out?"

"Don't know much about her. She was new to town. Moved here to Belo from Congonhas about four or five months ago."

Gilberto made a note. "Did she make any friends while she was here?"

The man shook his head. "She kept to herself. She was a hard worker."

"You never saw her flirting with a customer?" Ubaldo said.

The barkeep stared at the ceiling for a while and then frowned. "There was someone, now that you mention it, but it wasn't like that. She was just being nice."

"Who was this person?"

"Don't know.  Haven't seen him since."

"Can you describe him?"

The barkeep scratched his bald head.  "Not really.  He had some money, you could tell from the fancy wristwatch he wore."

"But you don't remember what he looked like?"

"What else is there to notice?"

Gilberto slid a folded *cruzeiro* bill across the counter.  "You sure you don't remember?"

The barkeep snatched up the bill.  "He was too old for her."

"So he wasn't a boyfriend?"

"Who knows what he offered?"

"If you ever see him come back here again," Gilberto said, pulling one of his cards from his wallet, "call me at the station."

\* \* \* \* \*

"Who is Catarina?"  Roz bolted up in bed later that night the instant she heard Gilberto return home to their apartment from his shift.

There was a pause of silence.  Then footsteps as he approached the bed.

"Are you still awake, *meu amor*?  You didn't have to stay up for me."  He placed his gun in the drawer of the night table where he always kept it when he was off duty, and sank down onto the bed.  "But I'm glad you did."  He reached for her arm under the sheet and kissed her fingers one by one, then her palm, working his way up her wrist, the inside of her arm—

"Stop that."  She pushed him away and propped up on her elbow to stare at his shadowy outline in the dark.  "Did you hear

146

me? I asked you a question."

He rolled away from her, slid off the bed, and padded into the bathroom. He must've turned on every water faucet in there from the sound of so much gushing water. She jumped out of bed and followed.

"Come back here," she said, her heart suddenly pounding with alarm. What was wrong with him? Usually, he could never contain his excessive tenderness.

Maybe it was the glow from the nightlight that turned his nutmeg face into a stranger's. She flicked on the light over the sink. The cinnamon of his eyes turned to rock hard candy.

"Gil, what's wrong?"

"Nothing." He ran water over his face, disappeared to the toilet, reappeared with his fly unzipped.

*Catarina.*

"So it's true," she said.

He swished his belt from his pants like a whip and stomped back into the bedroom.

*Their* bedroom. Not Catarina's.

Roz followed and watched him sling his clothes over the bedpost. "Who is she?"

"She, who?" He turned his back on her and slapped his bare feet across the tile floor.

"Where are you going?" She eyed the tight curves of his cheeks as he disappeared down the hall.

"I'm hungry, okay?"

"I'm talking to you, okay?" *Jerk.* Why had he suddenly grown so cold?

No reply. She heard the refrigerator door open and close. She thought about chasing him down, forcing the confession out of him.

Catarina. A former girlfriend? Or maybe not so former. He'd say, wouldn't he? If it was over, he would just say so. But then, what did she really know about Gilberto? She'd married him too fast. Because he'd promised to help her run away. After accidentally killing that oily-faced man who'd been stalking her. She'd thought at first he was her roommate's pimp. Turned out, he was much more than that.

She hadn't meant to kill him. But no way was she going to not fight back, nor hand over her hard-earned money. No one owned her, not like the way men had owned her mother. She wasn't going to turn into her mother. She felt as if she'd never really had a mother. There'd been a time when she'd hoped Anabela might have fit the role. That was before they'd met.

As for Gilberto, she hadn't *made* him run away with her. It just happened. And she let it.

It wasn't like they were newlyweds in love. Theirs was a marriage of convenience. He got her body, and she got to play the part of Rosalinda da Costa.

It was better than the alternative. Prison, if she survived.

Even if she ended up with Gilberto's mother and the rest of the da Costas as a bonus.

So Catarina shouldn't matter. Why did she?

\* \* \* \* \*

March 29, 1959

Gilberto's knuckles ached as he gripped the steering wheel of his Fairlane and struggled to keep his attention on the road before him. Seven weeks had passed since Fatima Souza's death; three, since Angela Cardaso's. He'd spent most of his time going nowhere, and now he had two more places to visit—Congonhas as well as Sete Lagoas—and they were in opposite directions.

This morning he was heading to Sete Lagoas alone. It was his first opportunity to question the uncle who'd confirmed the identification of the body from *Carnaval*.

The uncle, Pedro Pires, had nearly fainted upon viewing Fatima's body, his brother-in-law Ben had reported in the morgue. As soon as Uncle Pedro could walk again, he'd hastily left, returning to the fresh air of his modest *fazenda*, a ranch in the planalto near the small town of Sete Lagoas. Gilberto had respectfully allowed time for the body to be examined, released, and finally buried with a proper funeral before pushing for an interview.

Ubaldo had resisted wasting more time to drive with him all the way out to Sete Lagoas. What was the point of interviewing the uncle now? Both of the victims, Fatima Souza and Angela Cardaso, had died from illegal abortions. A crime, sure, but it wasn't as if they had a serial killer on the loose. Their time would be better spent, Ubaldo had argued, tracking down the assholes who'd done the sloppy procedures. Fatima's uncle wouldn't know anything about that, since the girl had run away from home. It was pointless going there.

Gilberto disagreed. The presence of acid in both victims' vaginas told him that their killer was more than just a clumsy abortionist. Their target was an abortionist who didn't care if he killed the mother along with the fetus.

And then there was that other victim—his first wife. It hadn't been an abortion that had killed her, but the end result was the same. Her death had a possible connection to all of this, on account of the cult factor, and he couldn't get it out of his mind. Ubaldo called him obsessed, and maybe he was. But Roz's mention of her name the night before had scared the shit out of him.

He pushed that episode from his mind and focused on the macadam stretching before him. It was a good road out here through open *cerrado*—the Brazilian savanna—unmarked and barely wide enough for two vehicles to pass, but then, they rarely did. It was more likely that he would get caught up in the midst of hump-backed zebu cattle being herded across the road by their attending cowboys.

But he was lucky, and he didn't encounter any delays along the road. He made it there in under an hour. He'd sent a message the day before to expect him, and now he followed the information that the uncle, Pedro Pires, had written down in his statement, about how to find his ranch house on the acreage of his *fazenda*. Where the red dirt track turned off the highway, the terrain was flat enough that the ruts weren't too bad. Gilberto guided the Fairlane slowly over them, and soon, the ranch house came into view, looking like a cement block squatting under a pair of towering bottle trees. It's what he'd always called this type of tree because it was shaped like a fat beer bottle.

Pedro Pires stood in the vast plain of red dirt before the house. He was a rugged-looking man, wearing a leather hat and boots. The sleeves of his white shirt rolled up to callused elbows, and a red kerchief tied around his throat. The lines of his haggard face pulled down, whether from grief for his niece or the hardness of a *fazendero's* life, Gilberto could not tell.

Gilberto offered his condolences, and Pedro Pires gave a nod of quiet acceptance. They sat together on a bench under one of the trees with a homemade brew while the *fazendero* told the little that he knew.

Fatima had always been a quiet child, the daughter of his wife's sister. When the girl's father abandoned the family, Fatima and her mother came to live in one of the sheds on Pedro's *fazenda*. Two years ago, they'd buried Fatima's mother, the victim of a snakebite, and now Fatima, the victim of another type of snake.

"Can you tell me who were her friends, *Senhor*?" Gilberto asked softly.

"The girl, Irmã Furtado. They were like this." Pedro Pires twisted one of his fingers tightly around another. "I hear she ran off, too."

"Any boyfriends?"

"None that she dared to tell me about. If not for that Irmã, our Fatima would still be here with my wife and me today."

Gilberto made a mental note to ask Irmã about this. The times he'd pressed her further about Edgar, otherwise known as Picapau the street kid, she'd made it sound as if *he* was the one who'd found Fatima without any help at all from Irmã. "You think Irmã Furtado was a bad influence?"

"I don't think. I *know*. She's the one who took Fatima with her for days at a time. I am pretty sure they went to meetings of cults. Some cultists came through here a couple years ago, and Irmã was always a believer. Fatima became one, too, thanks to her friend. She was eager to grasp at anything after losing her mother at such a tender age. My wife and I did what we could for her, but it wasn't enough."

Unease twisted through Gilberto's gut. The girl had seemed so eager to go with him, away from Dona Mariana's pink house. But if Pedro spoke the truth, then what had Gilberto done by bringing her into his home? He must somehow prevent Irmã from also leading Roz to the cults.

"Is it possible," Gilberto asked slowly, "that your niece met someone at one of those cult meetings?"

Pedro Pires shrugged. "She met someone, because someone gave her a *figa*. She tried to hide it from me, tucking it under the collar of her blouse, but I saw it."

"Did you ever ask her where she'd gotten it?"

"Sure. She said it was Irmã's. That she was only borrowing it." Pedro grunted, maybe a laugh. "It was a lie, of course."

"Where did she claim that her friend got it?" Gilberto asked.

"From one of the cousins who came to the funeral of my wife's sister."

"And the cousin's name?"

"Edgar. Mariana Pena's son."

Just as he'd suspected. Picapau the street kid was also the son of the dona of the cult house. Edgar Pena.

In the end, Gilberto thought all the way home to Belo, Ubaldo might've been right again. Gilberto had actually learned very little new information from Pedro Pires. He'd already known about the friendship between Fatima and Irmã, but he hadn't wanted to know about any bad influence on the part of Irmã. He suspected that the uncle's grief had twisted such perception, because Gilberto had seen Irmã's fear himself. She was too frightened to be the girl Pedro had described, someone who was capable of leading Fatima astray.

Gilberto also believed that the uncle was wrong about the

*figa.* He'd seen Irmã's reaction when he dangled the charm before her stricken face. It had belonged to her friend, and not to Irmã, he felt certain. He would bet anything that Picapau, the street kid thief also known as Edgar Pena, had acquired it from one of his thefts and then given it to the girl he was trying to impress—Fatima.

But there was even more that Gilberto was still uncertain about. He was no closer to finding the butcher who'd killed Fatima. He had no idea if that abortionist was the same one who'd killed Angela. How many were there in Belo? Perhaps Gilberto would've apprehended him by now if he'd listened to his partner. It wasn't for nothing that Ubaldo was a third generation police officer. Sometimes Gilberto thought he would never measure up.

By the time he made it back to his desk at the station, his thoughts had returned to Roz, where his thoughts usually roamed these days. She made him feel like a giddy youngster, inflamed with zest and passion—and then there was the night before. Her question about his first wife had taken him in a chokehold. Was it wrong of him, as his mother claimed, to let Catarina slip from his mind, replacing her memory only with the crime that had taken her away? He didn't even feel guilt for that. Perhaps he should find his rosary and say some prayers.

No, he would let his brother, Francisco, handle that. Being the elder brother, Francisco should've been the one to take over the family business of mining, but he'd escaped to the priesthood, leaving Gilberto to assume the responsibility. It was hardly fair to expect Gilberto to handle the mines, when he'd been called to a mission, too, and it drove him with equal fervor. For justice. And yes, vengeance. He had little faith in the world and the evilness that tried to consume it.

Back at the station, he sat down heavily at his desk, already weary, and the day had hardly begun yet. Squeaking his wooden chair, he turned to unlock his desk drawer, sift through his folders, and pull out his paper to write up his report about Pedro Pires. Another document to add to his collection. How far off course he'd veered from the investigation he was supposed to be conducting into the Gonzaga kidnapping case last December.

As Ubaldo would no doubt point out.

A commotion in the communal room of police officers and their desks pulled Gilberto's attention away from his report. Speak of the devil. Ubaldo strode across the cluttered room, carrying himself with an air of cocky confidence, plowing through the room like a barge through a wake. He headed straight to Gilberto's desk with a grin on his face. He was the cat who'd caught its mouse.

"Hey, man," Gilberto said, "what are you doing here on your day off?"

"Got a surprise for you." Ubaldo perched on one corner of Gilberto's paper-littered desk. "I wanted you to be the first to know."

"Oh, yeah?" Gilberto laid down his pen and looked up at the radiant face of his partner, free of sunglasses today.

"I decided to take your advice, since marriage seems to agree so much with you."

"You're getting married?"

Ubaldo grinned and nodded.

Gilberto leapt from his chair and embraced his partner. "That's wonderful news! Congratulations. Who's the lucky bride?"

"Relax," Ubaldo said. "I haven't met her yet."

"Oh." Gilberto's handshake slipped away, and he sank back into his chair.

"But I will," Ubaldo said. "Soon. You'll see. Maybe you'll introduce me to that sexy, new girl in your apartment building? Let's go get a beer and talk about it."

Gilberto shook his head and picked up his pen. "Wish I could, but I've got reports to fill out. You know how it is."

Ubaldo pointed to the open drawer beside Gilberto. "I see you're busy as usual with your pet project."

Gilberto scowled, bumping against the drawer to close it. "Who likes this shit?"

"Not so fast." Ubaldo slid off his perch and came around to open the drawer again. He reached inside and pulled out an enlarged black and white photo of the room where Angela Cardaso, the angel, had died. "Have the reports come in from the lab yet about the contents of those little bags we found there?"

"The lab is backlogged. Ben says I have to be patient."

Ubaldo let out a hoot. "I thought your brother-in-law was a smart guy."

Gilberto let the insult pass. "The photos don't show it, but those bags were different colors, as if that meant something. But the contents all looked the same, like tealeaves."

"Have you considered that's what it is? Tea?"

"You want to be the one to test it?"

"Thanks for the offer, but I prefer my drinks a little harder."

"The bags were tied up with green string," Gilberto said. "We're still waiting on lab reports about that, too."

Ubaldo's finger stabbed at the photograph where a small,

unmarked box of sanitary pads was shown lying on the floor. "How about this? Any progress yet on tracking down the place where she bought this?"

"Do you realize how many places sell that stuff for women? Not just in a drug store."

"You find the right drug store," Ubaldo said with a knowing wink, "and you'll find the place where she hooked up with your abortionist."

Gilberto grunted. "That's a lot of legwork, and it takes time. You could do some of it. You're on this case, too."

"It's my day off, remember? I get to go have a beer." Ubaldo sauntered around the open drawer and then paused, bending down to pick up another photo, this one encased in a plastic sleeve. "Hey, what's this? It's her, isn't it? The Yankee?"

Gilberto snatched the photo from his partner and tossed it back in the drawer. "Don't disrespect her. You know her name."

"Why do you hide her picture?" Ubaldo said, reaching for it again.

Gilberto blocked his arm. This was exactly why he'd avoided introducing his partner to his wife. He'd known that Ubaldo would take too much interest in Roz, and he didn't want any extra attention directed her way. It was bad enough that Gilberto had found these photos of her on the dead body of that gangster who'd been following her in Denver. Neither of them could've afforded the questions raised had the locals been brought in, and besides, the scum didn't deserve better. So Gilberto had taken the photos and buried the body in the snowbank of a remote canyon of the mountains, a place where no one would find him for a long time. In the meanwhile, he didn't need Ubaldo digging into the matter.

Just when Gilberto thought he'd succeeded, Ubaldo lunged again for the photo. In their tussle, a handful of file folders spilled out of the drawer, too. A small plastic bag dropped out from the mess, falling onto the floor.

"Dammit," Gilberto said, scooping up the bag, which contained the aquamarine ring.

# Chapter Fifteen

March 29, 1959

**By the time Roz** woke up that morning, Gilberto and his gun were gone. Irmã made coffee, the Brazilian drip-method way, and then steered clear of her, sensing trouble in the air. Roz sipped and brooded over their argument.

It wasn't an argument if he hadn't engaged.

He hadn't even given her the satisfaction of a shouting match.

She didn't care if he had a relationship on the side with Catarina. Now that she thought about it, that would explain his long absences "at work." Really. She told herself over and over she didn't care. But she didn't believe herself. Apparently she *did* care, just a little, and that's what made her mad. Not Catarina, not really. She and Gilberto had made a deal, dammit. He was the only one who knew the truth about her past. It was only fair that she knew his.

Never mind that he didn't know all of her truth.

She flung the morning newspaper away and thought.

The newspaper. She was getting pretty good at picking out information from the paper. Good enough to...

She sprang out of her chair at the kitchen table and grabbed her leather bag from the bench where Irmã kept placing it each time Roz carelessly let it drop onto the floor. It was bad luck to leave your purse on the floor, Irmã had warned. You could lose all your money. That would be ironic, Roz thought with a snort. She'd never had money before, and now there was enough, thanks to Gilberto, that she didn't have to worry ever again about losing it. That didn't mean she didn't.

Digging through the purse's contents, she found Teresinha Prado's business card and held it up to read once again. She studied the telephone number for the language institute where the da Costa cousin used to teach English classes until Anabela interfered.

Hurrying to the icy air of their bedroom, she slipped on a housedress, a shapeless shift of blue gingham, and pocketed the business card. She ran a comb through her fake blonde hair and darted out through the front door of the apartment, into the sterile hallway of cold cement. Across the hall were two smaller apartments, one where the new woman with the briefcase had moved in, and the other belonging to Silvia, the neighbor who owned the only telephone and television set in the entire building.

She marched over there now, knocked on the door, and asked Silvia in her slightly-better-than halting Portuguese if she could use her telephone. Yes, it regarded her husband, and it was a matter of grave importance.

"Everything is important," Silvia said, "when you are a da Costa."

Silvia harrumphed, but she also nodded and pulled the door open wide, bobbing the rollers that wound tightly in her graying hair. She wore a thick, terrycloth robe, and fuzzy slippers on her feet. Her sleepy gaze traveled up and down the length of Roz's dress, ugly but suitable for the part of housewife that she played. She stepped aside and invited her in.

The room was orderly but plain. Two stiff couches lined against one wall facing a television set that was turned on to a picture of static, awaiting the next broadcast, whenever that would be. At both ends of the couch line-up were doily-covered tables. A radio on one table played a soft, sensuous bossa nova, and a telephone sat on the other table. Silvia crossed over to the radio, but made no move to turn it off, nor the television. She stood there with her arms folded against her chest as she watched Roz.

Roz pulled the business card from her pocket and dialed the number. She looked up and smiled at Silvia as the receptionist answered with the name of the language school.

Using her uncertain Portuguese, Roz gave another false name—Barbara from Buffalo—she was good at making up names—and asked to speak with Senhorinha Prado.

Silvia tipped her rollered head sideways and frowned while the receptionist put Roz through. It was just as Roz suspected. Teresinha hadn't stopped working there.

They agreed to meet for *cafezinho* later that day to arrange the details of a private class.

\* \* \* \* \*

Roz took the bus downtown. She knew the way quite well by now, and she even knew the particular coffee shop, having been there before, for lessons with Luis. She wondered if this was a common venue for language lessons. Next time, she would ask Luis if he knew Teresinha.

The linoleum-covered tables were filled with couples or

groups. Only one table had a woman sitting alone, but she had hair so red that it almost flamed blue. It couldn't be her.

Maybe it could.

The red-haired woman looked up and caught Roz's sweeping gaze. "Barbara?" she said, waving her over to her table.

Roz's stateside characteristics—whatever they were—must've given her away. Today, she must remember that she was Barbara. She only hesitated a couple of seconds before gathering her strength of will and winding around the tables to the redhead's.

They shook hands over introductions, and all the while, Roz couldn't take her eyes off the redness of her hair.

Teresinha smiled. "It's natural."

"Sorry if I was staring," Roz said. "I just didn't expect... You know, yourself being Brazilian and all."

"My family traces its origins back to the first Portuguese settlers."

"Oh yeah. I understand that you're a relative of the da Costa family. They're pure Portuguese, aren't they?"

"Who told you that?"

"My husband. I guess...the da Costas are pretty famous around here."

"Only to some," Teresinha said. "Who's your husband, anyway?"

Roz felt her cheeks grow warm. "Look, I wasn't being completely honest with you. You see...I'm not really from Buffalo. And the truth is, my husband *is* a da Costa."

A tiny flame of satisfaction flickered through Roz for having confessed the truth, but before she could take pride in her confession, Teresinha yanked her shoulder bag from the back of her chair and started to rise.

Roz lightly touched her arm. "Please don't go. I have no one to talk to. It's going to take me forever to get past the language barrier. I feel so alone in this place."

Teresinha sank back down to her chair with a sigh. Her eyes softened with compassion. "Okay, Barbara. I can stay a little longer."

"That's not really my name, either. I knew your receptionist wouldn't put me through to you if I'd given her my real name. I'm Rosalinda da Costa." *Not exactly true, either.*

Teresinha's eyes widened, and she gaped at her, speechless. Apparently, Roz's reputation had preceded her.

Roz quickly went on. "I can hardly speak my husband's language, although I'm beginning to learn." *And the family has to know it by now.* "His mother hates me. All I want to know is why. Maybe fit in with the family some day. All I ever wanted was a family. A place where I could belong."

"What do you want from me?"

"The truth, that's all. When I first called, it was just for some lessons. I didn't know where to start, but then my husband— Gilberto—came home with your business card." Roz dug in her purse and pulled out the card once again, thrust it across the table for Teresinha to examine. "Now I wonder if you're even the one who gave it to him."

Teresinha shook her head.

"Don't tell me," Roz said. "That must be Anabela's handwriting."

Teresinha shrugged and pushed the card back across the table, as if it had stung her.

"Why did she do it?" Roz said. "She set me up, and then

what happened to you?"

Teresinha glanced nervously over her shoulder. "I was told not to come in that day."

"But why wouldn't she let you teach me Portuguese?"

"Who knows? One doesn't question Dona Anabela. If she finds out I'm even talking to you now, I could lose my job."

"That sounds too harsh, even for her. What's it to her, anyway?"

"Naturally, she's concerned about your marriage to her son. She only wants the best for him."

"And she thinks I'm not good enough for him." That was true, but Roz had hoped it could change.

"No, of course not. A mother worries, that's all. She has the family to think of, too."

"So if she keeps me from learning his language she thinks that'll break up my marriage?" The woman was even more twisted than Roz had thought.

"I didn't say that."

"But you implied it. Catarina has something to do with this, doesn't she?"

"I didn't say that, either. Look, I have to go. I have a class soon."

"Who's Catarina?"

"You should ask your husband that."

"I tried already. He wasn't talking."

Teresinha sighed and rose, scraping her chair backwards, goosing Roz's spine with the screech. "You didn't hear this from me, understand? But I think you have a right to know. Catarina was...a friend of mine. And she was his first wife."

Roz felt her heart skip a beat. "Was?"

"She's dead. Brutally murdered around five years ago."

\* \* \* \* \*

That night, Roz stayed awake again, lying alone in bed, waiting until she heard him drag into the apartment. Lying on her side, with her back facing him, she listened to the familiar sounds. The chink of the gun going in his drawer. The rattle of his belt buckle. His feet slapping the tiles. Water running through the bathroom pipes.

When she was sure he was gone, she rolled over, reached across to the drawer, slid out the gun, careful not to touch the trigger. So this was how it felt in her hands. Cold. Hard. A killing machine.

As was she.

No. She hadn't used a gun on that man, her stalker, although he'd deserved one. She'd struggled, fighting him off. He'd fallen backwards and hit his head on the bathtub. Less efficient than a gun.

She was holding the gun when his footsteps pattered across the bathroom. Then stopped in the doorway. She heard his breath suck in, and she looked up from the bed.

"Just don't move," he said in a throaty whisper. No purr. "Let me have it."

Well. The gun certainly got his attention. "I found out about Catarina today."

He slumped against the doorway.

Still holding the gun, she said, "Are you going to tell me about her or not?"

Silence.

"Why won't you talk to me? You're the only one I can talk to."

"Why you want to open the past?" His grasp of English seemed to break down.

"Secrets get in the way between us."

"She's no secret."

"Your mother seems to think she is. She didn't want me to learn your language because of her, isn't that right? I'm guessing she doesn't want me to take Catarina's place."

"No one can take her place. You and me, *meu amor*, we make a new place only for us."

"We can't make a new life on secrets. We had a deal."

"We still do. Just give me the gun."

Oh, God, the gun! Was she still holding it? While demanding answers of him? How had that happened?

"Lay it down. Easy now."

She'd never wanted to touch the thing, and now her fingers twisted around it. *Ewww*. Killing machines belonged to the past that she was leaving behind. She wanted to shake the gun off her fingers, but then it would go off, and oh God...

"Careful, *meu amor*."

Her hand trembled as she set it on the bed beside her, and her fingers quivered as she unhooked them. Freed, thank God, both hands flew to her face and covered her mouth. She hadn't meant to. She hadn't meant to. She hadn't... What had made her? What was wrong with her?

Gilberto pounced on the gun and checked it. Yes, it was empty. He always removed the bullets.

But he could've slipped up. Just once.

As she had.

She let out her breath. Hated the damned thing, living in

his nightstand drawer. "I'm sorry she died, Gil. Did they catch the bastard who did it?"

He shook his head and collapsed onto the bed beside her. He was shaking all over. The mattress shook, too. The fine, rippling muscles of his chest heaved, as if he were a broken man.

"Gil," she said, sliding closer to him, encircling him with her arms, feeling her own body shake along with his. "I've got to know. Did the bastard do it with a gun? Is that why you keep yours beside you at all times, even here in the bedroom?"

He looked up at her. Tears streaked his face. "A knife. Someone cut my son from her belly."

Roz shrank back.

"They took my son. They left *her* on an empty hillside to die."

"*Não.*" She breathed the word. She took his hand in hers and clung to it. Leaned down to cover his hand with kisses, to hide the tears flooding from within. Her old grief surfaced, snapping apart her stitched-together heart.

She'd stolen the information out of him, just like the bastard had stolen his son. She only hoped to God that she and Gil could heal together.

They would turn their lust into a child. That would give them a new start. Because Roz was *not* Catarina. Catarina's fate would not happen to her, and yes, a child would finally put the past behind for all of them.

But only if the baby survived.

# Chapter Sixteen

April 17, 1959

**The road to Sete Lagoas** stretched before them under a simmering sun. Gilberto squinted straight ahead at the dusty streak of pavement, only slightly aware of Irmã beside him. She'd scooted as far away from him on the bench seat as possible, hugging the door, her head turned to face the passing scenery of the *cerrado*. It was dried-out dirt, spotted with scraggly shrubs, grasses, and a few haphazard trees.

Haphazard described his wife, too, on whom his thoughts kept straying. Roz had stayed behind in Belo today, doing only God knew what while Gilberto drove their maid to her little hometown.

He never thought that Roz would actually have fired his gun. But then, he didn't really know his wife. And furthermore, accidents happened all the time. Accidents, the result of far less provocation than what they'd experienced three weeks ago in the bedroom. With his breakdown and the consequent loss of his manliness, they'd put Catarina's spirit to rest. Ever since, the sex had never been better.

These days, he rested easier than he had during all of these last five, brutal years.

Ben had congratulated him over drinks in the pub last week.

And Sam noticed, too, even though they didn't always work together. The North American friend kept asking when Gilberto would get back to some serious police work.

It was true, Gilberto had coasted through these last three weeks, sometimes forgetting—no, not forgetting, *never* forgetting—but feeling less of a sense of urgency to follow through with the plan that eternally drove him. He hadn't forgotten that part of his plan required him to get the needed information from Irmã about the cult that had killed his first wife. Instead, he was going about its acquisition in a more careful manner. He wanted to let both the girl and Roz settle into their new situation of having each other.

And then there was that matter of trust. Pedro Pires had suggested that it had been Irmã who'd led Fatima Souza astray before she'd died in the alley during *Carnaval*.

When he'd noticed that Irmã started singing to herself as she went about her daily chores around the apartment, he thought she was growing comfortable enough with them that the time had finally come. And then he'd waited some more, until she asked for a weekend away, so that she could visit her family in Sete Lagoas. He'd offered to drive her there. Not only would it give him the long-awaited chance to tease information out of her but he would also get to see where her family lived, so that he could return another time to question them as well. Irmã could catch the bus back to Belo at the end of the weekend.

But, would she?

He threw a cautious glance at the girl at the other end of the Fairlane's front seat. She looked nervous enough that he feared she might spring from the car at her first opportunity when it slowed. He wondered if she planned to come back at the end of her little vacation. It was now or maybe never.

"Have you been happy working in my home?" he asked, breaking the silence that had grown between them.

"Oh, yes, *Senhor*. You and the *dona* are very good to me."

"Are you glad to be away from Dona Mariana's house?"

Her voice dropped to a whisper. "I am very grateful, *Senhor*."

"You are a hard worker. You deserve this time off. How long has it been since you've seen your family?"

"Too long."

"You came to the city with Fatima, your friend. How long has that been?"

She squirmed against the door handle and did not answer. He knew the answer—since the first of the year. The question was meant to ease into more serious matters.

"You were a good friend to her," he went on.

"We went to primary school together," she said timidly.

"I will find who did that terrible thing to her."

"Thank you, *Senhor*."

"But I need some help."

She fidgeted some more.

"Will you help me?" he asked softly, "as I've helped you?"

"I do not know anything that would be of any help."

"You may think it's not much, but it is something. And it may actually be very helpful. Will you try? To honor the memory of your friend?"

She dipped her chin in a brief nod and twisted her fingers together in her lap.

He smiled and said, "What made the two of you decide to leave home, the only home you'd ever known?"

"There wasn't much future there for either of us. After her mother died, Fatima only had her Uncle Pedro. And she'd never had a boyfriend before. Edgar made her feel special—"

"Do you know if he has another name?"

"He has no other name. When he brought that gift of the *figa* necklace, Fatima couldn't say no to him."

"But you weren't so sure, were you?"

"She didn't know what to do after she got pregnant. Her uncle would've kicked her off the *fazenda* if he'd found out."

"The boy could've married her."

She snorted, and her laughter seemed to loosen the words from her. "At least he didn't disappear, like they usually do. He wanted her to run away with him, although he didn't say anything about marriage."

"And that's what she did."

"What else could she do? He knew a place where she could go."

"Dona Mariana's place."

"He called it a 'Temple for Lost Women'."

"Lost?"

"Didn't you know? I thought you knew. You said you were looking for a lost friend that day you came to the *dona's* house, remember? That's why I opened the door for you."

"Uh, right," he said with a cough. "But you didn't believe Edgar."

She shrugged. "Who could? The words were too fancy for him to speak. It was some hidden cult we had never heard about."

*Banned, without doubt.* Banned groups were an off-shoot of a cult trying to become a religion. They started by gaining a foothold in the countryside.

"Does this cult have a name?" he said.

"They call themselves 'Umbrotamba'," she said, "and they worship some goddess called the Lost Daughter."

Gilberto gripped the steering wheel until his knuckles whitened. A slow simmer rose from deep inside him, and he held his breath. He couldn't trust himself to speak. He'd never had a name before, a name attached to the cult that had stolen the attentions of his first wife. Was this it? Umbrotamba. Not an actual religion, but a cult. If that's the group she had joined, did it mean that Catarina had felt lost? How was that possible, given the comfortable life he'd given her?

"We wanted to believe him," Irmã continued, "but it sounded too good to be true. He told her she could join, and one day have an important place with them, maybe even become a priestess, and I think she believed him. Fatima was ready to believe anything. She'd follow even the smallest shred of hope. I wasn't so fast to believe."

He let out his breath and summoned a comment. "But you believe lots of...things." Superstitions, he meant. His voice sounded too rough, even to his own ears.

She nodded. "Anyway, she was my friend. I had nothing to lose by going with her. Looking out for her. Except, it turned out that I didn't do such a good job of that after all."

"You did the best you could."

"It wasn't enough." She turned her face away from the window and glared at him with the force of tiny piranhas.

"Don't blame yourself," he said, feeling the heat of her stare on his right ear as he focused on driving.

"I shouldn't have gone out that day," Irmã said. "I should've stayed with her, kept her from leaving. She ended up never coming back."

"How could you have known she wouldn't come back?"

"I should've known. She made me leave with the other girls on the samba truck. When we came back in the early hours of morning, she was gone. I never saw her again after that. So I don't know what happened to her, and I am no help at all."

"What about Edgar? Was he with her?"

"He was supposed to meet her at *Carnaval* in the center, but he said she never showed up."

"If you thought she was missing, didn't you go to the police to report that?"

She sucked in her breath. "What good would that do? Besides, Edgar told me she'd gone home to Sete Lagoas, and he'd go there himself and bring her back. But when he didn't, I sent a telegram to Uncle Pedro. Let him file the report. I was too afraid."

"I would've helped you if you'd come to the police station."

She sobbed, and her words sounded strangled. "I didn't know then, but...that day you came to the *dona's* house, *Senhor*, and you showed me her *figa*, I guessed right away that Edgar had probably known she hadn't gone home as he'd said. He'd been lying to me all along. That's why I agreed to go with you to Dona Rosalinda. What will he do to me if he finds me?"

"He won't," said Gilberto, "because I won't let that happen. But I can't do anything more until I speak to Dona Mariana. And one thing you must promise me: you will never speak to Dona Rosalinda about Umbrotamba."

Her head shook as her fingers twisted the fabric of her skirt. He didn't know if she'd heard him or not.

\* \* \* \* \*

Ever since the night of Gilberto's confession, a sense of well-being flowed through Roz's veins like nectar. The more she thought about her new goal, the better it seemed. A pregnancy would complete her change of identity.

A pregnancy would also bring some happiness to her husband after having suffered that horrible tragedy of Catarina and the baby. At least she hoped it would make him happy. She wanted to make him happy. She wanted to make *herself* happy. It would be the first real time in her life for that to happen. As a bonus, Roz's pregnancy would earn her a genuine place as one of the family, rather than an interloper's. Language acquisition alone would never have done it. But a child would.

Most every night, she stopped using her douche after love-making.

Now that the family knew about her growing grasp of the language, she'd begun attending family functions. She never missed a weekly dinner, nor any of the receptions and social galas. Anabela mostly gave her a cold shoulder and hollow smiles, but one thing at a time. Roz was even attending Mass, taking her place alongside the da Costas in the family pew. She mouthed along the recitations while Francisco Junior, who looked nothing like the rest of the clan in his long robes, led in his monotonal voice from behind the pulpit.

It wasn't her voice that mouthed along. How could it have been when she didn't know the ritual? Chills shuddered through her on such occasions, thinking that it was the ghost of Catarina who was in the process of taking over her body.

Impossible! Roz didn't believe in the supernatural.

At least, not the same way that her maid, Irmã, did.

So, the day that Gilberto drove Irmã to her hometown for a weekend visit away with her family, Roz saw her chance. She would finally pick out the pet that she and Gilberto had talked about—not a dog, but a bird, which would need less attention. It was a start. Irmã was superstitious about birds, never liking to watch them on their weekly visits to the market together. If the maid were with her, she'd surely try to talk Roz out of her plan. Roz didn't need the scrutiny of the little maid, who somehow always seemed to know everything that Roz thought and did (even though her Portuguese wasn't *that* good, not yet).

Watching from the bedroom window, she waited until the fishtail-finned car pulled out of the garage and drove away, out of sight. Then she gathered up her handbag and fled outside, tiptoeing past Silvia's door and running down the stairs before her neighbor could realize she'd left. Out on the street, she felt someone's gaze upon her back. Silvia, no doubt, peering at her through the shutters of her window. Roz shrugged and kept hurrying, heading toward the street where she could flag down the bus.

At the corner, she paused to glance over her shoulder. Half a block behind her, she spied the silhouette of a man with a cane. She couldn't recall ever having seen someone like him before in the neighborhood. Despite his heavy size, he ducked quickly behind a bush. Deliberately out of her sight? Or was he visiting whoever lived behind those bushes? She slipped around the corner, and then skirted the edge of the ravine. If she were to follow the path through its middle, it would've been a shortcut to the bus. But she'd promised Gilberto that she wouldn't go that way. And she had to admit, that dead, vacant area surrounding the ravine gave her the shivers.

She couldn't shake her goosebumps, even on the bus.

When she finally alit downtown, the autumn sun warmed her, and she felt free of watching eyes. The smell of oranges heralded the *feira* before she caught sight of the gates to the open-air market. On her weekly visits here with Irmã, the maid always led the way through the maze of bins and display trays, chatting with vendors as she chose the vegetables, fruits, and grains they would need for their meals. Now Roz was on her own.

She darted around customers and past the canopied stalls in the central area. Moving through the hum of voices, she rounded a bend and worked her way past the sizzling smells of grilled meat. Behind the snack bar, where there was less of a crowd, were the animals—birds, mostly, and also monkeys brought from the Amazon. Amongst their chirps and chatters, she usually always lost time back here in this corner of the market while Irmã completed the shopping.

Larger birds, not in cages, had had their wings clipped, so that they couldn't fly away, but she was drawn more to the smaller birds. She paused beside one giant cage to watch the mass of parakeets bob and weave inside, mesmerizing her with their movements and dusty smells of feathers. It was hard to decide which one to take home with her.

Suddenly a shriek brought her out of her trance and made her look away. An agitated macaw hunched atop a post, eye to eye to a man who stood there, facing the bird. The man was so thin that his flesh appeared to stretch over his bones. The knobs of his elbows protruded as he swung his arms and shuffled back and forth, watching the bird, maybe imitating the bird. He certainly appeared just as agitated. The bird lifted its wings, ruffled its feathers and rattled out its call, "*A-ra-ra!*"

The vendor had told her once before that these birds were called *araras* because that's what they said. Now, the thin man stopped shuffling and spoke back to the bird, making cooing sounds as if in bird language. The vendor appeared behind him, carrying a cardboard box with holes punched out. In all the times Roz had admired the birds, she'd never actually seen anyone purchase one of these *araras*, but now it looked as if that's what this man planned to do.

Fascinated, she stepped closer to watch the transfer of the bird into the box. The *arara* shrieked again, and suddenly the thin man jerked his head to one side, catching sight of Roz, throwing her an accusatory glare. She froze in her tracks. His eyes were glacier blue, and his hair a shade of copper. He didn't look very Brazilian to her, but there was something faintly familiar about his features. He reminded her of that language teacher—Teresinha—and... The round shape of his face resembled Gilberto's!

But this wasn't her husband. Startled, she stumbled and gave him a placating smile that felt more like a grimace.

He frowned at her and then turned back to the bird, holding out a finger, as if he meant to poke it. Squawks erupted from the bird. With the speed of a cobra, the vendor pushed past Gilberto's look-alike and grabbed the bird by its feet. He uttered a stream of scolding words as he wrestled the bird off its perch and into the box amidst a flurry of flying feathers and more shrieks.

Roz, not wanting to draw any extra attention to herself for

the disturbance, backed away. She wondered if this buyer was related to the da Costas. Another cousin, perhaps. She had a hard time believing in the coincidence that had brought the two of them together to the same place. Was it possible that he'd been following her? To report back to Anabela? She blended into the busy stream of customers, increasing her distance from the animal corner. She decided to wait until after the da Costa cousin left, and then she'd return to pick out her parakeet.

From a nearby section of the market, she could keep an eye on the birds in the distance. Pausing beside a row of cane-woven bins and burlap bags, she breathed in their earthy smells.

"What do you desire?" said a vendor in Portuguese who squatted behind a bag of what looked like crushed twigs.

"What is this?" she asked, pointing. It looked like sprigs of herbs but smelled more like tealeaves.

He replied with a stream of information that she didn't understand, except that it was something medicinal from the Amazon.

"I'm sorry," she said, "I don't understand."

He gave her a look of sympathy and repeated what he'd said, but she didn't understand it any better the second time. She spied a bin of rice nearby and asked for a kilo. They could always use more of this staple at home. Irmã served them rice with every meal.

While he scooped the grains into the bag she'd brought, she stole another glance across the way, toward the birds. The vendor over there was still trying to tuck the *arara* into the box. A new arrival had appeared, holding the box steady while the vendor closed its flaps and the thin da Costa cousin watched idly. She recognized him from her day at the pool with the family.

The man with the potbelly, thick, gray chest hair, and slick, black hair. She struggled to remember his name. He'd spoken Portuguese with an accent, as she did. Now she remembered. He had a foreign name, too. Klaus Hoffman, the doctor.

How convenient that he'd appeared just now to assist. She didn't know what it meant, but she didn't like coincidences. She paid for her rice and left. Her bird would have to wait for another day.

# Chapter Seventeen

April 18, 1959

**Long before the sun** rose, Gilberto crept out of the warm nest of his bed, leaving Roz alone yet again. During the trip to Sete Lagoas the day before, he'd noted for future reference where Irmã's family lived and had returned to Belo that same day. Today, he was ready to finally confront the fledgling cult.

By the time he made it across town to Dona Mariana's pink house, the sun was about to rise. There'd been no point asking Ubaldo to join him, given the unholiness of the hour. Besides, he would have to have called his partner from Dona Silvia's telephone, and the neighbor was already irritated enough with him. He'd tried to get a telephone wired to his apartment, but so far it hadn't happened. He refused to ask his mother to pull her strings for him.

From behind a bush, he watched the house. The window with the burned-down candle was shuttered closed. Soon, he heard the faint squeak of a door, just as Irmã had assured him would happen. According to the girl, Dona Mariana went out each morning with the sun, hunting fresh eggs and digging for roots and gathering her special ingredients for the potions she brewed for the initiates.

Watching the door to the house, he waited for the *dona* to

emerge into the thin, rosy light of dawn. She didn't appear.

He remembered that Edgar Pena had slipped away through a back door while Gilberto and his partner had surveilled the front. Now Gilberto ducked through the bushes, circling around to the back side of the house. He made it there in time to see a woman wearing a white bandana on her head, making her way slowly in a rambling course down the hill. She carried a basket in one hand and a stick in the other, poking the bushes. He could follow her and risk an encounter with a snake, or he could wait here by the back door for her return. Irmã had said it didn't take her long to do her morning rounds, maybe half an hour. Sometimes less. He decided to wait.

Next to the back door, a single window shuttered closed. This would be the room he hadn't been able to see the day he'd spoken to Irmã through the front door. He leaned close to the window, listening through the slats of the shutters for any movement within. He heard none. The girls that Dona Mariana sheltered as initiates should be moving about their morning duties, but there were no sounds of voices nor footsteps. The only sounds came from the roosters outside, announcing the day.

He glanced over his shoulder at the hillside view of the city in the distance and bushes in the foreground. He thought of this area, near where Catarina's body had been recovered, as no-man's land. Now, only a solitary chicken pecked the ground beneath a bush. Dona Mariana was not in sight.

In two quick strides he was back at the door, pushing against it. It opened with a grating creak. He paused, holding his breath, waiting for several heartbeats to be discovered, but no one stirred. He breathed a sigh of relief that apparently no one else was awake inside the *dona's* house at the moment, needing a sanctuary.

He slipped inside.

The shadowy interior of the shuttered room was sliced with a bar of golden, morning light that slipped in with him through the crack of the opened door. This back room seemed to be used for multiple purposes. A cot with rumpled bedding stood against the wall nearest the door, and a small, pink box sat on the floor beside it. From having grown up with sisters, he knew about those unmarked boxes of sanitary pads. It was a necessary box to find in a house of women.

Except, the women didn't seem to be here.

He ducked through the doorway into the other room. Empty. He'd expected to find cots of women, semi-conscious in the drug-induced depths of sound sleep, but no one was here. The room held no furniture. No initiates.

Nothing, except for an altar assembled against the far wall. An icon statuette of a woman's bare breasted figure with a bulging belly stood about a meter tall in the center of candles and flower petal offerings and shredded twigs. The long, blue feather of a parrot's tail lay across the base of the statuette.

The feather might as well have been a dagger plunging through his heart. The memory of the dead bird at his door, the morning of the day Catarina had disappeared and surely had been murdered, flashed through his mind.

He turned away from the image and the altar and quickly returned to the back room. Breathing deeply to still the hammer of his heart, he was running out of time.

Against the interior wall stood a stove and sink, and he strode swiftly past them. A large, wooden table took up the center of the room, and the edge of a stool peeked out from underneath. In the corner of the far side of the room, a stack of boards and cement blocks assembled into homemade shelving where there were dented pots and pans and utensils, mis-matched plates and cups of tin and chipped ceramic, burlap bags of grains, baskets of fruit, and tin cans of food. Larger cans and boxes sat on the floor beneath the shelves. He lifted the lid of one can with a scar of rust along its side and reeled backward from the smell, reeking of something rotten. He shook his head, wondering about the filth that must also contaminate the nearby food supplies. It wasn't much of a shelter for anyone here, let alone a supposed temple for lost women. If anyone ate contaminated food, they would be lost permanently. No wonder Irmã had been eager to leave and was now flourishing in his household.

The door squealed behind him, slamming against the wall, and a gruff voice shouted. "You!"

He whirled around, holding up his hands to show that they were empty. The wide girth of Dona Mariana blocked the sunlight flowing into the room through the open door. She dropped her basket and lifted her stick, shaking it at him.

"It's all right," he said. "I mean you no harm."

She advanced on him with her stick, her feet pounding the wood of the floor. "I'll show you who can do the harm."

He circled around the table, keeping it between them. "*Senhora*, I came here looking for you. I only wish to speak with you."

She stopped her advance, but she didn't lower her stick. "Why?"

"You have been highly recommended, for the way you treat your girls."

"Who told you that?"

*Who, indeed?* He thought fast. "A friend. A lost friend."

"Who is your friend?"

"She came to you, seeking your help, and you took her in."

"Of course I did. It's what we do. If you want to speak to the spirits for your friend, you'll have to come back later, the proper way."

"I only want to speak to you. No spirits."

"What do you want, then?"

"Information. For my friend. She...has a little problem growing inside her belly and needs to get rid of it. They tell me you know where she can go."

"Who tells you?"

"A skinny kid from the streets. Mustache. Sharp nose. Goes by the name of Picapau."

Also known as Edgar Pena, the dona's own son. Though Gilberto couldn't reveal that he knew about their personal connection. It would arouse too many suspicions, and he still hoped for information from her, information that would lead him to the abortionist.

"Ah." She lowered her stick. "My little man told you that?"

"He said you could arrange it."

"Then he lied to you."

"It's not you?"

"This is a law-abiding house. It is only me. You can see that for yourself. Tell your friend to go somewhere else."

"Where should she go?"

"That is for her to figure out. The boy shouldn't be saying such lies."

"Maybe I misunderstood? Then, perhaps I should speak to him again. Do you know where I can find him?"

"You bring my girl Irmã back, and then maybe I'll tell you." She lifted her stick again. "No need to look so surprised. I know you're the cop who stole her. It's on your face who you really are. You think I'm blind? Where did you take her?"

His blood chilled. This was the moment when he wished Ubaldo were here with him. His partner would turn the tables on this woman, putting the fear of God in her, telling her she'd better shape up or else face the consequences.

"Somewhere safe, *Senhora*," he said softly, still holding his hands up.

"Impossible." She whacked her stick against the table. "My girls are safer with me than with the police."

"You can trust me. I follow the rules." Most of the time. "I am da Costa with the *Policía Civil*. May I show you my badge?"

"I don't want your badge. I want you out."

"Where are the rest of them?"

"They come when they need me. As will Irmã."

Something collapsed inside of him as he thought that maybe the girl would be better off if she didn't return from her vacation with her family in Sete Lagoas. "*Senhora*, one of your girls died already. Surely you don't want to see any more of them die."

"No one dies until the spirits wish it."

He wavered a bit as his knees momentarily lost the strength to hold him up. Had the spirits also targeted Catarina, wishing her to die? He'd failed her by failing to honor the spirits.

Mentally, he crossed himself, and he turned his attention to the basket she'd dropped on the floor. "But sometimes," he said, motioning to the basket, brimming with miscellaneous gatherings, "your offerings don't satisfy the spirits."

She stared at him for a long moment, as if speechless, not

knowing how to deny a possible mistake on her part. Finally, with spittle dribbling from the corners of her mouth, she said, "You have no right to break in to my home. Your captain will hear about this."

Gilberto nodded solemnly, edging around the table. He couldn't argue with the facts, but even she must realize the uselessness of her complaints.

"I'll let you off this time," he said, moving closer to the back door. "But just remember that we will be watching this house of spirits for any funny business."

He slipped out the door faster than he'd entered.

# Chapter Eighteen

April 24, 1959

**There was something...some** force that seemed to want Roz to become Catarina. Pregnancy. What else could explain her increasing irrationality?

Just when she'd figured that her wild thoughts must be the result of a hormonal upheaval, her period had started.

She'd marked her calendar with a red "x," feeling a tiny twist in her heart.

It was too soon, she told herself, to achieve her goal of a pregnancy, but that didn't ease the pain.

Tonight, as she lay in Gilberto's arms, she realized once again that she hadn't douched. To get up and do that now would ruin this moment of divine contentment.

She was an expert at ruining moments.

"I would hate to close the shutters at night," she said as her heart continued to patter from the excitement of their recent lust. "The breeze feels so delicious."

"We don't have to, my love. We are high enough above the ground that we don't have to worry about thieves."

"Irmã tells me that nothing stops thieves if they want to get in, not even bars on windows. They can still crawl through. Gil, I think that's what happened to the fur stole. We must've had a thief, and he came inside while we were sleeping." She was sorry about its loss, but she didn't need the stole, really. His arms felt warmer and smoother than any fur.

"Is that what worries you?" He released her and sat up in bed, his head resting against the backboard. "No need to worry. It's safe at my mother's house, where there is a climate-controlled room for storing furs. It keeps the moths out. Isn't that a better place than here?"

Roz frowned, not caring about moths or the stole. It was a matter larger than that. She'd thought she'd heard Anabela talking about it at the pool the month before, and Roz had meant to follow up with her questions to Gilberto, but the matter of Catarina had come between them first.

"But how did the fur get there?" she said. "We both thought it was here. In one of the boxes. Before Irmã moved in. Remember?"

"*Mãe* must've picked it up one time when she was here."

"But when was she here? Did she come over one day when I was gone but you were here alone?"

"It doesn't matter anyway."

"But it does. You didn't tell me she was here. Or that you were, either. I always try to be home when you're home."

She wasn't sure why it bothered her, that Anabela had been here while Roz was out and Roz hadn't known about it. It felt as if her private sanctuary had been invaded, like that time when Anabela had pushed her way in, uninvited. Almost as if Roz hadn't been present then, either.

"I might not have been home at the time," he said.

Roz wrapped the sheet tightly around her. Then that meant that Anabela had somehow gained access to the apartment and had helped herself to the fur, as if anything that belonged to any da Costa really belonged to Anabela. And never to Roz. There was no such thing as privacy around Anabela.

"But how is it possible," Roz said, "that she would've gotten in without our being here? Did she climb up the railing like a thief?"

He laughed. "My mother? Of course not."

"Then how did she get in?"

"Isa probably let her in."

"Isa?"

"I trust my sister. You can, too."

"It's not a question of trust," Roz said. Of all of the da Costas, Isa was the one Roz trusted the most. "It's your mother. You always let her decide things for you." *Control*, she meant. He always let his mother control him.

"*Meu amor*, you don't understand. *Mãe* can't do everything by herself. Isa manages this building for the family. We own it. Didn't you realize? How else could you and I have been lucky enough to find an apartment on such short notice if it wasn't already one of the family's assets?"

Roz felt a chill creep along her spine.

* * * * *

April 30, 1959

Roz kept reminding herself in the days that followed that the family was on her side. Well, maybe except for Anabela. But the truth was that not everyone was out to get her. While there was that shadow who kept following her around town on the occasions when she went out alone, he'd never approached her. She didn't know it was a "he," since she'd never actually seen anyone, except that one time when she'd glimpsed the heavy man with the cane. And once there'd been the barefoot boy at the bus stop. Once did not turn either of them into a stalker. Whoever was shadowing her seemed merely curious about her activities. Was keeping tabs on her. He'd not harmed her. If he'd been hired by the father of the dead man in Denver, he would've made his move by now. She'd been in Brazil four months already, and no serious damage had been done. Therefore, she reasoned, whether correctly or wrongly, whoever was following her couldn't be from Denver. And the creep from Ohio was too stupid to venture to another country. Probably instead it was someone who worked for Anabela. He could be one of her hired guards, and if so, then he would be reporting back to Anabela about Roz's movements.

But she couldn't figure why her mother-in-law would care so much about what Roz was doing every day when she went out. It must be her way to control the family. The thought alone left Roz with a breathless feeling of suffocation. It was time to give Anabela something to think about. Time to lead her astray.

Roz decided to let Helen take her round town, showing her where to shop. It wasn't as if Helen was her *friend*, just because her husband, Sam, was Gilberto's. The fact that Sam was an American cop did nothing to ease Roz's mind. She'd tried to steer clear of him and his questions about what she'd been doing in Denver, but... Would she ever truly put her past behind her once and for all?

Roz had never had a real friend before. Helen was as close as she'd ever come. There was no language barrier with her, nor a career that kept her busy, as with Isa. But whatever special magic it was that glued friends together, it just wasn't there for the two of them. Trips out with Helen always left her feeling tense.

Roz actually felt more comfortable with her maid, Irmã. She'd returned from her weekend visit to her family more dedicated than ever to make sure the da Costa apartment was a safe place, a haven for good luck. She placed tubs of rock salt in the corners of the rooms. On Fridays she wore white dresses, even though she was always scrubbing something on her hands and knees. And she always insisted they enter and leave through their own door to the apartment, even though both front and back accessed the central hall only a few feet apart from each other. That way, they couldn't accidentally leave through a door through which they hadn't entered. Which would bring them bad luck.

Maybe it was Irmã's tireless superstitions that gave Roz a false sense of security, she didn't know. At least it worked for now.

Until the gemstones changed everything for her.

* * * * *

May 14, 1959

It started with another argument.

"But what do you really know about Sam?" Roz asked one evening over supper of leftover *feijoada*, after Irmã had retired to her room. The maid always kept their supply of bean stew well stocked in the refrigerator.

"He is my friend, what is there to know?"

"Is it normal for a 'friend' to stalk his friend's wife?"

Gilberto tipped his head sideways, giving her that puzzled frown that meant he didn't recognize the woman who sat opposite him at the little square table. Well, sometimes she didn't recognize herself, either. But she knew this: today on her walk, she'd caught another glimpse of the man with the cane. Seeing him more than once confirmed in her mind that he was the elusive shadow she'd sensed following her these last few months. And he had the same blocky shape as Sam.

"Don' worry about Sam," Gilberto finally said.

"But how can you be so sure?" She wasn't sure, either. Up until now, she'd convinced herself that her shadow was one of the da Costa family's guards. But when she actually saw him, she thought it looked as if it *could* be Sam. It wasn't so far-fetched, because she'd been suspicious of Sam from the first time she'd met him. Most important, the fact that she'd seen her shadow today gave her a sense of vindication. Her paranoia was not just a figment of her imagination. There really was someone trying to keep tabs on her whereabouts.

Gilberto rose, kicking back his chair. He left his unfinished plate of supper on the table and stormed down the hall to the bedroom. She held her breath, listening. And then she heard it, the faint scraping sound of the night table's drawer. He was checking the presence of his gun.

She sprang out of her chair and marched down the hall after him. Her voice rose as she burst through the bedroom door. "I wish to hell you'd keep that somewhere else."

"Is to keep you safe, *meu amor.*" He gave her his puppy dog look and slid the drawer shut, gun inside. "If someone bothers you, he has to get past me, first."

"There *is* someone, Gil. You have to believe me."

"Is not Sam."

She ran out of the room, not understanding his blind devotion to his friend. Was it because they were both cops? Although, Gilberto had never actually admitted that's what Sam was. Nonetheless, Gilberto *was*. His profession as a detective should make him as suspicious as she. She stormed into the bathroom, slammed the door shut behind her, sank down onto the commode and cried.

\* \* \* \* \*

May 15, 1959

The next morning, after Gilberto left for work, Silvia tapped on her front door. "Phone call for you," her neighbor said, sounding bored.

It was Helen. She had a babysitter lined up and an appointment to see her favorite jeweler. She could be here in forty-five minutes to pick up Roz. Did she want to go?

This was an opportunity Roz couldn't resist. If Gilberto wouldn't do anything about Sam, then Roz would have to find out for herself. Maybe Helen was the way to the information she needed. Besides, Roz's spirits had lifted this morning because the argument the night before hadn't produced another migraine. In fact, Roz hadn't had a headache for quite some time.

Helen's favorite jeweler, Guilhermo Machado, did business from his home in one of the more modest residential sections of town. He spoke English well, making it easier to do business with him, which was why Helen liked to order her custom jewelry from him. Helen explained all this in the car as they drove across town, but Roz kept trying to steer the conversation back to Sam.

"So, what does your husband actually do here in Brazil?" Roz saw no other way, except to be blunt.

Helen laughed and lifted one gloved hand from the steering wheel. She flicked the air, showing her opinion of Roz's silly question. "He's an adviser, like everyone else assigned to Belo."

"But what does he advise about?"

Helen pulled the car to a stop at the side of the street and switched off the engine. This street was cobbled with mismatched rocks, each one about the size of her fist. "His specialty, same as anyone else. That's why all of us are here, you know."

Not Roz. Unless she counted hiding as her specialty.

Helen climbed out of the car and stepped onto a sidewalk, which butted up against a wall a little taller than the tops of their heads. "Well, maybe except for the missionaries, but then, their specialty is God, I suppose."

"I just wondered how our husbands ever met," Roz said.

"Oh, that." Helen laughed again and led the way to a gate. Its iron bars offered a glimpse into a courtyard garden of palm fronds spilling over each other. "You realize, don't you, that we only want to help this country achieve standards like the rest of the western world? Sam's specialty happens to be policing."

Roz took in a long, slow breath of flower-scented air. The confirmation felt like a punch to her stomach, although it shouldn't surprise her. She just didn't understand why Sam's policing should include tailing her. Had he been hired by the

Denver connection, just because he was already here?

She discarded that idea as fast as it had come to her. A friend of Gilberto's couldn't possibly be a corrupt cop. Still, the thought had touched her mind.

A maid led them through the lush garden and into a square and sparse living room. The only furniture was a couch, a chair, and a coffee table. Roz and Helen sank down onto the vinyl couch, and Guilhermo spread out velvet-lined trays of gemstones before them on the table. The dim bareness of the room faded to the background as the jewels took center stage. There were tourmalines in their range of colors from pink to green, topaz in their various shades of gold, royal purple amethysts, red garnets, miscellaneous beryls, and blue aquamarines—all the kinds of gemstones mined in this state, in various shapes and sizes, but only the best quality. Guilhermo's stones, he explained, came from the da Costa mines, the best of the best. He had the privilege of knowing the family well. The *Senhoras* could trust him.

"Lovely," Helen said with a gasp, "but I'm only shopping for aquamarines today."

As Guilhermo cleared away the other trays, Helen turned to Roz and explained. "You see, they are the most valuable stone. Brazil gave a gift of them to Queen Elizabeth upon her coronation, and so everyone wants them now."

Roz sucked in her breath, but not because of the beauty of the gemstones. Guilhermo smiled appreciatively and went on to explain even more about them. But Roz wasn't listening.

Her gaze fixed on the blue stones sprinkled like spilled candy across the velvet. This was the same stone as the one in that ring she'd found, the one in Denver that she'd told Gilberto had belonged to her grandmother. No wonder he'd taken such an interest in it. He'd warned her that the ring was worth far more than what the pawnbroker offered. He knew about such things, being a Brazilian whose family was in the gemstone business.

Had the stone in that ring originated from here?

Too bad Roz didn't have it anymore, to ask Guilhermo about it. She'd ended up taking the pawnbroker's money, needing the cash. Finders keepers. Now she wondered if she'd done the right thing. Right or wrong, it had brought her here.

# Chapter Nineteen

June 17, 1959

**Eight weeks since the** last red "x" marked her calendar, Roz sat in the front seat of Isa's boxy Mercedes. With gemstones on her mind, she only half-listened to her sister-in-law as they rode out of the city. Isa drove, bubbling over as usual with her wide smiles, while Roz replayed in her mind the family's poolside discussion with cousin Jacinto. There'd been some problem at their mine. Roz had tried to follow up with Gilberto, not successfully, and couldn't pursue her questions because the right opportunity had never materialized. She'd ruined enough moments with him as it was. She suspected the ghost of Catarina was really to blame.

The visits to the jeweler's with Helen had brought it all back, and she'd pestered Gilberto for more information. Finally, he'd handed her off to his sister Isa, who arranged a visit to the mine. And now at long last, the two of them were on their way.

The ride was bumpy enough along the main road, but nothing compared to the dirt trail that turned off into rolling hills. They called it a road. Roz's stomach lurched in her belly each time the car crawled into and out of the ruts, kicking up a cloud of dust as they bounced along through the brush.

"Because of the mine we have to keep the road in good

condition," Isa explained along the way, as she shifted furiously with each dip and turn of the road.

Was she joking?

Isa went on. "And we are lucky it's dry season now. This car never comes out here in the rain."

Red dirt showed through thirsty-looking bushes that mostly dotted the landscape instead of trees. The bushes would be too scrawny to hold back a sea of mud washing down hillsides during rainy season. Such emptiness didn't match Roz's idea of lush tropics, the way it had been in Rio. Here in the interior, there was a sense of rawness that she liked. It agreed with her frame of mind.

"The road has to stay good enough for the bus to get through," Isa said, her voice a wavery vibration from this patch of washboard. "We have our own private bus to bring the *garimpeiros* to and from the mine each day to work."

Roz knew by now, having listened to enough family conversations, that *garimpeiros* were a kind of Brazilian miner, who worked independently—in other words, whenever they felt like working. It was one of the family's challenges to find a steady supply of miners to dig through ore, exposing the veins of gemstones.

After half an hour of bumping along the road, a cyclone fence with a roll of razor wire on top came into view and ran alongside them for another mile or so until they finally came to a gate and a guardhouse. Roz sighed with relief, feeling as if her bones kept rattling in the aftermath of the bumpy ride. A man with a rifle waved them through, and they crunched into a graveled flat area, where they parked between a Jeep and a bus, both covered with red dust. This was the bus used for the mine's private shuttle, Isa explained. It looked so beaten up that Roz suspected it had been retired from some rural school district. Beyond the parking area, heavy equipment littered the base of a hill rising before them. A pit, looking like a giant bite out of the earth, sank into the left side of the hill. It was a hole large enough to swallow all three of the parked vehicles, and then some.

Isa climbed out of the car and shaded her eyes. "Where is everyone? *Mãe* worries that the *garimpeiros* are stealing from us. Is that why no one is working?"

Roz followed her out onto the thin layer of gravel. Among the equipment before her, an ore cart sat empty on a set of rails that disappeared into a dark tunnel opening into the hill. Its dark, rounded arch looked like a cave. She shuddered from the comparison. It brought on unbidden memories.

"Let's go find Larry," Isa said.

"In there?" Roz shrank back. There'd been a cave in Ohio where she and her little sister Janie had been trapped, turned into helpless, simpering victims, at the mercy of the gods of darkness. And the rapist. Janie hadn't made it out alive.

"Not there. Anyway, we can't go inside the mine without a guide. It's the rule." Isa led the way past equipment toward a shed, positioned to overlook both the pit and the mine entrance. Its tin roof reflected a blazing light that cut into Roz's head. She'd wanted to visit the facility and see where the gemstones came from, but that didn't mean she'd expected to go *inside* a tunnel that looked like a cave.

Isa pounded up three wooden planks and pushed through a thin door, calling, "Larry?"

Roz, feeling the beginnings of a headache throb in one

temple, followed more slowly. She wondered if this Larry was the same one who'd been mentioned at the pool. He'd found something and had become a problem.

Inside the boxy shed, a bear-sized man dominated the cramped space. He jumped up from behind a wooden table, spilling black drops of *cafezinho* across the papers littering its surface. Isa introduced him as Larry LeCain, the general manager the family had hired the previous year. He happened to be from the United States. Unlike Roz, he still didn't speak much Portuguese beyond the basics. He didn't need to, not with his assistant who spoke some English and dealt with the employees. The assistant was yet another da Costa cousin.

"Sure am glad you came," he said, shaking Roz's hand in a grip so tight she thought her knuckles would crack. He looked to be about Gilberto's age, somewhere in his thirties, but she couldn't be sure. A baseball cap shadowed his brow, and bristly stubbles covered the lower half of his face. A smell of sweat spiked the close air of the shed, suggesting that his rumpled coveralls hadn't met a washer in over a week.

Was that the problem? Roz suppressed the urge to wipe a residue of grease from her hand. "Thank you for letting me come for a tour. I've been wanting to see this place ever since I came to Brazil."

The shadows on his face broke apart in a pleased grin. "Well, it's a dandy. This old mine has given us plenty of reliable veins of the highest grade."

"I only hoped to see how the gems are processed," she said. "I didn't actually expect to go *inside* the mine."

"Oh, you'll want to poke your head inside. Get a feel for the place."

Isa interjected in Portuguese. "Why is there no one else here besides you? Why aren't the miners working?"

Larry scratched his head, pushing his cap back from his brow, and spoke to Roz, as if Isa weren't standing next to him. "Uh, I guess she's asking about the miners. *Mineiros*, right? Well, as you can see, they're not here." He spread one thick arm in a sweeping arch. "Never mind what you may have heard about our bread and butter vein running out on us last week. Nothing to worry about. We'll find an even better one real soon."

The wide smile that usually defined Isa's face slid to a narrow line, as thin as her full lips could form. She frowned, and the likeness to Anabela startled Roz.

Isa spoke slowly, deliberately, in the few words of English that she knew. "They. Are. Where?"

Larry shifted, and his boots squeaked the peeling linoleum of the shed's floor. "It's those damned spirits again, you know? They control everything about the miners. Maybe even the mine itself. Ask Jacinto about it. He's a little wet behind the ears, but he thinks he knows everything, thanks to those fancy ideas he got from the diamond mines in South Africa. But here? He thinks the miners think that the spirits are not happy. My assistant can't talk any sense into them, but it's stupid, I'm telling you."

Roz tried to summarize in Portuguese to Isa, who responded with a frown and one word: "*orixás*."

Spirits.

"Yeah," Larry said, "that's what he calls them. And the miners can't work in the mine until it gets fixed. That's where Jacinto is at now, trying to fix the problem his way." He'd said all this to Isa, as if she understood him, and then turned to Roz.

"Back home our miners are superstitious, too, but nothing like these *garimpeiros*. I've got another idea for how to bring them back, and it don't have anything to do with spirits."

"Like what?"

"I hear that I can get my hands on some good smokes, know what I mean?"

"No. Are you talking about drugs?"

"You didn't hear it from me. You ladies want some coffee?"

Larry set up folding chairs for them and squeezed coffee through a cheesecloth funnel. When they all sat down with their tiny cups of sugared coffee, he said, "Rio is where you'd expect to find that funny business about spirits and voodoo and all. Not here. Not in my mine." He slurped noisily.

"Well, technically, the mine isn't *mine*," he told Roz, avoiding Isa's steely look. "You know what I mean. As long as they hired me to take charge, it might as well be mine. The rest of the world forgets about you in a place like this, here in the central interior of Brazil. Makes it a great place to..."

"To what?" Roz asked when his voice drifted away, lost in thought.

Larry flushed. "Hell, it's a great place to mine. Yes, to *mine*. These mountains are full of gemstones. Arizona can't hold a candle to this place."

"Arizona? That's where you're from?"

"Me?" He snorted. "Naw. Got some experience there, though. Mining. That connection is what got me this job. Some relative of Dona Anabela's, y'know?" He turned his attention to licking the last drops of sugar from his cup, then said, "You ladies ready to get started?"

They followed him outside to a bin of hardhats sitting next

to the shed. Larry plopped one over his baseball cap and sorted through the rest until he found a couple that looked so clean they probably had never been worn. He helped Roz and Isa adjust theirs to fit, and then strode across a field of weeds to the edge of the pit.

"This here is where the *garimpeiros* usually sift with pans. When they're working, that is. They're not like our unionized miners from back home, but these guys are good, no question about it. They pick through loose rubble that all looks the same to most eyes. Not to theirs. They can instantly spot the raw pieces that have broken loose from one of the veins. You ask me? I think they're looking for something more than tourmalines."

"Like what?"

Larry shrugged. "Just a feeling I get. There's something haunted about them, the way they work, like they keep one eye and ear open to some spook they half expect is gonna grab them from behind. I guess the spooks actually got 'em this time." He laughed half-heartedly.

"Where are they?" Isa asked again.

"That's the question, isn't it?" Larry said. "I think they figured the dona's mine was all done. Played out, and it was time to move on. You ask me, they're wrong about that. There are plenty of gemstones in these mountains. I can almost smell 'em. There's another vein, and we're gonna get to it real soon. Maybe a better one. New variations always bring a good price on today's market. Anyway, the men were all here this morning, up until Jacinto came out and talked to them. After that, everyone took off. Didn't even wait for the bus driver. 'Course, they don't have much of a home to go back to in the *favelas* where they live. They scattered somewhere out there to the four winds."

Larry squinted at the surrounding scrub brush.

"Where do they go out there?" Roz said.

Larry shrugged. "Who knows where? They probably got places to hide. I'll bet you they're doing a little mining on the side." His gaze rolled furtively to Isa. "Don't tell the boss, y'hear?"

Roz stepped carefully over the rails that disappeared into the tunnel. She took up the rear position behind Isa and Larry, who stopped beside the dark entrance. Even from outside, Roz could smell the damp earthiness of the interior of the mine. Isa gazed into a box sitting on the ground next to the rails.

"See what I told you?" Larry said to Isa. "This is what Jacinto brought out. Look, I know he's a cousin and all, but I'm telling you, this ain't going to work. It's not how we're gonna find that new vein."

Isa stared into the box, frowning and shaking her head at Larry. She hadn't understood his words. Roz hurried to catch up.

"This is a bad idea," Roz said in Portuguese to Isa. "Maybe we should come back another day."

"Yes, it's bad," Isa said. "Take a look."

Inside the box were several bottles of beer and an orange, cut into small pieces.

"It explains everything," Isa said. "Why our shipments are down. The gemstones have run out, and the *garimpeiros* think it's the work of the *orixás*."

Roz didn't see how this explained anything. "What do oranges and beer have to do with any problems here?"

"They are an offering to the *orixás*, to bring the miners better luck."

Like those burning candles, flowers, and shells Roz had seen on the beach in Rio. They'd been offerings, too. She'd made a promise there, offering herself to Brazil, but she didn't intend that offering of herself to mean going inside a cave.

She pulled off her hard hat. "I'll wait for you guys out here."

She wasn't about to stir the demons of her past, bringing them back to mind. She'd put her past behind her. If only she could believe that.

Sue STAR and Bill BEATTY

# Chapter Twenty

June 24, 1959

**The basement office** at the morgue always made Gilberto shiver. It seemed he was coming here far too often. This time, he didn't have enough energy left to fight the waves of cold, and his body felt numb to the chemical smells wrapping around him. He wondered how his brother-in-law could spend so many hours working down here. It was a tomb that hadn't been sanctified with the rituals honoring death.

Having no resistance left, Gilberto sank down onto the metal chair Ben had unfolded for him and waited, as instructed. He'd done a lot of waiting these last few days, chasing down interviews of the hospital personnel and also the woman who'd brought her sister there, too late. In between, he'd only snatched small doses of sleep. Now, his eyelids fluttered shut while Ben scribbled furiously behind the mountain of papers on his desk.

"This time of year," Ben said, jolting Gilberto from his slump, "we see more deaths." Ben's voice slashed the air along with the scratching sounds of his pen. "It's the season of weddings and also the season of crimes of passion."

"Each death is one too many," Gilberto said, "but in this case, the passion came before. It only led indirectly to this crime." He scrubbed his face with the palms of his hands, unsure if he made sense anymore. He couldn't rub away his tiredness.

Ben grunted. "Crimes keep me employed."

"Have you had a chance to take a look at the body yet?"

Ben waved at the stack of folders on his desk. "You try to go away for a few days of fun surrounding the Miss Brazil pageant, and look what you come back to."

Gilberto yawned. "I know. The work never ends."

"Tell that to Anabela," Ben said. "We missed you there, at the pageant."

"Are you crazy? You can't expect me to go." Gilberto had met his first wife at one of the beauty pageants. They were important social events that his mother never missed.

"The women thought..." Ben searched for words. "They thought Roz might have enjoyed going."

Gilberto scoffed. "*Mãe* has to learn to accept Roz for who she is. She can't turn her into another Catarina, no matter how hard she tries."

"That doesn't mean your mother will ever forget Catarina."

"Of course not," Gilberto said, "but Catarina belongs to the past. If *Mãe* can't accept that, then she should at least consider Klaus's feelings. He must resent seeing anyone try to replace the woman he considered as his own daughter."

"Really? I didn't think Catarina ever liked him. In fact—"

"What she liked or not didn't matter. She treated him with the respect a father deserves. Besides, she had no memories of her real father. But all that is in the past. Let's bury it and be done with it. Roz is all that matters to me now, and I don't want to see my mother interfere."

Ben burst out laughing. "Good luck with that, man."

"First of all," Gilberto said, chuckling along, "Roz won't let

*Mãe*—or anyone—decide anything for her."

"From what Carlota tells me," Ben said, "I can imagine. Although, my wife reports that she is making good progress with your bride. Apparently, your Roz has a better understanding now of the dynamics of Brazilian families and has agreed to help prepare the twins for the domestic roles your mother insists they have."

"Roz agreed to that? I don't believe it. Besides, no one, not even Roz, could succeed with such a task. She and Carlota would have better luck taming a jaguar."

Ben chuckled. "You're right, she is nothing like your first wife."

"Nothing."

"But she knows, doesn't she? About Catarina, I mean."

"Of course. How could any man keep a thing like that from his wife?" Gilberto hadn't meant for Roz to find out the way she had. He hadn't meant to keep the information about his first wife from his second wife. It was just that he hadn't been able to talk about it. Not to anyone. This was the first time he'd opened up this much, even to Ben. He was finally pulling through his darkest days, and Roz deserved all the credit for having led him through.

"Right." Ben tilted his head and gave Gilberto a thoughtful, sympathetic gaze.

"Look," Gilberto said, trying to keep the growl from his voice, "are you going to tell me about this latest case?"

Ben cleared his throat and chose a folder from the stack of papers on his desk. "My assistants did a preliminary examination while I was away." He studied the papers maddeningly slowly. "Ieda da Cunha, twenty-three years old. It seems that she died of septicemia. Infection, most likely from unsterile equipment, and it spread to her blood. There were also traces of acid and abrasions of the vagina. We've seen that before on the other victims."

Gilberto lurched out of his chair and paced the room. Yes, they had. He wondered if the signature of acid and abrasions meant that this was the work of the same abortionist to whom Dona Mariana had sent Fatima. But Angela hadn't been one of Dona Mariana's initiates, he was sure of that, based on what her neighbor, Joana Morango, had told him. There hadn't been enough hours of the day left over in Angela's workday to spend any time praying to the *orixá* spirits. Most likely, there was more than one hack, which complicated Gilberto's hunt. How many butchers were out there, and could he ever get rid of all of them?

And now there was Ieda. Ieda's sister sadly hadn't known where Ieda had gone for the procedure, but she *did* know about the mysterious bags of medicinal herbs. Ieda had brought them home from the *feira*. Different vendors set up there frequently, and Gilberto had quizzed all who were there. None of them remembered—or claimed to remember—the young mother with three kids and no husband. No means to support another child. Ieda had been another lost woman. Perhaps that had attracted her to Dona Mariana's pink house, the "Temple for Lost Women." The sister didn't know about any cults.

Ben sighed. "When you find this guy and take him out of operation—and I know you will—ten more just like him will replace him."

Not if Gilberto could help it. He was lucky to have Sam's help in this regard. His North American friend, Sam Clinton, was advising the police department about "effective" interview techniques. Hopefully, they would deter criminals once and for all from ever carrying on their butchery.

*　*　*　*　*

Somehow, Gilberto made it through the rest of the long day, and at the end of shift, he was no closer to finding the killer abortionist than before. Ubaldo had ducked out of the station early, as he usually did, leaving Gilberto to tidy up the day's paperwork. The promise of Roz's soothing magic guided him down the long hall and out the front door.

Sam caught up to him in the parking lot and clapped a hand on his shoulder. "Hey pal, tough day? You look like you could use a drink. What do you say?"

"I need to get home."

"Hey, just one."

Gilberto didn't have enough strength to resist anymore as Sam steered him to the sidewalk. His friend was a head shorter, but he was all muscle, and he nudged him along the block, all the way to the pub that was a favorite for off-duty officers. Even though the pub was open-air, giving it the feel of a non-committal place, where passers-by could stop for a quick drink on their way home, a cloud of cigarette smoke engulfed him as they entered the cordoned area. They ordered pints of beer from the covered bar and then carried them to the first available table, a round two-top outside the perimeter of the awning.

"You want to tell me about it?" Sam said.

Gilberto sipped froth and then leaned heavily on his elbows. "No."

213

Chatter buzzed around them, as the tables filled with customers. Only a couple tables were left empty, toward the back. In the far corner he spied the towering head of his partner, Ubaldo, in earnest conversation with a golden-haired man, whose back was turned to Gilberto. No surprise. That's why Ubaldo had been so eager to leave work early. He and his companion laughed and raised their pints, and then Gilberto caught a glimpse of the profile of Ubaldo's drinking partner.

Jacinto. One of Gilberto's cousins. The one who'd recently returned from the diamond mines of South Africa. Roz had asked him about some "problem" regarding Jacinto, but he'd avoided her questions, rejecting such a possibility.

Gilberto ducked his head over his pint, wondering how he could escape the social obligation of exchanging greetings with his cousin. It was all he could manage, just to sit here numb with Sam, letting the brew loosen the troubles knotting his mind. Anyway, what was his cousin doing here? He hadn't realized that Jacinto and Ubaldo knew each other, but then, Belo was a small town at heart. Now he wondered if his wife was right and his cousin really did have some problem he didn't know about.

"Someone you know?" Sam said.

"The guy I sometimes partner with." He took a slow breath while thinking briefly about his cousin. Should he also mention Jacinto to Sam? Probably not. Keep the family out of this. "You've met my partner. Ubaldo Ramos."

"I remember." Sam snorted. "The one with the chip on his shoulder."

"Best detective in the department." Gilberto took a long sip and wondered what was Ubaldo's business with Jacinto. A security issue at the mine, perhaps? If that was the case, then why hadn't his cousin come to *him*, instead of going to his partner?

Well, it wasn't his concern, but he couldn't help the doubts that kept resurfacing at the edge of his mind. Hell, if he had a choice of whom to ask for detective work, it wouldn't be Gilberto da Costa, either. He hadn't solved a case in almost a year. If not for being who he was—a da Costa—he surely would've been fired by now. He'd made no progress, hadn't even spotted Picapau the street kid, aka Edgar Pena, for nearly three months. He hadn't fulfilled any of the promises he'd made, with the exception that Irmã remained safe in Gilberto's household. For now. He'd gone back to Sete Lagoas to interview her family, but he hadn't learned anything. They'd vouched for their daughter's essential goodness, unlike the claims of the first victim's uncle, Pedro Pires.

The question was, who was lying? And where was Angela Cardaso's family? He hadn't found them in Congonhas or the friend with the goiter, either. But the question that burned him the most was the identity of the ringleader behind the butchery of abortion.

Then Sam's voice broke through his morose thoughts, bringing Gilberto back to the present moment. Laughter surrounded him. Passers-by swished past their table. Cigarette smoke clouded the air.

"You going to be at your mother's dinner party when that deputy from the Embassy visits town?" Sam said.

Gilberto grunted, grateful for the distraction. He wasn't accustomed to self-pity, but he simply couldn't abide his failures. "Not if I can help it," he said. "Roz doesn't like to go out much."

"Some of us don't have a choice. Ike is going to visit Brasilia soon, so the deputy in charge of arrangements is stopping over here, on his way there. All the big whigs of Belo will be at your mother's house."

Gilberto's gaze shifted toward the far corner. What were those two talking about?

Sam laughed. "All I hear at home is how Helen has to get herself dolled up just right. It's costing me plenty with all that jewelry she's buying. Can't you help her get a discount?"

"Ask Isa. She's in the business, not me."

"I'm surprised your family never pulled you in, too," Sam said.

"They tried plenty of times, believe me." *They got Jacinto, instead.*

"But you resisted."

"Yeah. Too much else to do. Too many assholes out there who need to be caught." Fatima Souza had gone to see one of them that day she never came back, but Gilberto was no closer to finding out where she'd gone.

"With some of our methods of..." Sam paused, as if searching for the word he wanted. "Umm, 'interrogation...' You'll have a good chance of eliminating problems. You won't have any worries after the prisoners get released."

"If we had more prison space, maybe they wouldn't get out so fast. But Kubitschek wants to build an entire city, instead of new prisons. And show it off to the world, besides."

"Brasilia is an amazing accomplishment. Have you been there yet? It looks like something from another planet."

"It might as well be," Gilberto said, "that far into the interior. The president will never persuade people to move so far away from civilization."

"He will, once the government relocates there next year.

You have a mighty big country to fill, and it has plenty of space for everyone to spread out. No need to cramp everyone up along the coast."

"Send the assholes out there to the interior. Headhunters will take care of them."

Sam laughed. "You believe those stories?"

Gilberto studied his friend silently, considering a range of responses. He didn't want to offend his friend, because they weren't made-up stories. The only question was where, exactly, the tribes were at the moment. With a shrug, he decided not to address the issue of belief versus fact. "If we send them far away," he said, "then maybe they'll stop making victims of poor, young, and pregnant women."

"Like Ieda da Cunha?"

"Yeah."

Sam carefully adjusted the position of his pint glass. "You know, don't you, that if she'd survived, she would've been arrested in the hospital."

"If I'd done my job better, she would never have had to go to the hospital to die."

"Look, pal, you can't blame yourself."

The hell he couldn't. "Who else, then?" He lifted his glass and swallowed a third of its contents in one gulp. "I'm no closer to putting her killer out of business than I was months ago. Hell, years ago."

When the dead bird had shown up on his doorstep, sprinkled with herbs, and his wife had been found dead hours later, her body mutilated, the fetus of their son removed. The bird sacrifice had made it look like the work of a cult. Umbrotamba.

"It takes time," Sam said softly.

"How much time? How many more women have to die in the meanwhile?" *Not Roz.* He couldn't survive if he lost her, too.

Sam spread his palms on the table. "Look at it this way. Sex is...shall we say, more open here in this culture. As long as abortion remains illegal in Brazil, some women are going to look for help, however they can find it. Naturally, there will be a few opportunists who step in and take advantage of the situation."

"More than just a few."

"They think they are offering a solution to the problem. They'd prefer that their patients live. All they really want is their money. They don't mean to kill. The deaths are collateral damage."

Gilberto nodded, then swallowed the last of his beer. There'd been too many deaths. While he'd been wallowing in self-pity. He scraped his chair backwards, nearly tipping it over in his unsteadiness. His vision was growing fuzzy from the spirits of smoke and brew. He had to clear his head. Roz was just the person to do that. And then tomorrow, he'd resume his search. He'd find that clinic even if he had to go door-to-door, building by building throughout the city. He would never give up.

# Chapter Twenty-One

June 25, 1959

**After Gilberto left for** work that morning, and after Irmã left to do some shopping, Roz turned up her radio and danced along with the music. She barely heard the knocking when it came to her front door. Uh-oh. It was probably Silvia, complaining about her noise, even though her neighbor was the one who watched static on her television screen and listened to its scratching sounds. Roz switched off the radio and went to the door.

"Who is it?" she asked in Portuguese, as Gilberto had instructed her to do, as if she wouldn't know to use caution. She'd come a long way, but she was still in unfamiliar territory. "Your new neighbor," said a woman's voice in the softly nasal sounds of Portuguese that Roz's foreign tongue couldn't fully imitate for the life of her.

Roz opened the door to a smiling woman who looked to be about her age. Everything was soft about her, besides her voice. Her face was shaped like a heart, and black hair fell in soft curls down to the rounded shoulders of her crisp, white blouse. The flowered pattern of her skirt flared out in soft gathers from a waist tinier than Roz's.

"I'm sorry if things got a little too loud," Roz said.

The new neighbor laughed and held out her hand. "What noise? I'm Marilia Iriri. I moved in to the apartment across the hall a few months ago, and Dona Silvia asked if we'd gotten to know each other yet. So here I am."

Her softness was everything that Roz was not, and in spite of Silvia's manipulation, Roz couldn't help feeling intrigued. "Please come in," she said, holding open the door. "I'm Rosalinda da Costa." After six months, the name finally felt natural.

Marilia practically floated inside, moving with the sensuous grace that Roz envied. By now, Roz knew the polite custom was to serve *cafezinho*, without even asking whether or not the guest wanted it. But Irmã was out, and Roz wasn't sure how she could make the coffee without abandoning this new arrival. She'd never had a real guest before. She didn't count the times that Helen or Isa had stopped by at the apartment, picking her up on the way somewhere. Helen was as foreign to Brazilian customs as was Roz, and Isa was family. So neither one of them counted as a Brazilian guest.

"You want a *guaraná*?" Roz asked instead.

Marilia laughed. "My favorite."

Roz laughed too. She also knew that it was the custom never to turn down anything that was offered, whether the guest liked the offering or not. Roz led the way to the alcove where the refrigerator sat, inconveniently distant from the kitchen, but that's where the plug was with the proper voltage. She pulled out two bottles of *guaraná* from the refrigerator, found some glasses in the kitchen, and then led the way back into the living room.

"I meant to introduce myself before now," Marilia said,

"because I know you're foreign, but they keep me very busy at work. Today I don't have to go to the office, and when I heard your radio I thought..."

Marilia's voice drifted into words Roz didn't understand. She wondered if her being foreign would always make her the newcomer, even though she'd lived in this building longer than Marilia. A twinge of guilt reminded Roz that she was the one who should've made the first move toward introductions, maybe with a plate of cookies to the new neighbor. Being Betty Crocker was just not Roz, no matter the change in her identity.

"Right?" Marilia said, breaking into Roz's confusion. "You're from the United States, aren't you? I've never met a *gringa* before. Tell me about yourself."

"There's not much to tell," Roz said, feeling the tightening of secrets spread through her. Rather, there wasn't much she was willing to tell. "I married a Brazilian and moved here. That's all. Now it's your turn to tell me about you."

Marilia's laughter made a tinkling sound. "My aunt tells me I'm too modern. She was scandalized that I found a job after school and wanted my own apartment. Since I'm not married, she thinks I should either live with her, here in the city, or go back to my small hometown and live with my family. But all that is boring. A career is so much more interesting, don't you think? I'll bet you have a career, too. Don't all *gringas* have one?"

Roz shrugged. "I left all that behind. I was going to be an actress."

"Really?" Marilia's eyes widened to mascara-ringed circles. "I love movies. Sometimes they let me write reviews of movies for the newspaper."

"The newspaper?"

"That's where I work, didn't I say? I bothered them long enough until they finally gave me a job. It's a start, but they won't let me do any important reporting. Not yet, that is. All they let me do is write about things they think women would like. What kind of soap to use, stuff like that. I have to save movies for my days off. Like today. We should go together. All the latest movies come here, and we have nice theaters."

"I know. I've already been. It's one of my favorite things to do."

They chatted on about favorite movies and actors, losing track of time slipping by. They checked the newspaper, chose a movie, and rode there together on the bus. The warmth of the promise of friendship stayed with Roz long after the credits played and they'd returned to their separate apartments. After one short day, Roz knew that Marilia was going to be the first real friend she'd ever had.

\* \* \* \* \*

Gilberto started his renewed search with a visit to the drugstore where his former father-in-law worked. He'd tried his best to avoid Klaus during these last five difficult years of investigation into Catarina's murder. His late wife had never fully bonded with her stepfather, regardless of her filial duties, which had made interviewing Klaus all the more difficult. But since Klaus had lived in the neighborhood at the bottom of the hill where Catarina's body was found, the interviews had been necessary. Ever since that awful time, Klaus's presence only helped remind Gilberto of the blinding pain he'd suffered. Now he couldn't put off a visit any longer.

It was a small shop, just inside the Contorno, the avenue that formed a ring around the city. The original planners thought the city would end there, with an expected 150,000 in population, but these days, the city had exploded to 700,000. Now, the ring street only separated the business side of the city from newer quiet residential areas, such as Barroca, where he and Roz lived in one of the da Costa family-owned properties.

The lime green storefront took up little more space than the width of the glass door. A bell on the door jingled as Gilberto entered the air of antiseptic smells. A narrow aisle led from the front door, through the depth of the building toward its back wall. Glass-topped counters lined the sides and far end of the aisle, separating customers from the products that crowded onto shelves the length and height of the walls. Shoppers had to wait until the clerk could retrieve a specific item for them.

At the far end of the store, Klaus looked up from his position behind the counter, where he was helping a customer. His thick, black hair slicked back, its darkness contrasting starkly with his white smock. He scowled at Gilberto and bent back down over his task of measuring out a powdery substance for the customer, a young woman.

While Gilberto waited, he strode slowly along the aisle, peering at the gaily-wrapped packages and labeled bottles lining the shelves. The tops of larger items were barely visible from where they sat on the floor behind the counter. One such item looked like the head of a statue. Gilberto leaned across the glass surface of the counter for a better view. A statuette of a woman with bare breasts and a large belly sat there. It was like the one he'd seen on the altar at Dona Mariana's house.

"I'll be with you in a minute," Klaus said, his tone of voice snapping off his words.

"Take your time," Gilberto said, backing away from the counter.

The young woman customer appeared to be in her early twenties, close to the same age as the women whose deaths by botched abortion he was investigating. His gaze traveled to the pots of dried leaves and powders that Klaus dipped into, releasing earthy, pungent smells into the air. He spooned them into small cloth bags, each one a different color, and then tied them up with green string.

Similar to the nearly empty bags he'd found in Angela Cardaso's room. And there was green string in the waste bin of Ieda da Cunha's bathroom.

Unease spread through him, wondering how widely used among druggists were these particular bags and string. He also wondered about the power of these natural drugs. They would've originated from the Amazon, easily available through the *feira*. Klaus, or his boss, had probably acquired their supply from the open-air market, and then resold them here in the shop. And more importantly, Gilberto felt a rumble of disquiet over possible reasons why this poor, young woman wanted such drugs, along with the helpful advice of a druggist.

When she finally paid for her bags of drugs and left, sweeping past Gilberto, he noticed the goiter on her neck. Goiters were not so uncommon here. Just because this young woman had one didn't necessarily make her the friend of Angela Cardaso, whom her neighbor Joana had told him about. Still...

"Wait, *Senhorinha*," Gilberto called. But the door slammed shut behind her.

"Now then," Klaus said, tapping the counter impatiently. "Have you finally brought me some news?"

Gilberto rushed to the door and pushed it open, but the woman had disappeared from sight. He turned back to Klaus. "Who is she? Do you know where she lives?"

"Where's your warrant?"

Gilberto sighed and crossed the store to face the irritating man. "I was hoping for a little cooperation from you. Perhaps you've heard about the rising number of deaths from illegal abortions?"

"The only death that matters to me is my little girl's." Klaus narrowed his eyes, aiming his gaze at the golden band on Gilberto's wedding ring finger, one of a matching pair he'd ordered from Guilhermo Machado. "Apparently, you've forgotten."

Gilberto could almost feel his blood simmer. Just because Catarina had respected her stepfather had never made her Klaus's "little girl." Furthermore, Klaus had always made Gilberto feel inadequate that the police—his own colleagues—hadn't yet found her killer, let alone arrested anyone. And finally, he hadn't forgotten. Would never forget. Roz helped ease him through the darkness of his days. The reference to the distraction of having a new wife was only meant to get a stir from him. It worked.

"With your cooperation," Gilberto said through his clenched jaw, "I might be able to bring you the news one day of her killer's arrest." He pulled the photographs of the victims from his shirt pocket and spread all three of them on the counter before Klaus. "Did any of these women ever come into your store?"

"Where did you get these?"

"I took them."

"They let you do this?"

"It's my job."

"Brazilians don't like it much," Klaus said, "having their photographs taken."

"These women are past minding, since they're dead."

"And you think they died from illegal abortions?"

Gilberto nodded.

"Catarina didn't die from an abortion," Klaus said with a scoff.

No, but her death had been caused by the butchery of removing the fetus, same as any woman's death from a botched abortion. Gilberto couldn't discuss the particulars of a case with a civilian, and certainly not with Klaus, even though that investigation had been closed long ago. He hoped it would be reopened as a result of a breakthrough on his current cases, which he feared wouldn't remain open and active much longer— unless another death occurred. Gilberto's mission now was to prevent further deaths.

"That woman who was in here just now," Gilberto said, instead of responding to the bait Klaus had tossed at him, "what was she buying?"

"Why don't you run after her and ask her yourself?"

"I thought you might save me the trouble. What are those drugs for?" He pointed at the open pots before Klaus.

"What makes you sure they're drugs?" Klaus resealed the pots and slipped them beneath the counter.

"This is a drug store. What else could they be?"

Klaus motioned at the open shelves along the wall with his thick arm. "We sell other items besides drugs."

"Such as...?"

"Look around. We offer a full array of items for any medical problem. You tell me what you need, and I will find it for you. Maybe a little something to help you get it up?"

Gilberto growled as he snatched the photos from the counter and stuffed them back into his pocket. "What I need is information. What was your customer buying just now?"

"You saw her. It's for her goiter."

"What she bought didn't look like iodine."

Klaus laughed, but no mirth sounded. "Forget it. The offerings for *orixás* work like medicine, too. No need to worry."

"You sell spiritual items here." It wasn't a question. Gilberto had seen the icon statuette behind the counter.

"We are a full-service shop in matters of health."

"Including abortions?"

"They're illegal."

"That doesn't stop them from happening," Gilberto said. "Do you have any clients who ask where they can find one?"

"Why would I know about something that is illegal?"

"Perhaps you know another druggist who does know. Perhaps your own boss? You have colleagues in this business. They must offer a variety of special 'medical' services."

"What you're looking for is a hospital," Klaus said.

"There are some services that hospitals won't provide."

"What are you accusing me of? Come out with it."

"Have you ever heard of Umbrotamba?"

Biting off his barrage of retorts, Klaus straightened. Tugged the hem of his smock across his belly. Stood back a couple steps from the counter, as if heading for the narrow entrance to the back room. "Never," he finally said. "Are you suggesting that's who killed my girl?"

"We don't know yet, but we're working on it."

"The hell you are. You're too busy enjoying your little honeymoon, aren't you? You only care about the Yankee. Not your own people."

The vehemence in his words felt like a hot wind blowing in Gilberto's face, and now he was the one to step back. "You don't know."

Klaus gave him a smug look that read as if he disagreed. But Klaus had no idea. Gilberto had found Roz only because she'd had Catarina's ring. Because someone had brought it to Denver for her to find. He slammed through the door and set off for the next drugstore on his list.

# Chapter Twenty-Two

June 26, 1959

**Ten weeks since the last** red "x" on Roz's calendar, and she knew the rabbit was going to die. Tomorrow she had an appointment to see the family doctor, whether or not it was too soon. She had no idea if it was or not, but tomorrow was the day. Tonight, nothing else mattered. Not even Anabela. Because Roz was going to achieve her goal. Her identity would change so completely that no one could ever haul her back to her old life and make her pay for all those past mistakes.

"You look radiant tonight, *meu amor*," Gilberto said in the car on the way out to the family estate for the weekly dinner.

She couldn't tell him yet. Hadn't expected feeling like a silly schoolgirl, out-of-breath excited about the prom. It must be the hormones. A part of her old brain protested at losing control, but she told it to shut up. She was here to stay.

She smiled at him. "This...what we planned...you and me... it's going to work."

"I know." He smiled back. "You are not sorry for your part? Maybe sorry that you came here?"

"I'm only sorry that...things have been difficult. Me." She scooted closer to him and nestled against his arm on the steering wheel. She'd mouthed off to this gentle, kind man too many times, but the truth was, that the permanence of her move here

229

had terrified her. Her smart mouth had covered up her fear. She understood that now, and she no longer felt afraid. At least, not that much.

"We will not talk about any difficulties in the past but only look ahead to our future."

"Agreed." She sighed and massaged his thigh.

The road climbed a hill in open country. At the top, it rounded a bend before meeting the stone wall that surrounded the da Costa estate. Gilberto pulled the car off into the grasses at the side of the road and turned off the engine.

"Why are we stopping?" she said, pulling away from him and looking around. There was no traffic out in this wild place. No houses, no people. She and Gilberto were alone, except for a couple of cows on the other side of bushes.

He took her in his arms and murmured as he covered her with kisses. "You are so beautiful, *meu amor*." He pushed her down to the vinyl bench seat.

"We'll be late."

"Shhh," he said, and then nothing mattered anymore except for the passion of the moment.

She really did feel like a schoolgirl. She'd felt it once before. In Ohio, at the drive-in when she was sixteen with dreams of Hollywood. The flame had already ignited within her—until her mother's boyfriend found the boy.

What had gone before was over. Now, here... Time stopped.

Later, when time started again, she caught her breath and smoothed the tousled locks of her hair, overdue for another chemical treatment. Too much mousy brown showed through the blonde streaks. Her linen sheath dress was hopelessly wrinkled. Anabela would probably believe it was due to Irmã's faulty ironing.

Gilberto started up the car again and pulled out onto the empty road. They must've traveled a mile or so alongside the stone wall that surrounded the da Costa estate before they came to the guardhouse by the gate to the driveway. The guard wiggled his eyebrows at Gilberto when he opened the gate and waved them through. He seemed to know about their stop back there at the bend in the road at the top of the hill. Perhaps that spot had seen many couples before.

The driveway rolled another half-mile through low, scrubby hills. Behind one of the hills, she caught sight of a lake, its water glistening under the late afternoon sun. "Is that where your brother had his accident?"

She regretted the question as soon as it left her mouth, as his face turned a shade darker and his shaggy eyebrows furrowed together. His head dipped in a curt nod.

Gilberto had explained to her once, shortly after she'd met most of the family, that Tonio had almost drowned in one of the ponds on the property. They hadn't thought to secure the ponds on account of the threat of schistosomiasis. Nobody went in the water because of those snail parasites, but Tonio hadn't known. He'd been a curious kid of around seven or eight when the accident happened, not too long before Francisco Senior shipped off to war. Those were years of tragedy, and the family still didn't like to talk about them.

Roz dropped the further questions from her mind—did they know if Tonio had also contracted the dreaded disease? Anyway, the little lake disappeared from sight as the mansion came into view.

They parked the Fairlane in a rounded parking area at the bottom of the hill where the house soared. Two Mercedes, one belonging to Isa and the other to Carlota, were already here. Roz's reference to the brother's accident might've dampened Gilberto's spirits, but nothing could spoil Roz's mood. She wondered as they climbed out of the car and started up the long steps if Doctor Ben had come along tonight to the family dinner. Would he be able to spot her pregnancy in the glow of her face? The twins, Olivia and Elvira, hadn't left a car out front, since they still lived at home with their mother and would continue to do so until they married.

They wound up through the hillside flower garden and ducked under flaming red leaves of poinsettia trees. When they made it to the landing at the gemstone-studded entryway to the mansion, Roz reached for Gilberto's hand and clung to it. She didn't like the way his mother made her feel this way. Uncertain. In need of extra support. She'd always been able to handle herself just fine.

Okay, maybe she'd made a few mistakes along the way. She didn't need anyone pointing them out to her.

Gilberto patted her hand, and then the butler opened the door for them, lifting his chin as he whisked them through the marble halls of the house. He flung open French doors to a terrace that stretched across the back of the mansion and overlooked a sea of green. As always, the wide blades of grass had been meticulously trimmed. The family looked up from their pre-dinner cocktails as Roz and Gilberto stepped out into the fragrant air of flowers. In the distance, birds sang and trilled.

"Even by Brazilian standards," Carlota said, stiffening as if a rod in the back of her dress held her up, "it took you long enough to get here."

"Did your car break down?" Isa said with a wide, soft smile.

The twins giggled and whispered to each other.

Anabela's gaze roved up and down Roz's rumpled linen.

Gilberto greeted his mother with a kiss, which started the round of kisses for all, and then he asked his sister, "Ben is working late again?"

"When isn't he?" said Carlota.

By now the family knew that Roz could understand most of what they said. Maybe it was just her imagination, but their conversation sounded more guarded around her these days, more stilted. Anabela pinched her thin lips together, looking as if she might burst from whatever was pent up inside her that she really wanted to say. When she finally spoke, it was in short spurts rather than the fluid whisper-purrs of the rest of them.

"As I was telling your brothers and sisters before you arrived," Anabela said (Roz wanted to interrupt, asking where the brothers were, but she bit her tongue), "I shall expect everyone's help for our gala event, when we welcome the ambassador."

"*Mãe*," Gilberto said, "it's not the ambassador who's coming, but one of his deputies."

Anabela flicked her wrist. "Anyone from Rosalinda's Embassy of the United States is someone we need to entertain properly. As hosts, we will take great care of him."

Roz's hand hesitated over the glass of champagne on the attending maid's silver tray. Perhaps her mother-in-law intended to make the deputy initiate a background check, searching for the dirt on Roz: her own past as Linda Armbrust. Anabela would not rest until she found it, and then what? Ship her back to the States?

Not with a baby on the way. Roz smiled to herself and

sipped her drink. She shrank away from the rest as their voices rose with anticipation. There would be a *churrascaría*, Anabela announced, with special ovens brought in to grill skewers of sixteen different kinds of meats. Carlota would oversee the additional staff that would be required to pull off an event with a guest list nearing two hundred, and Isa would be in charge of house decorations. When Gilberto's name was mentioned, Roz looked up from her glass and shifted closer to pay better attention.

"Gilberto," Anabela said, "you will be in charge of the additional security we will need. Can you ask your friends at the police station to fill in?"

"No," he said simply, thrusting one hand into his trouser pocket while the other hand tipped his glass of caipirinha to his lips. Roz recognized the stance as his stubborn stance. It would be interesting to see if Anabela could change his mind.

"But my son," Anabela said in a honeyed voice, so fake that it sounded as if someone else spoke through her, "we desperately need more security. Do you not care about all the break-ins we've had on the estate recently?"

"That's why you hire guards."

"But there's too much land for them to cover effectively, and the walls aren't high enough to keep thieves out who are determined to get in."

Gilberto shrugged. "Hire more guns."

"Of course, my son, that's what I mean to do. But you have the better contacts in that department."

"Your walls should be higher," Carlota said, "and you should add broken glass on top."

"For now," Anabela said, "I just want to hire more security.

If you won't do it, Gilberto, then I shall have to ask Jacinto. He'll do it."

A touch of pink crept up Gilberto's neck, rising from the collar of his white dress shirt. Roz wondered why her husband didn't seem to like his cousin. She couldn't recall that the two of them had ever appeared at the same family events. At least, not since she'd been here, half a year now.

All this talk about security was making her feel less secure. She scanned the grounds around her—the stretch of green grass before her, the row of buildings beyond the gardens, and in the distance, open fields of wild grasses. She saw nothing amiss, but she wasn't sure that she would recognize trouble if she saw it. She'd never even been sure that the shadowy man with the cane she'd spotted had actually been following her these past few months. More likely, he was just someone from the neighborhood, and she was imagining the shadows. She was finally safe now, but even so, she took a few steps closer to Gilberto's side.

Then suddenly, an eruption of bird squawks sounded from across the lawn. *A-ra-ra!*

Human voices called, and footsteps scuffled. The disturbance was coming from the cluster of buildings across the lawn. They were guest houses and separate apartments, including one for Tonio, and farther out were quarters for all the staff. Roz had never formally been introduced to the disabled brother, but she'd seen him from afar at times when the family gathered out here on the back terrace.

Anabela lifted a silver bell from a nearby table and jangled it. The butler appeared moments later, and Anabela instructed him to find out what was the cause of the commotion. Surely the servants realized, Anabela scolded him, that the family was not to be disturbed.

He went away, and soon, maids scurried back and forth, between the kitchen doors at the far end of the house and the guest houses. There were enough buildings clustered together and sheltered discretely behind trees and flowering bushes, that altogether they resembled a village. Roz imagined it took a large staff to run a place like this. Tonio's quarters were also over there, somewhere. His condition required round-the-clock staff to care for him.

"What's going on?" Roz whispered to Gilberto. Slapping noises drifted across the lawn. They sounded like flapping wings.

*A-ra-ra!* cried the birds.

"Tonio's upset. It's nothing to worry about. His nurses will give him something to calm him down."

"What do you mean?" Her voice rose. "What are they going to give him?"

"Shhh."

"Drugs? Is that what you mean?" Her heart pattered as she remembered back to her mother, who'd spent most of her time in drugged-out semi-consciousness. Roz hadn't been able to stand it then, and she couldn't stand it now. "Has anyone thought to find out why he's upset?"

"It's impossible to communicate with him," Gilberto said. "We're doing the best we can, by keeping him here, but maybe that's a mistake. Maybe we should've sent him to an institution, instead."

"Or just kill him with drugs," said Roz. She pulled away from Gilberto and marched across the terrace into the grass.

Voices argued behind her, but Roz kept going, stomping through the thick grass. Its blades tickled her toes through her open sandals. She didn't look back.

She reached a dirt path on the other side of the grass and stopped one of the maids scurrying back and forth. "Where is he?"

The maid pointed over her shoulder and mumbled her apologies to the *Senhora*. Roz followed her pointing arm, and soon she came to a wire birdcage, standing on wooden pillars and as big as the bathroom in her apartment. Inside the cage was a trunk with a branch, where a blue and yellow macaw danced nervously back and forth.

Roz stopped suddenly and gaped. A man who must be Tonio stood next to the cage and sobbed openly, with loud, dramatic *boo-hoos*. She recognized the tall, thin man, and not just because he looked like a gaunter version of Gilberto. She'd seen him a couple months ago in the *feira*, while watching the vendor stuff the *arara* into a box. Next to Tonio stood a plump, middle-aged woman wearing a white smock. She draped one arm about his shoulders, and he kept shaking off her arm.

"*Boa tarde*," Roz called. "Are you the nurse? What's going on with Tonio?"

The nurse nodded, shrinking away from Tonio and giving Roz a wide-eyed look of horror. "I'm sorry, *Senhora*," she said, almost sobbing, too. "He got away from me when one of the maids mentioned the birds. He went crazy, but I'll get him calmed down soon, I promise."

"What about the birds? Has something happened?" Roz stepped closer and touched Tonio's shoulder tentatively.

Startling at the touch, he brushed her hand from his

237

shoulder and drew himself upright to look at her. An unruly lock of coppery hair fell over his eyes, which were astonishingly blue through the stream of his tears. Except for the eyes, he could've been a thin, less muscled version of Gilberto. She gasped, and so did he. As if he recognized her.

He snuffled loudly and said, "You... You did it."

Her rejected hand covered her mouth as she stumbled backwards. "What? What did I do?"

The nurse looked over Roz's shoulder as footsteps pounded the path behind her. Gilberto's arms encircled her protectively, and his voice snapped as he questioned the nurse. "Did he hurt her?"

"No, *Senhor*," the nurse said. "It was a simple mistake. Someone left the door of the cage open. We didn't keep their wings clipped, and one of the birds has escaped. Your brother is devastated. He treats the birds like his best friends."

A chill crept down Roz's spine. Tonio must've seen the truth in her soul—she was as much a prisoner as the bird. Perhaps that was why he thought she'd set the bird free.

# Chapter Twenty-Three

July 10, 1959

**The bird had escaped**, and the rabbit had died. Now Roz feared the worst for her unborn child, on account of the cramps.

The morning she awoke with cramps, it had only been thirteen weeks since that last red-x day on her calendar. An unlucky number. Ever since then, she and Gilberto had acted like rabbits themselves, the way they'd gone after each other. Not to mention all the car rides over bumpy roads. And then there was the anxiety Anabela tried to lay onto each of them about her stupid party. The woman didn't seem to realize that the trouble she was going to was for an embassy deputy and not for the ambassador himself. Who was this deputy, and why did he matter to anyone else, someone who had nothing to hide in her past?

Today it would finally be over. Tonight would be the party. They were expected at the estate at midday, to oversee the last-minute set-up. Anabela wanted more pairs of hawkish eyes to help her hover over the extra staff she'd hired.

Well, Roz would see about that. She'd awakened this morning with the most back-wrenching cramps she'd ever experienced, and Gilberto had already left for work. Marilia was away at work, too. Irmã dripped some coffee into a tiny cup, filled half with sugar, but that didn't help. Roz considered crossing the hall to Silvia's apartment to ask to use the telephone. But whom would she call? Gilberto? He didn't even know about the baby. She wasn't sure why she hadn't told him yet. She'd been waiting for the right moment, and with Anabela's overriding frenzy, that right moment had just never happened. Now she didn't even think she had enough strength to make it across the hall to Silvia's.

Instead, she decided to go back to bed, and she barely made it there before collapsing. She fell asleep as her head touched the pillow.

\* \* \* \* \*

*A-ra-ra!*

*She is a bird with streaming blue feathers, flying free...*

*The currents carry her, and she soars over shimmering mountains, and their shimmer becomes the sea.*

*Her stomach rolls with each swoop and dive.*

*Beneath her flight, candles burn. Their flames singe her feathers with dripping moisture.*

*She swoops closer to the sparkles beneath her. They are not the sea, but glittering stones. Gemstones...*

*A box of beer and oranges sits beside a deep, dark hole. The darkness sucks at her, and she is falling... Falling...*

\* \* \* \* \*

*Oh!*

The cramp stabbed her awake from her dream. Stretching

against the pain in her lower back, she curled up into a fetal position beneath her sheet. Something warm slicked between her legs.

She rolled out of bed and aimed herself at the bathroom. Doubled over on the balls of her feet, she staggered as if stepping on spikes. She barely made it there before another cramp overwhelmed her.

The clot of blood finally passed, draining her body of pain's lead weight. Waves of residue pain, mere echoes of what it had been, thrummed through her. She collapsed in a ball, sobbing, her tears flowing, mixing with the blood.

"Irmã!" she cried.

She shouldn't have had that ride out to the mine in Isa's bumpy car. All this was Roz's fault. It was always her fault. Just as it had been her fault with that first one, back in Ohio. Both times, they'd only been helpless fetuses, but this time it was different. Was this one payment for the first one? What happened to this one now, after being flushed down the toilet like a bundle of unwanted tissue in a heavy flow of blood?

It wasn't unwanted tissue, not like the first time. It was a fetus, and it would've grown into a child.

"Irmã!" she cried again, and this time hasty footsteps scurried, answering her call from the other side of the door.

"*Senhora*?" Irmã knocked on the door. "Are you okay?"

"Call Gilberto."

\* \* \* \* \*

She sobbed in Gilberto's arms the rest of the day.

"*Meu amor*," he kept whispering to her over and over,

stroking her. "Everything is okay. We will try again when it is safe."

It was a hell of a way for him to find out, she thought, sniffling.

He put her back to bed, after Irmã had changed the sheets. Wearily, she closed her eyes and watched the blue and yellow bird flit past under her eyelids. Voices whispered somewhere in the darkness. Swishing, scrubbing sounds came from the bathroom. The toilet flushed, and her baby was gone, leaving her empty inside. It wasn't right, sending a baby into the sewer.

She drifted...

Or maybe she slept...

Or maybe she flew away with the bird...

Later... (How much later? There was something she had to do... Somewhere she had to go...) More voices.

"*Meu amor.*" Fingers stroked her, slowly pulling her from the depths of the black hole that had swallowed her. Gilberto.

"Gil," she said. Her voice croaked, sounding like a stranger's to her own ears.

"My brother is here to talk to you."

"Tonio?"

"Of course not. Francisco. But only if you want to see him."

"Like this?" God, she was a mess, her face caked with tears and snot, her body crusted with bits of dried blood.

"You are beautiful, my love."

"He's too late. For last rites." She choked on tears.

Gilberto recoiled, and through her blurry vision, she noticed for the first time that haggard lines etched across his face, aging him at least ten years. Those lines on his face tightened, as if she'd slapped him.

More tears slid down her cheeks. She hated herself. Why did the wrong words always erupt from her?

"Give me a little time to clean myself up and change. Can he wait?"

\* \* \* \* \*

The *cafezinho* smelled ready by the time Roz limped slowly out to the living room. Irmã had left the pink box handy for her in the newly scrubbed bathroom, and now the pads crinkled with each step, sawing at the tender flesh of her thighs. The two brothers sat at the tiny table, which someone had shoved up against the window. Both of them sprang to their feet as she entered the room. Gilberto dashed to her side and helped her to the couch.

Francisco followed more slowly, hovering behind Gilberto, as if his collar leashed him to God, preventing him from ever getting too close to an earthly being. Gilberto fussed, tucking pillows around her, lifting her feet gently to the cushions. Then he darted away, toward the table where her *cafezinho* awaited. In his absence, Francisco watched her silently.

It was hard to believe that he was a da Costa. He had none of Gilberto's cuddly teddy-bear qualities, nor the harsh hawk-like features of his mother and elder sister. He was a featureless shadow shaped like a man.

"Hello, Francisco," she said. "It's kind of you to stop in, but shouldn't you be at your mother's party?"

He dipped his chin, raising more shadows around his head, and mumbled. "It is not God's plan."

Should she call him "father"? She couldn't. "Anabela

243

planned her own party, not God."

The shadows fell away from him as he peered at her with a glimmer of fire in his eyes. Fire for the sinner. Yes, they were Anabela's eyes, after all.

Then the flash was gone, as fast as it had appeared.

Suddenly, Gilberto was there, thrusting the tiny cup of coffee into her hands. "My love," he said soothingly.

Francisco cleared his throat. "It is not always possible for us to know His plan."

Roz sipped the warm, sweet brew, feeling its strength charge through her. "Don't tell me that God could've planned shit like this."

He was trying to tell her in his own way that she'd had nothing to do with what happened. She was not in control, never in control. The mistakes of her life weren't her fault. But he was wrong.

What it meant was that *her* plans had failed. This time she'd lost control.

She would make sure that it never happened again.

# Chapter Twenty-Four

July 23, 1959

**Roz lost her fire** along with her baby. After the initial waves of grief, visits to the doctor, and avoiding the family, her days rolled by with emptiness. She didn't want anyone's pity, and that included Gilberto. He and Francisco kept her loss secret from the family, although his brother would probably call it something else, having to do with the confidentiality of confession.

But she hadn't confessed to her sins, even though, oh lord, she had enough of them.

The official reason for her withdrawal from the family was that once again, she had become too indisposed to attend social occasions.

She canceled her language lessons with Luis, even though she hadn't yet learned all the verb tenses he thought she should know. She spent her days prowling the streets of Barroca, her neighborhood, imagining where the sewer lines ran underground. She followed their courses, and sometimes she found them leaking into the areas of vacant land, where vultures gathered. Was this where her baby's remains had been swept?

She decided that the ravine in the vacant area two blocks downhill from her apartment building was her baby's grave, and she returned there once per week to memorialize him with flowers and sometimes an offering of oranges or mangoes. The baby had been a little boy, she was as certain of that as she'd been that first time in Ohio when she'd lost her little girl. She'd been paying ever since for that mistake, and now the vultures watched her with suspicion. She tickled with goosebumps and the sensation of being watched.

And finally today she caught sight of the boy to whom she'd given bus money. She was sure this child was the same one, although she only caught a fleeting glimpse of his bare feet as he kicked up dust, darting out from behind a bush and disappearing over the crest of a hill, in the general direction of the nearby *favela*. She had a disorienting moment where she saw him as her own baby, grown to child size. Her baby had been flushed here, and now he'd grown into a child. A collapsed cardboard box was his home. His food was what the vultures left behind as scraps. That's why he'd been watching her. They were connected by blood.

\* \* \* \* \*

August 6, 1959

Each week, Roz turned down Marilia's request to go to the movies. Instead, she had to bring food to the vacant lot, although she never told anyone that's what she was doing. She left the bundle of leftovers wrapped in a cloth napkin atop a rock. Each following week when she returned, the food was gone, but the napkin remained, blown into a bush and bearing smudges of dirt. She saw no traces of the boy again, but she hadn't lost the sensation of being watched.

Vultures eyed her hungrily.

She realized in a flash of lucidity that the birds were the ones who'd probably been devouring her food. Today she missed coming to her private memorial. Instead, she and Marilia went to the movies together, stopping afterwards for a *cafezinho*. The review practically wrote itself.

\* \* \* \* \*

August 12, 1959

The *feira* took over an entire city block with a jumble of market smells of citrus fruit and frying meat. It was a place where Roz could wander anonymously through chattering crowds because no one cared who she was or where she, the obvious *gringa*, was from. In Belo's central market, she was just another one of hundreds of shoppers, pushing past the bins of grains and stalls displaying vegetables that looked so misshapen they might've come from another planet. She had no idea what they were. Irmã would know. The maid usually did the shopping for their daily food needs, but today Roz had wanted to come alone instead. Irmã had been asking too many questions about why they needed extra food, and then, where did all that extra food go?

As always, Roz's first stop at the *feira* was to see what Amazonian animals were displayed in the cages for sale today. Two *araras* lined up on a branch, looking like a swing set without the swings.

Seeing them reminded her of Tonio and his dismay at losing

one of his birds. The family—meaning Anabela—had decided that a thief had slipped past the hired gunmen on the estate and must've stolen the bird. Roz thought her mother-in-law must be even more paranoid than she was. Anyway, what was the fuss? These birds were too opinionated, too forcefully cranky for Roz's tastes.

Something smaller was more to her liking. She'd almost bought a parakeet before, but she hadn't been able to decide which one, and then Tonio and Klaus had interrupted. Her heart hadn't been in it since then, as the pregnancy had consumed her, and the baby...

But now she was ready. On her way to the parakeets, another cage caught her attention. Tiny green parrots the size of her fist danced back and forth, performing for her. Lovebirds. One of them, the tiniest, blinked at her with a penetrating stare while his cagemates shrieked. For small birds, they had the most piercing cry.

The quiet one dipped his head, studying her shyly. He looked like a Jorge to her. She liked the sensuous, somnolent way the name sounded, like the sea rolling in and out: *Zzzhorhhh-zzhe.*

*Take me home with you,* Jorge seemed to say.

She glowed inside—from the attentions of the bird, for heaven's sake. She liked the way he bobbed back and forth, batting his eyes at her, telling her in his own way that he was her friend. That must be it. She'd never had a friend before Marilia, not a real one, that is, and now she had two. As a friend, Jorge promised to help her heal from the inside out. That seemed to be what he was saying to her.

In the end, she bought the little parrot and a cage and took Jorge home with her.

As soon as she saw Irmã's dismayed face, she realized that she had forgotten to buy the vegetables and fruit.

"*Senhora!*" Irmã said, ticking her tongue with a scolding sound. "Now what have you done?"

"I've bought a pet. The *dom* and I have been talking about getting a pet."

"But it's a...a bird!"

"Yes. Birds can be pets, too."

"No. Birds belong outside. If you bring a bird into the house, you bring death along with it."

A bubble of panic stirred within Roz. Was that true? She looked at her new friend, who was busy picking at a splinter on his wooden perch. "Oh, Irmã. He can't do that." Could he? It was true that her baby had died, but that was before Jorge. "He's just a bird."

"I cannot stay in a house of death," Irmã said, folding her arms across her chest.

Panic rose from the bubble, spreading through Roz. She couldn't lose Irmã! How would the household function without her?

"If I put his cage on the open windowsill," Roz said, "then he wouldn't really be inside the house."

That would solve the problem in more ways than one. Jorge on the sill would be better than a burning candle. He was her promise of healing.

\* \* \* \* \*

August 20, 1959

Through the late days of winter, Gilberto could not focus. His mind felt scrambled; his drive stalled. He was a disservice to the women of his universe, and now this, the summons from his mother. They were to have a private lunch today at *O Clube*. Gilberto would find no excuses not to be there. He would not fail her again.

She'd wanted to send her chauffeur to fetch him from the station, but Gilberto had won that battle by promising to come. He would never have lived it down from Ubaldo, had *Mãe's* chauffeur plucked him out of the station like a scolded schoolboy.

And now he was here, pulling the Fairlane into the parking lot of *O Clube*. But he sat in the car long moments after turning off the engine, drumming his fingers atop the wrapped steering wheel, thinking it over. Or maybe he was just reluctant to go in.

He had been visiting pharmacies for nearly two months, and still that impossible task was not done. He had not found the druggist who admitted remembering even one of the three victims. And now the captain threatened to close the cases of the kidnappers and the abortionist, claiming the official reason was a lack of evidence. But Gilberto suspected the real reason had more to do with complaints lodged against him. Dona Mariana had already been to the station, seeking an audience with the captain as she'd promised to do after the way Gilberto had bungled his interview with her in the back room of her pink house. Lucky for him, the captain didn't believe the dona's accusations. Who could? The idea that Gilberto was controlled by some gang dealing illegal drugs was ludicrous. Besides, he was a da Costa. The dona should know better than to tangle with them.

Nonetheless, the captain had privately instructed Gilberto to back off.

Klaus had been to the station, too, shortly after Gilberto's fruitless visit to his pharmacy. Gilberto still had not found Angela's friend with the goiter, nor the mysterious older man with whom Angela had made an acquaintance at the pub where she'd worked, nor had he found anyone who admitted knowing Angela in her hometown of Congonhas. He had not found the source of Ieda's drugs, and the labs had not yet finished their report, concluding about the ingredients of the residue found inside the cloth bags. With such lack of progress, Gilberto might as well not have shown up to work each day. Perhaps he should take some time off, as the captain had suggested. Maybe a few days in Rio with Roz. But the captain's suggestion was just a polite way of telling him he would soon be fired. How many more hints did he need?

There'd also been phone calls from Denver.

And Ubaldo could no longer partner with him. He'd been assigned to another case, but he wouldn't tell Gilberto what the new case was. He didn't have to. Gilberto suspected it had to do with Jacinto. But when he pressed Ubaldo for more information, all he told him was that he had a new girlfriend. Gilberto should listen to the captain and leave it alone.

To top it off, Roz's growing depression turned his off-hours into time spent calming her delusional fantasies. Forget about his needs. Everyone was nervous at home, including Irmã, who was understandably nervous about that damned bird. Gilberto didn't recall ever agreeing to a bird. How could a bird replace a dog?  His question hadn't even produced an argument as it would've done in the old days, at the mention of the slightest challenge to Roz's opinion.  But then, Roz was not the same woman as the one he'd left Denver with, or rather, hadn't been able to leave Denver without.  He'd meant at first only to keep an eye on her, find out why she'd been in possession of Catarina's ring, in case she'd known anything about that and about his missing son.  That's why he'd gone to such lengths to bring her here.  He hadn't meant to fall so hard for her.  Was it possible that maybe she'd fallen for him just a little bit?  Now, at times, he thought maybe she was...yes, maybe just a tiny bit *louca*.  No, that wasn't true.  It was only a violent depression that colored everything, that was all.

Because of Roz, he'd been determined to make the streets safer.  For her, he'd meant to track down the butchers once and for all.  And yet he hadn't.

He sighed and reached for the door handle.  Best to end this morass of self-pity and get the meeting with *Mãe* over with.

Anabela had reserved a private room behind the main dining room of the clubhouse.  The ceiling was taller than the room was wide, making the single round table look dwarfed, despite the way it was laden with linen cloths, crystal, and china.  It still looked small, matching the way Gilberto felt.

He sighed and took his place opposite his mother, who was already there, studying her gold and gemstone-encrusted wristwatch.

She frowned and turned back to her plate of palm hearts without looking up.  "You're late."

"I told you I'd be here."

A waiter appeared, placing a plate before him.

"With you, my son, one can never be sure."

"I'll take that as a compliment."

"It wasn't meant to be, although your father would've been proud of you. You are stubborn, as was he."

Gilberto grinned.

The waiter fussed around the room, refreshing their water and pouring their wine. When he finally left them alone, she said, "Francisco told me."

Gilberto chewed in silence, considering his many possible responses. Finally, he spoke. "He shouldn't have. It doesn't concern you."

"Of course it does. It's my grandchild. And that woman lost it."

"*Mãe*, you know her name."

"Rosalinda."

"She prefers Roz."

"And that, my son, is part of her problem, to deny who she really is."

Unsure what his mother meant by that, he steered the conversation back to its topic. "You don't know how hard of a time she's had over the miscarriage."

"What about me? Do you think it is nothing, all that I have been through?"

He shook his head and murmured soothing acknowledgements of his mother's trials over the years. God knew, she'd seen enough, too.

"I know a few tricks," she said, eyeing him. "I might have been able to help, but now it is too late."

"Yes, too late."

"But not for the next child. I will send over some

supplements she must take. And in the future you will keep me better informed, you understand?"

Was there a future? He looked up with the tiniest glimmer of hope shining through.

His mother went on. "If Rosalinda is to be your wife, then she must respect my wishes and follow my advice. If she is to carry my grandchild, then you will have to quit that job of yours. I tried to warn her in the beginning, not long after you thought to introduce her to the rest of us, that your police job would only create unforeseen, shall we say, problems. But she didn't listen to me."

"She didn't understand very much Portuguese back then."

"Perhaps she'll listen now."

He shrugged.

"Don't either of you understand? It is your job that is to blame for the loss of my grandchild."

"My job? It is our police work that will turn Brazil into a modern country. That is the only way we can catch up to the rest of the world. My job is important."

"Of course it's important, but let others do it. Your family needs you more than that ugly business needs you. Your father didn't understand, either. He thought he had to personally fight everyone else's battles, and he lost. You will not lose, my son."

Gilberto swallowed hard, remembering his call to justice, the drive he'd nearly forgotten. No, he would not lose. He would never abandon his mission to rid his city of the evil that threatened them all, taking fine men such as his father. It was his purpose in being, and he'd nearly forgotten—until now. "Thank you, *Mãe*."

Her lips twitched, indicating a smile. "You're welcome.

And you'll thank me again once you quit that job of yours. So will Rosalinda."

"I don't think so. And she likes Roz better."

"Do you take me for a fool? I know what she thinks. And I also know all about the one called Linda."

His fork clattered to his plate.

She chuckled softly and reached across the table to pat his hand. "Don't look so surprised. I have my resources, you know that."

# Sue STAR and Bill BEATTY

# Chapter Twenty-Five

August 28, 1959

**Roz counted the days** until the upcoming getaway holiday to Rio that Gilberto had promised her. It would be perfect timing for trying to make a baby again.

She pulled out the suitcase from under the bed and threw an armload of negligees into it. Rummaging through the drawer of her dresser, she found the string bikini.

Adding it to her bag, she remembered that midnight festival to *Iemanjá*, the *orixá* goddess of women and fertility, which she'd seen taking place on the beach shortly after arriving in Brazil. It was hard to believe that more than half a year had passed since then. She wondered if that celebration could only occur on New Year's Eve. But what difference did the exact timing make? Roz didn't see why she couldn't make her own ritual with her own offerings whenever she happened to go to Rio. Copacabana's waters were the same seawater as always, weren't they? Those waters should still cleanse her, regardless of the timing, as they had cleansed the souls of the women who'd walked into the sea last New Year's Eve. It should be all about the ritual, Roz decided, and not the timing.

She would need the proper offerings for her private ritual, and that's where she'd needed help. Irmã would supply them for her.

Roz had sent the maid alone to the *feira* with instructions to find the various seeds and herbs and flowers and whatever else she might need, perhaps the right candle or two, along with the weekly shopping. With Irmã gone for a while, Roz let Jorge out of his cage. Bringing the little bird home with her had been the right thing to do, despite any opposition. Jorge showed her that she was in control of her own decisions. Besides, he'd helped distract her from her despair of this last month and a half since losing the baby. She'd almost lost herself, too, drowning in all that despair. But Jorge and his antics coaxed her out of that black pit and made her laugh. His favorite game was to fly from one end of the apartment to the other, shrieking at her to chase him. She turned on the transistor radio to help cover up his noise.

For such a little bird, the flap of his wings sounded like the rustle of fabric, the way Irmã shook out newly laundered sheets. Sitting atop his cage, eyeing her, Jorge fluttered his feathers, gave her a shrill titter, and soared away, just as she reached to touch his tufts of down.

"You want to play, do you?"

Setting off through the apartment after him, she wondered whom she could ask to take care of the little troublemaker while she and Gilberto were away in Rio. Certainly not Irmã, who was planning to visit her family at that time. Even if the maid stayed behind here, alone in the apartment, she'd never agree to care for the bird.

But then, Jorge would be no trouble at all as long as he stayed in his cage. Roz couldn't bear to cage him in all the time. Birds needed exercise as well as anyone. They needed the freedom of flight. Sometimes Roz felt like a caged bird, and so she could sympathize.

He perched on a coat hook by the front door and watched her approach. Just as she reached out, offering her hand as a perch, he squealed and took off again. *Chase me!*

"Come back here, you little scamp." Whirling around to start after him, she heard the light tapping of familiar footsteps on the stairs outside her front door. Marilia. Of course. Roz would ask her friend to care for Jorge while she was gone.

Roz watched the bird disappear into the kitchen, and then she opened the door a crack. "Marilia, can you come in for a minute?" she asked, then hurried to switch off the radio.

When she turned to face her friend, Marilia stood just inside the door, breathing heavily. Her cheeks were flushed. All that from running up one flight of stairs.

"You're home early from work, aren't you?" Roz said, suspicious.

Marilia shrugged. "Not really." Her glance slid to the floor. "I only have a minute."

"Come on, you can tell me what's going on." Roz softened her voice. "Did something happen at work?"

"Sort of." Marilia lifted her chin. A small grin tugged at her lips, freshly applied with hot pink lipstick, a shocking contrast to her complexion, as dark as a three-month tan. "A visitor came to the office today, and already he wants to take me out for a drink later on tonight."

"A visitor?"

"Don't look so worried," Marilia said. "He's really nice."

"But he's a stranger."

"Not anymore. Come on, you've got to help me. I have nothing to wear, and my hair looks like shit." Marilia giggled

259

and covered her mouth.

Roz laughed, too. She knew something about makeovers. "Okay. Let's find something to drink, and you can tell me all about him."

"There's not much to tell, except he's very handsome. And he says he knows your husband."

"He told you that?" Roz came to attention on her way to the kitchen. The hairs stood up on the back of her neck. First, the guy must've already known, even before he met Marilia, that Roz was her friend. And if he also knew who Roz's husband was, then he didn't sound much like a stranger to her. No, she didn't like this at all. It was entirely too much information for a casual visitor to know about someone unknown. "What's his name?"

"Ubaldo Ramos. Maybe you already know him, too? The four of us could go out together sometime. To a movie, perhaps."

Roz came unglued from her spot as a shaky sort of relief swept through her. She yanked open the refrigerator and stared blankly at its contents. "Maybe."

"It would be fun," Marilia said.

Roz still hadn't met Gilberto's partner. It seemed to her that her husband was deliberately preventing that from happening. She reached for the pitcher of orange juice Irmã had squeezed that morning and felt as if worms crawled through her intestines. "Why was he at the newspaper office today?"

"Don't worry. He seems really nice. What does Gilberto say about him?"

"You're right. Gilberto has nothing but praise for him." Which didn't make sense. Why would Gilberto keep her from meeting his wonderful partner?

Jorge shrieked from the top of the kitchen cupboard and flew away to a lampshade in the living room.

"Oh!" Marilia said, ducking. "Is that a bird? Shall I help you get it out?"

"No, it's okay. That's Jorge."

"But he's not in his cage."

"I let him fly around while Irmã is gone. He needs some exercise."

Marilia's eyes widened as she watched the little green streak dart from one corner to another. "How interesting."

"You're not afraid?" Roz found glasses, poured the drinks and led the way to the couch.

"Why should I be? He's so little."

"My maid says that bringing a bird into the house brings death."

Marilia laughed. "That's just an old-fashioned superstition. Nobody modern believes that anymore."

"I'm glad you think so, since I was going to ask you to take care of him while we're away." But she wasn't entirely glad that Marilia felt so modern. Otherwise, she wouldn't have accepted an unchaperoned date with a man she'd just met.

\* \* \* \* \*

September 1, 1959

Four whole days had passed since Marilia's date with Ubaldo, and Roz was dying to know how it went. Except, she hadn't seen her friend since then. Marilia had gone home to her village for the weekend, while Roz's promised trip to Rio was postponed. When she asked Gilberto what Ubaldo had surely told him about the date, he'd claimed not to know anything.

She knew that he knew. He must.

Roz felt stymied by her lack of information, but she knew what she could do, and no one could stop her. She would take food to the barefoot boy in the ravine. Anyway, she needed to get out and get some fresh air. All she had to do first was to search the kitchen while Irmã wasn't looking. The maid was busy scrubbing laundry on the washboard in the little utility room off the kitchen. While Roz scooped leftover rice into a napkin, heavy footsteps shuffled in the central hall of the building, just outside her front door. This time she didn't recognize the slow, deliberate footfalls nor the way the floor vibrated slightly. Then a knock sounded.

She wrapped the napkin into a ball and held it behind her back as she moved closer to the door. "Who is it?"

"Klaus Hoffman," said a man's guttural voice. He coughed and cleared his throat.

Roz remembered the overweight doctor with slick, black hair, whom Isa called "uncle." She'd first met him at *O Clube*, and again a few times at Anabela's estate, when he'd also passed through, on his way to check on his patient, Tonio. What was he doing *here*?

She pulled open the door and said in Portuguese, "How nice to see you."

"The pleasure is all mine," he said in English with a grin that pulled tightly across his cheeks. He held a small, plastic bag, which he lifted in her direction. "I brought you something."

Roz pulled the door open wider and invited him in. Behind her, she heard the door to Irmã's quarters slam shut.

Apparently, there would be no *cafezinho*. Roz decided to ignore the customary offering of a beverage. He was a foreigner here, too, just like her. "Please have a seat, Doctor Hoffman," she said, waving him toward the couch with one hand while she continued to hold the napkin of rice with the other, behind her back.

"Klaus," he said. His gaze took in the little apartment. Bypassing the proffered couch, he strode to the kitchen table where he set down his plastic bag. "Your mother-in-law asked me to bring you this."

Roz backed into the kitchen and dropped her napkin onto the counter. "What is it?"

"Just a few tealeaves. She is concerned for your health."

"That's nice of her to be concerned, but there's nothing wrong with my health."

"Isn't there?"

"Why, no. Should there be?"

"Perhaps it is nothing, but nevertheless, tea won't hurt you." He dipped into the plastic bag and pulled out three cloth bags, each one no larger than the palm of her hand.

"That depends on what's in it," she said, stepping backwards. If it had been Anabela's idea, then she could imagine something like ground-up lizard tails. She grimaced.

"It's nothing like that," he said with a laugh, as if he could read her mind. He held up the bags one by one, which were of different colors. "Yellow is for the sun. You make tea from this mixture in the morning. Blue is for rain, you take at noon. And black is for night. You drink this before bed."

"And they do what?" she said, skeptical.

"They make you strong." He demonstrated with a fist,

263

flexing his muscles.

"And Anabela thinks I'm not strong?" She chuckled.

"You should listen to your mother-in-law. She always knows best."

Roz wished she could believe that. "She seems very sure that there's something wrong with me."

"She worries, that is all. Dona Anabela has been through more than any one woman should ever have to endure, including the loss of her husband, and the loss of her children..."

Tonio, he meant. And there'd been a child who'd died at birth. Certainly not Gilberto, nor any of the others. "Is this what you give Tonio, too?" Roz said, pointing to the tea.

Klaus laughed in his throaty way, sounding more like a cough. "Certainly not. The best we can do for that one is to make him comfortable within his own little world. But the future, ahhh! All of Dona Anabela's hopes must rest with her grandchildren. This is why she only wishes for you to be fertile."

Roz tipped her head sideways, studying the colorful bags. *"That's* what this tea is for?" Fertility. Perhaps she'd misjudged Anabela.

\* \* \* \* \*

October 13, 1959

The rains of rainy season had started up again, and the trip to Rio was cancelled. Her husband couldn't get away from work, but Roz didn't care. Another rabbit had died.

She told Jorge, the lovebird, that she knew these tests didn't work quite that way. The rabbit would die regardless of the results. That's why she had to be certain before she went for the test. She didn't want to be responsible for the needless death of a rabbit. She wanted Jorge to understand.

This time, Roz couldn't wait to tell Gilberto the news. Maybe that had been her mistake before, waiting too long to tell him. She wouldn't make the same mistake again.

Being an expert by now about the different bus lines, she could find her way anywhere in town. She caught the bus in front of the family doctor's office, and after a couple of transfers and a drenching downpour, she ended up at the police station where Gilberto worked. Generally, she avoided this place. Even though Brazilian police had nothing on her, it was still the police.

The gray, stone building smelled of rain-soaked cement and reeked of law enforcement. Walking inside immediately tamped her spirits, but on this day, she wouldn't let anything weigh on her heart.

She couldn't remember exactly where his desk was amidst all the busy activity of coming and going. She scanned the officers bent over their desks, but she couldn't find Gilberto's tousled head among them. He must be out, doing whatever detectively duties he did during the day.

Okay, she would wait. She had all day. Time no longer owned her.

She found a chair and watched the bustle sweep around her.

Sometime later, a tall, well-filled-out man with a movie-star air of suaveness, stopped by her side. He smiled a twisted smile as he thrust out his hand, grabbing hers with an enthusiastic shake. A scent of limes drifted from his hand. "Ubaldo Ramos," he said, as if it was obvious she knew his name and that he was identifying himself, rather than speaking in code.

"Ah, so you're the one." She studied him curiously, wondering why he'd disappointed Marilia. Her friend had never gone into details, once Roz had finally pressed for them, only to say the date hadn't worked out. She'd brushed off Roz's questions as unimportant. Roz suspected he'd tried to force himself on her.

"Yes, everyone wants to work with me." He winked.

"I believe you know my friend, Marilia Iriri."

Ubaldo coughed and rubbed his nose. "Are you here to find Gilberto?" He spoke carefully and slowly in a heavily accented English.

"Yes," she said. "Have you seen him? I'm his wife."

"I know. He speaks of you all the time."

She figured that he'd spotted her as if she wore a placard identifying her nationality. That's what must've triggered his awkward attempt to speak her language. Whatever it was, they were obvious characteristics that shouted at the world: *Look at me! United States person!* And yet, everything that she wore, including her makeup and her undergarments, was Brazilian. How did they know? Sitting still in the uncomfortably hard wooden chair could not demonstrate that the muscles in her body didn't move in the same sensuously rhythmic way that Latin muscles controlled the movements of a Brazilian born and bred body.

Her child would be born that way!

"Where is he?" she said, switching to Portuguese. Her Portuguese was better than his English, and she felt herself sing inside with the small victory of language.

"Come with me." He curled one finger for her to follow him

266

through the maze of desks and people.

She followed, trying to match the swing in his hips, more sensuous even than Gilberto. It was as if he walked on a cushion of air, while Roz had to fight for balance against the pressure of the earth. How did he do that? She would have to learn.

He led her to another wooden chair beside a metal desk cluttered with papers, which she thought was Gilberto's, although she couldn't be sure. She'd only been here a couple of times, and all the desks looked alike.

"Will he be back soon?" she said, sitting down.

Ubaldo perched on one corner of the desk, wrinkling the papers that lay there. He shrugged. "With him, who knows? He is always chasing some idea, instead of what he should be doing."

"What do you mean? What ideas?"

"Oh, you know," he said, carefully extracting the papers from beneath him. "He's got some idea about some cult. He's been chasing after illegal cults ever since... Well, never mind. That's not important. What *is* important is the victims."

"Victims?" Her heartbeat sped up.

"No worries, *Senhora*. They're not like you. They're women in trouble."

"Women? Trouble?"

Ubaldo laughed. "Your husband seems to think that if he can break up the illegal cults, it'll solve all the women's troubles, but of course he's wrong. He hasn't been with the *policía civil* long enough to know better. But you can trust me. I promise I will cover for him while he is off chasing his windmills."

"What do you mean? Is he neglecting something?"

Ubaldo leaned low across the desk and whispered. "Family

matters. The mine is losing money, and your husband should be the one investigating. Instead, they asked me to do it. They know I'll get it done. Know what I mean?"

"No, actually."

"Well, never mind." He glanced at his wristwatch and swore. "I'm late for a meeting. If you'll excuse me, *Senhora*?"

"Of course." She watched him saunter back across the room, pausing at several desks along the way to pat his colleagues on the shoulder, as if he wasn't in a hurry at all. He must've wanted an excuse to get away from her, leaving her questions unanswered. What on earth had he meant about the da Costa mine? It hadn't run out of gemstones. And what was it that Gilberto should be doing about the mine instead of what he was doing? And what, exactly, was that? Who were those women in trouble? She hoped he wasn't including Marilia in that.

Cults. Roz was pretty sure by now, from the bits and pieces that she'd learned, that burning candles indicated cults.

Narrowing her eyes in thought, she watched Ubaldo make his way slowly past the desks and eventually fade through the doorway. She crossed to the window and caught sight of him again, as he emerged outside. Now he hurried, bouncing down the steps of the building. He splashed through puddles towards the street corner, where a heavy-set man stood under an umbrella, apparently waiting for Ubaldo. With a mustache so thick that it covered the expression on his face, and the black umbrella shadowing the rest of his face, the man meeting Ubaldo was hard to identify.

Roz's angled position peering through the window didn't help her get a good look at him. She wasn't sure, but she thought he looked familiar. Maybe he only reminded her of someone.

Helen's husband, Sam... Yes, that was it. He was Gilberto's friend, and she'd only met him a couple of times. He consulted with the police here, Helen had told her. Ubaldo apparently knew him, too.

She watched as the two of them walked away together down the street, Ubaldo with his floating gait, and his companion with a limp.

She didn't remember that Sam had a limp. This person wasn't Sam after all, not unless he'd recently hurt himself.

But now she wondered about Ubaldo's mysterious behavior regarding this meeting and furthermore, why the issue of trusting him had even come up. Unless it meant that Gilberto was involved in something he shouldn't be doing. She hoped it didn't have anything to do with a cult.

\* \* \* \* \*

October 30, 1959

As the days of October wound down to an end, Roz's occasional migraines started up again. She had to remind herself that it was almost Halloween. There were no pumpkins on people's doorsteps, no costumes of witches and princesses in storefront windows, nor piles of dried autumn leaves to walk through. Instead, the rains picked up with regular frequency and increasing intensity, and Roz covered Jorge's cage with a blanket. Sometimes, she even brought Jorge in from the windowsill, but only after Irmã had finished her daily duties and retired to her room behind the kitchen.

"Did you see anything interesting today from the window?"

she whispered to the bird each night when she brought him in.

He chortled softly, as if he didn't want to alert Irmã, either.

It wouldn't do to let Irmã know that the bird was inside the house, and as long as she didn't know, Roz reasoned, then the household must remain safe from death. Roz didn't believe in all those superstitions. At the same time, she didn't want to upset her maid. If that happened, then what?

Neither the rains nor the possibility of a watching shadow could stop Roz from taking her daily walks. Her umbrella offered a limited bubble of protection, but the mud and ruts that washed through the hillside roads made walking more challenging. Walking was good for her body, which also meant it was good for the growing baby. The rains didn't stop the vultures, either, from their normal activity. They continued to glare at her from the vacant areas, as if blaming her for imposing limits on their scavenging. Besides, she only brought scraps of fruits and vegetables, intended for the barefoot boy.

They wanted meat.

She hadn't seen the boy again since July, and it crossed her mind that perhaps she'd only imagined him, given the fragile state of her mind back then when she'd lost the baby. Now that she was pregnant again, she laughed at herself for ever having considered that the boy was her own grown child. How silly of her. Of course he was not.

But if she hadn't imagined him, then she wondered where the boy had gone. He'd disappeared somewhere into the city. Maybe to an orphanage? Or to a temporary shelter during rainy season?

She asked Irmã about this, one day when she returned from her walk, whether there were such places where the child could've gone. The maid—whose costume today was a white dress, not because it was the day before Halloween but because it was a Friday—looked up from her work at setting the table for dinner. Isa and her latest boyfriend were to join them tonight.

"He's probably a thief," Irmã said, "and he's run away to hide."

The maids of the neighborhood knew such things because they often met during their breaks and gossiped about the neighborhood. Roz had overheard them numerous times through Jorge's open window. Usually their talk concerned the problem of thieves. One of the maids—Ester, from the blue house across the street—was the best informed of them all, in all matters of the neighborhood.

"You must stop leaving the shutters open," Irmã said with a shake of her head, "as you do for that bird. Open shutters invite thieves in, and that's why the boy has been following you."

"But he's just a child," Roz said.

Irmã rolled her eyes. "You may think that's what he is, but the best thieves are small. That's how they climb through the bars on windows."

Bars were only on the ground level windows, not on upper levels, where her apartment was located. There was no convincing Irmã that the barefoot boy was just an innocent child. The maid was certain that he'd been the one behind the recent rash of stolen *figas*, those good luck charms that only brought good luck if they were a gift—or if stolen. Irmã knew, she claimed, because she'd had a friend once whose boyfriend had given her a *figa* on a necklace. It represented twice the luck, because it was both stolen and a gift.

Of far more timely importance, however, was the report

from the maid across the street.

"Ester," Irmã said, laying out the plates, "saw a man who is new to the neighborhood. Twice. The same man."

Roz tensed, as she always did when she thought a stranger might possibly be taking an interest in her activities. And this one was. She knew. Because two times made it intentional. Not a coincidence. Her paranoia was flaring again, but she couldn't help herself. "What was he doing?"

"Walking back and forth on our street."

"Maybe he was lost?" Roz said. She wished that was the case, but she didn't believe it. It wasn't likely that someone would pass through this neighborhood, at the end of the bus line. It was a destination, rather than a place to pass through, on the way to somewhere else.

"He had a camera," Irmã said, shaking her head. "So all of us went inside our houses and hid."

"You didn't want him to take your pictures?"

Irmã's hands shook, and the silverware rattled. "No, *Senhora*. If your enemy gets his hands on a photo of you, he will take it to the local *macumbero* who can then do with you whatever he wishes. You could even die."

A knot twisted inside Roz, and it was far too soon for it to be the baby kicking. She had plenty of enemies from her past who would gladly consult a witch doctor. That's who a *macumbero* really was. A witch doctor. She thought she'd escaped her enemies by now, but she'd been wrong before.

"You can't really believe that," Roz said, taking the silverware from Irmã's shaking fingers and hastily placing it around the table. She wanted to tell the maid that her belief was just a superstition, and that didn't make it true. But was it?

"Oh yes, *Senhora*." Irmã's voice raised in pitch to a whine. "I know of it happening before. I beg of you. Do not let the man take your photo."

"Okay," Roz said. It was better to soothe her maid with agreement rather than try to convince her that her fears were not real. That was a losing battle. "What does he look like, so that I can avoid him?"

"Big, like this." She held out her arms, pantomiming the shape of a bear. "Wears a hat and carries a cane."

"Because...he has a limp?"

Irmã nodded.

"What about a mustache? Does he have a mustache?" Her fingers shook.

Irmã frowned. "Yes, I think so."

Roz dropped the silverware with a clatter onto the table. A knife bounced off and landed on the floor. Why would the man who looked like Sam want to take her picture?

Irmã sucked in her breath and covered her mouth with her hand. "Oh no!"

Roz bent down to pick up the knife. The description sounded like the man with the cane she'd spotted before. He could also be the limping man Ubaldo had met. He'd carried no cane that day, and he wasn't Sam. She was sure of it, much as she distrusted that American cop friend of Gilberto's. Sam didn't limp.

"*Senhora*, no! Leave it!" The maid scooped up another knife from the table, knelt, and laid it carefully across the fallen knife on the floor. "When a knife falls to the floor," she said, "it means there will be a fight. But I have fixed it now, by crossing the fallen knife." She stood up and smiled.

Roz wished that she could feel as assured as Irmã that the foretold fight—whatever fight—had been averted. With a bird of death in the house, the outcome of such a match didn't look good. A pain throbbed behind her temple, wondering who the fighters would be. Was one of them the same man whom Ubaldo had met, Sam's look alike?

# Chapter Twenty-Six

December 13, 1959

**Roz shifted on the** wooden bench of the family pew, trying to find a more comfortable position. Its polished surface felt extra hard today, here at Mass. The priest's melodic voice, warbling through the rituals, along with soothing whiffs of incense usually produced a hypnotic state for her.

And then the cramps started.

Roz had taken the bus downtown to the cathedral to join the family in their pew. She'd come alone because Gilberto had to work, no matter that it was Sunday. The plan was that after Mass, she would ride with Isa out to the family estate, and Gilberto would eventually meet her there.

The cramps changed her plan. *God, no!*

Roz stared across the rows of the faithfuls' faces, searching for Francisco in his robes up there behind the altar. He'd been with her the last time this happened, and now he felt like a tenuous link, something faint for her to hold onto.

Isa, who sat next to Roz in the pew, leaned close and whispered in her ear. "What's wrong? Are you okay?"

Roz moaned softly and cradled her belly, only recently beginning to swell. "Nooo."

Isa's eyes rounded and her voice rose a notch. "Is it the baby?"

She and Gilberto had finally told the family their news about the baby, only at the start of advent, having waited until then to match their joy with that of the Christmas season. They were all to celebrate tonight at the family estate.

"Can you take me home?" Roz said.

"Of course. Let's go."

As Isa helped Roz stand, Anabela, who sat on the other side, laid her hand on Isa's arm and whispered something. Roz couldn't understand, because the pain in her lower back consumed all of her attention. She felt the puzzled stares on faces as Isa guided her down a side aisle to an exit.

"The car is not far," Isa said, once they were outside. Luckily, it wasn't raining at the moment. Heat rose in sauna-like waves and coated Roz with sweat.

It seemed to take forever, walking gingerly to the car. Driving through downtown streets. Roz closed her eyes and leaned her head thankfully against the padding inside the car's door. Each stop and start felt like a punch to her belly, vibrating through her body along with the tightening of cramps. Finally, their drive smoothed out, and she opened her eyes. They were leaving the city behind.

"This isn't the way home," Roz said.

"*Mãe* said it's better to take you to her house. You can rest there."

"But—"

"Don't argue," Isa said, turning with a look that drilled into Roz. "You need a nurse. You won't get one at the hospital, even if I were to take you there. *Mãe's* house is the best choice. She told me so back there in church, as we were leaving, and I agree. We have our own medical staff at the house for Tonio, you see, and it's better than the hospital. Our people can help you."

Pains crashed over Roz, sweeping her along their course, dominating any will to resist.

\* \* \* \* \*

She dreamt of the bird that night as people rushed in and out of the room where she slept around the waves of pain.

No, what awakened her were the birds' cries. And voices murmuring in the haze surrounding her. Someone tilted her head up from the pillow and spooned a vile-tasting liquid down her throat.

She spat it out.

But whoever had done the spooning was stronger. His hands came at her again, and they weren't gentle.

She swallowed.

Time whirled around her, blending in a torrent of pain. Her body writhed and twisted, wringing the baby out like laundry.

It finally passed.

She caught a glimpse of its bean-pod shape in the puddle of blood before hands wrapped up the mess in a sheet and carried it away. She screamed, "Nooo! Don't flush it!" And then cried herself to sleep.

The bird in her dreams carried her away to a safe place. A sanctuary where she could heal, and no one could hurt her again.

\* \* \* \* \*

When her eyelids finally fluttered open again, the face of a hawk was peering at her. She gasped and blinked. Its sharp beak and piercing gaze resolved into her mother-in-law's face. Anabela.

"Where's...Gilberto?" Roz said in English, too tired and numb to think, to pull any Portuguese words from her mind. And then the word she'd needed washed over her, instead of another wave of pain. *Onde?* Where? She held her breath, waiting for cramps to squeeze through her, but nothing came. Their aftermath swept her with a numbing combination of relief, heaviness, and exhaustion.

"He's not here," Anabela said, biting off her words.

Obviously. A faint flame of the old irritation flickered through Roz, and she struggled to sit up. "Where is he?" she said again, this time in Portuguese. "I need him here with me."

Yes. She *needed* him.

"It's that job of his," Anabela said with another snap.

"What will become of the baby?" Roz said. Had she dreamed the rolled-up sheet? The flushing of unwanted tissue?

The memory of the sewer pipes leaking into the ravine below her apartment, guarded by vultures, haunted her.

"There is a place," Anabela said, "in the family plot, for my grandchild."

*A grave.* Roz sank back onto her pillows with an odd sense of relief and an even odder sense of a bond with her mother-in-law. Anabela seemed to understand her need for a proper burial. Not a flushing into the sewer.

"None of this would've happened," Anabela said, "if my son had agreed to my offer in the first place."

*An offer?* Roz wondered what kind of an offer could've

prevented her miscarriage. Was it something Roz had not done, also? She should've drunk the tea. It had been Roz's fault both times before. And this time, again. She hadn't done whatever was right. Whatever she should've done, it would've protected her baby better. She wasn't a very good nurturer, she decided with a sigh. "What offer?"

"He could've had one of the apartments on my property. There is one available next to Tonio's."

"You wanted us to live here? On your estate?" Roz didn't follow. Maybe it was a language issue. Maybe it was the mess of her body and mind. "How would living here have kept me from losing my baby?"

"We have nurses here," Anabela said, "and Klaus provides them with whatever they need."

The thought of living here, so near to Anabela, instead of in the cozy little apartment in Barroca, sent a chill through Roz.

Anabela went on. "Together, they could've stopped this new tragedy from happening. But now we bury my grandchild, instead. Perhaps my son will finally learn to listen to me."

Roz hoped not. She would've been a prisoner living here.

\* \* \* \* \*

She stayed as Anabela's prisoner until a commotion in the hall outside her bedroom awoke her. Gilberto's voice both cried and shouted, "Why didn't someone tell me?"

Women's voices murmured a hasty response that Roz couldn't make out. Then the door slammed open, and footsteps pounded across the floor to her side.

"*Meu amor*," he whispered, falling to his knees. He caught

her hand in his and lifted it to his lips. "How do you feel?"

Sobs overcame her, and tears streamed down her face. She opened her mouth to tell him it was her fault, and she was a fool, but all she could do was hiccup and shudder within his tight embrace. Finally she found her voice again, and she said, "I-I lost the baby. They didn't tell you?"

"Hush, my love, it doesn't matter. I am here now."

"Will you take me home?"

Instead of answering, he scooped her up in his arms and lifted her from the bed. He strode through the house with Roz in his arms, kicking doors out of his way. His mother tugged at his sleeve, flinging a stream of words at his back, telling him to put her back to bed, to leave women's matters to the women. It was better for Roz to stay here, Anabela pleaded, where she had access to Tonio's nursing staff. The hospitals were useless.

Gilberto plowed on, striding down the front steps with Roz in his arms. Anabela shouted from the front door that he was making a mistake. Didn't he want what was best for his wife?

"The only mistake, *Mãe*," he said over his shoulder, "is what you have done."

\* \* \* \* \*

Roz thought about his words all the way home. What had Anabela done? He must've been referring to the way his mother hadn't told him sooner about Roz's miscarriage. But what could Gilberto have done to stop it? Anabela had actually been nice for a change—in her own way. She'd tried her best to provide medical care for Roz, and now she was making arrangements for a burial plot.

The stronger Roz grew as the hours passed, the stranger that arrangement seemed. Not that she was complaining. She didn't want her baby washed down the sewer, as the one before, but what did they do with miscarried babies? Sure, a proper burial seemed the right thing to do.

And then what? How many times would Roz have to go through this? She feared that her past had ruined her body, and now she wasn't physically capable of carrying a baby to term. How many more graves would fill the family plot before Gilberto would turn away from her, and she ended up losing him, too?

She wondered if Catarina was there. In the family plot.

At home, Irmã fussed over her, making her a bitter-tasting tea. Something, she promised, that would help her body heal from its loss, so that she would be ready to carry a baby again, when the time was right.

The time had been wrong, this time, Irmã claimed, on account of the nearness of that bird in its cage. That's what had caused this to happen. Hadn't she warned her of death?

Roz shivered deep shudders.

Gilberto tucked blankets around her, fluffed her pillows, and murmured sweet nothings. "Not to worry, my love."

They would try again. Soon.

# Chapter Twenty-Seven

January 26, 1960

**Roz traced a new red** "x" on her new year's calendar. She and Gilberto had missed going to Rio yet again. Roz reminded herself that the timing of the Copacabana cleansing didn't matter. After a little more than a year here in Brazil, Roz's soul was feeling much cleaner.

If only Irmã would return from the *feira*.

Roz had lost track of the time while she and Marilia had been sitting in front of the static of Silvia's television set, waiting for a show to come on. They had an open invitation to watch the occasionally televised shows, and it was an amusing break from Roz's routine. But when the show was over and Marilia left, claiming that she had to get back to work on some article she was writing for the newspaper, Roz realized that Irmã was overdue from the *feira*. Another hour later, Roz barged into her maid's private room behind the kitchen. All of Irmã's clothes and personal possessions that had fit inside one battered suitcase were gone.

Roz felt both wounded and frightened. She'd taken in the girl, given her a place to live, cared for her, and now Irmã had run away. This was the thanks she got in return?

By the time night fell with its dazzling array of jewel-like stars, and the young woman still had not returned, a sickening worry spread through Roz. Irmã was out there, somewhere, alone in the city. Roz had failed Irmã as surely as she'd failed her little sister, Janie.

Janie was dead.

Gilberto finally came home to a leftover supper and tried to soothe her, but to no avail. Roz had worked herself into a state of feeling ill.

And Gilberto was no help. His mind seemed elsewhere, as if the maid's disappearance neither surprised him nor worried him. His lack of reaction fueled Roz, turning her anxiety to anger, especially when he kept quizzing her about Klaus's bags of tealeaves in the kitchen and the little vials of medicines he'd found tucked behind her makeup jars on the windowsill of the bathroom. Women's matters should be no concern of his. Besides, his own mother had supplied them, via the da Costa chauffeur. Why didn't he ask *her*, instead? And no, Roz had never taken any of the ghastly stuff. She didn't trust them with her memories of the awful medicine they'd made her swallow during her second miscarriage.

The next morning, Roz stayed in bed after Gilberto left, earlier than normal. She had no reason to get up and realized that Irmã had given Roz structure to her day. Without that structure, she had no direction. The plan she'd made a year ago to reinvent herself was a distant memory, and she was no closer to fulfilling it. She still had not been accepted by Anabela, and her identity was easily spotted amongst a crowd. She hadn't been very successful in shedding her old identity and even less so in blending in with a Brazilian crowd. She felt as if she still wore a neon sign that announced who she was.

All this, because of the loss of her maid. And more than that, Roz had let her maid down, after she'd helped her hide. Now Roz was on her own. Why had the girl betrayed her trust?

Roz spent the rest of the day replaying in her mind as many of her exchanges with Irmã as she could recall, searching for a hint about why the maid had left like that, secretly, without one word of goodbye. But how had she slipped out her back door with a suitcase without Roz's even noticing? She supposed the maid could've slipped out while Roz had been in the bathroom. But Roz remembered having spoken to the girl about possible items to buy at the *feira*. She'd handed her money. Had it been enough? Roz would've seen a suitcase then, and she hadn't.

Irmã must've taken the suitcase out earlier, when Roz wouldn't notice. She could've left the suitcase in the hall. But anyone passing through the building could've taken it, and Irmã had always been concerned about thieves. Roz hated thinking of the girl in the past tense. Or maybe Irmã had had an accomplice. Someone she'd given the suitcase to. Someone who'd been waiting for her.

She'd had a boyfriend.

Roz stewed about this the rest of the day, and when Gilberto came home that night, she told him her theory that Irmã had had a boyfriend. Except she didn't call it a theory.

"Do you know his name?" Gilberto asked, sounding more like a policeman than her husband.

Roz tried to remember. Irmã *had* mentioned someone. She didn't know if it was the boyfriend or not, but now that she thought about it, he probably was. "I think his name was Edgar."

Gilberto's face paled, and he drew up stiff, as if she'd said

"Catarina."

When he finally regained enough composure to speak, he said, "Have you met him?"

She shook her head.

"Did she say where he's from?"

She shook her head. Why was he quizzing her this way? It was like an interrogation. And what did it matter where he was from? The better question was where were they now.

He went on before she could protest. "The *favela*, perhaps?"

Roz squinted, which helped her think about it. She'd finally admitted to Irmã that she'd been taking food to the little barefoot boy in the ravine of the vacant area. But she was pretty sure the kid was from the *favela*. Why would a child be on his own? Even if he lived in a cardboard box, it would be with others. They begged by day and gathered in the *favelas* by night.

"Maybe," she said.

"You haven't been there, have you, my love?" He was frowning at her.

"You asked me not to go there, remember?"

His frown deepened. She sensed that this was going to blow up into an argument. They hadn't had a good one ever since the mention of Catarina had cleared the air between them. This was going to become a Catarina moment. Her frown went deeper than his.

His gaze searched her face and soul, and then he finally said, "Has she ever mentioned 'Umbrotamba' to you?"

"That's the cult, isn't it?"

"You know about the cult?"

"Not really."

"But Irmã talked about it?"

"She might've said something. What does it matter?"

He stared at her as if probing deep into her mind, and she felt herself tingle all over from his examination. A purple flush spread up his throat and into his face.

"Gil, what's wrong?" she said.

He let out a long sigh and finally spoke. "Nothing." Then he turned away, strode into the bedroom, and returned with the bulge of his gun in its holster under the waistband of his trousers. He headed towards the door.

"You're going out?"

"No worries. I'll be back soon." No added "*meu amor*," as was his usual.

"But you just got home." She felt rage steam through her. "You think you know where Irmã is, don't you? Why the hell don't you tell me?"

"Something I forgot to do. Don't wait up." He kissed her, a perfunctory, non-passionate kiss, and then he was gone, before her steam could explode into another question.

She was sure his departure had something to do with Irmã. She guessed he was going to extract their maid from the cult Irmã had called Umbrotamba. And since he couldn't wait until morning, she guessed that it had to do with a burning candle. Cultists burned candles at night. But would Irmã come home willingly with him?

\* \* \* \* \*

All the way across town in his Fairlane, Gilberto gripped the steering wheel and felt the cold, hard wedge of the gun dig against his lower back. He hoped he wouldn't have to use it.

But now he didn't know what to expect. Whom to believe.

He'd seen the little bottles of medicine in the bathroom, the ones that Roz claimed had come from his mother. And it was true, they looked similar to the supplies the family kept for Tonio at the house. They were drugs to help settle his brother those times when he reached an agitated state. *Mãe* must've sent some of them home with Roz after her last miscarriage.

When the light beams shone on the rutted road leading up the hill to Dona Mariana's house, he decided to park the Fairlane here at the bottom of the hill and walk the rest of the way. He didn't want to risk catching a wheel in a rut.

Trudging up the spongy side of the hill in the dark, he thought about the lies. Irmã had been seeing Edgar, the kid known as Picapau, despite her claims of friendship with Fatima. Irmã had been the deceitful one, just as Pedro Pires had suggested. She'd been lying—why? Was it for the same reason that she'd also broken her promise not to tell Roz about the cult? For what purpose? What else could it be but to indoctrinate Roz into the cult?

As they'd taken Catarina.

He hurried his step, and finally at the top of the hill, he paused to catch his breath. The dark of night surrounded him like a cloak, feeling strangely quiet. Below him in the distance twinkled the lights of Belo, but up here on the ridge above the city, all was dark. Granted, there was more vacant land here than the few scattered houses in this outlying fringe of the city, but what residents there were had turned off their lights. No one was taking advantage of this dry evening during rainy season to sit outside and smoke. Even the chickens had gone to bed.

As his eyes adjusted to the dark, he strode more quickly

down the path-like road, heading in the direction of Dona Mariana's house. Closer, he saw a faint light glimmer, piercing the dark. A burning candle.

Drawn to its tiny glow, he edged up to the side of the house. Pressing his back and his gun against the prickly wall of stucco, he crouched beneath the open window where the candle sat, flickering. Sounds floated through the window. The rhythmic thump of a drum. Low, soft moans wailed to its beat.

He straightened from his crouch and peered through the open window. Inside, the room with no furniture now shone with the lights of many candles and housed six...no, eight writhing women. They were half-naked in their loosely draped, white dresses. With their arms raised and their eyes shut, their bodies swayed to the beat. One of them—Dona Mariana—had fallen to the floor, where her body quivered and trembled. He scanned the faces of the dancing women, but he did not see Irmã among them.

A mixture of anxiety and relief swept through him. He blinked and searched the room again. Had he missed her?

The dona's white skirts splayed about her on the floor next to the altar with the bare-breasted statuette. The dark face of the dona outlined the white circles of her eyes, rolled back into her head. Her lips trembled and twitched, and her hamhock arms quivered, sparking against the floor as if with a life of their own. A magnetic energy flowed through the room, shaking the dona, pulling the women in their dance, and he felt some of it, too, tugging at him as he watched.

Tension drained from his muscles, and he closed his eyes, letting the other energy wash through him. For just an instant... He felt void of worries. Of doubts. Yes, even of fear.

*Não.*

He shook himself and opened his eyes. But even from that brief moment of the lure, he felt...strangely cleansed. He looked again.

Through the field of waving arms, he spied the drummer sitting with folded knees in one corner of the room. His eyes closed as he tapped out the rhythm on his bongo, but Gilberto recognized him. Picapau, that street kid who'd eluded Gilberto ever since rescuing Irmã. He was also Edgar Pena, the dona's son, and the boyfriend who'd sent Fatima to her death. Maybe now he was Irmã's boyfriend, too.

But if his guess was correct and the kid was here, then where was Irmã? Gilberto's gaze swept the room. This time, he saw a woman with a goiter on her neck. She was the same woman—he felt sure—whom he'd seen before in Klaus's drugstore. He was equally sure that she was the friend of the victim named Angela, and now he was growing more sure by the moment that this was also the place where the abortionist came.

* * * * *

January 27, 1960

When Roz awoke in the morning, Gilberto was still gone. He hadn't come home by the time she'd fallen asleep the night before, thinking about the gun hidden not so well beneath his trousers. But he'd come back during the night. She could smell the residue of his after-shave on the pillow. He had been here, and he hadn't awakened her. Now he was gone again.

She sprang out of bed, running through the apartment.

Jorge shrieked at her, agitated as he danced back and forth on the perch inside his cage. Roz kept running, checking the bathroom, the dining table, the kitchen. Yes, Gilberto had been here overnight. She spied the fresh crumbs he'd left behind on the table. And the box of cereal left out. The smell of orange peels in the trash. Irmã usually tidied up after him. Had he brought her back with him the night before? If so, that lazyhead maid was still asleep.

Roz dashed into the maid's quarters behind the kitchen. It was empty. No linens on the cot's mattress. No carefully folded clothes in the dresser drawers. No Irmã.

No Gilberto, either.

Jorge yelled, reflecting the anger that flared within Roz. She deserved to know what her husband was up to, if it had to do with Irmã. If he knew something about the maid's whereabouts, then Roz had a right to know. It would be better, anyway, if Roz went to her, instead of Gilberto, to find out why she'd run away. Roz knew all about running away. She was the expert at running away. And hiding.

Well, maybe not so very expert, since she still hadn't assimilated into Brazilian culture.

But she was close.

She'd be closer if Anabela hadn't opposed her every step of the way.

She gave Jorge a cracker and set his cage on the open windowsill for a little fresh air. That would calm him down. Fresh air would help settle her nerves, too, but she didn't want to be away from the apartment in case one of them came back. Irmã. Gilberto. She flounced around the place the rest of the morning.

After a bite to eat for lunch, she decided they weren't coming. Still, it wasn't raining, so she decided she might as well take her walk.

Outside the apartment building, she breathed in deep the sultry air. Across the street stood the row of houses, each one with a maid. Irmã had made their acquaintance. They knew everything that was happening in the neighborhood, Irmã had claimed. Maybe one of them—Ester—would know where Irmã had gone.

Roz decided to go to the house where Ester worked. It was the pink one, she was pretty sure. One of them where there'd been a break-in not too long ago. She stepped out into the street to head uphill in that direction, but then she noticed the vultures.

There were more of them than usual today, soaring and circling a short way from her apartment building. They mesmerized her the way their scrawny bodies dipped and their ratty wings flapped. She lost track of the time watching them, until one by one they dropped down from the sky to a landing nearby. It seemed to be in the vacant area another block away.

But Roz hadn't left any food there for the barefoot boy, not for several days. With her anxiety over Irmã, she'd forgotten. But the vultures had found something.

Roz's heart skipped a beat. A vision of Irmã flashed through her mind. God, she hoped the vultures hadn't found her maid.

She raced down the hill towards the vacant area, trying to talk herself into believing that whatever it was, it couldn't be Irmã. The maid had packed all her belongings and taken them with her. She'd intentionally left. Although, a robber might have waylaid her nearby.

Roz didn't want to think, either, that the vultures' feast could be the barefoot boy. Nausea rolled in the pit of her stomach, but she pushed the thoughts from her mind and kept running.

The flock of birds clustered on the ground in a black shroud and ignored her as she approached. This time she entered the empty land, following a path that led through scrubby brush, along the rim of the ravine in the center of this no-man's-land. The birds danced with hopping steps and bobbing necks. Rotting smells wafted with each flap of their feathers. As she approached, they fell back from their feast, far enough to reveal the long, thin and bloodied body of a young man.

# Sue STAR and Bill BEATTY

# Chapter Twenty-Eight

January 27, 1960

**Gilberto sat in his** Fairlane and watched the house where Irmã had grown up. Little more than a shack just outside the sleepy town of Sete Lagoas, it had been provided for the Furtado family by the *fazendero* for whom Irmã's father worked. He tended the horses that the cowboys used for herding cattle.

Gilberto had left the apartment early, long before Roz usually awoke. He should be home with her—there instead of here—but he had to be thorough in his search for Irmã. He tried not to think about those drugs he'd found in the bathroom back at the apartment. His mother had sent them, so they must be safe. Besides, Roz had assured him that she hadn't taken any of them. He told himself she would be okay by herself while he was gone. Finding Irmã was mostly for her, so he had to be here, in case Irmã had fled back to her family. He doubted that she had, since her goal had been to escape her modest origins, but he had to be sure. He sat in his car and watched all morning, replaying the night before in his mind.

Irmã hadn't gone back to the Umbrotamba house, as Dona Mariana had predicted she would. She hadn't run away with Picapau, either, since he'd been there the night before, and the girl hadn't. There had only been so much that Gilberto could've done. He'd been outnumbered by the women participating in that ritual, and furthermore, he had too much respect for the *orixá* spirits to break up one of their ceremonies, banned or not. Besides, it was the dona that he needed information from, no one else, and last night, she'd been the only one of the celebrants who was unconscious. He could've waited until she awoke and everyone else had gone away, but even awake, she wouldn't have cooperated. He was sure of that. He'd felt powerless to counter the forces of the *orixás*, once their ritual had begun. What else could he have done except leave? Irmã hadn't been there, not as a participant nor as a girl hiding in the back room. He'd checked there before slipping away, back across town to Roz and her warm bed.

And now it looked as if Irmã hadn't run away to her family home, either. He doubted there was another place she'd go in Sete Lagoas, now that her best friend, Fatima, was dead.

Gilberto watched the Furtados go about their daily tasks. He counted the siblings coming and going. There was no sight of Irmã.

It was almost noon when Irmã's mother was left alone in the house, and Gilberto finally approached her. He only succeeded in raising her alarm. The family hadn't seen Irmã since Christmas. All they'd learned then about her was their suspicion about a boyfriend, whose name was Vincente. Not Edgar. The mother had no information about her daughter's whereabouts, and Gilberto believed her.

The alarm that wailed from Irmã's mother felt contagious. Gilberto had lingered here too long, away from Roz. There was no need to stay here any longer. Roz was all that mattered. She'd become the important one, more so than the maid, and...

Yes, more important even than the mission of revenge that drove him.

The image of Roz's face, with her sensuous lips and teasing smile, filled his mind on the road back to Belo. She was his guiding star. Even away from her, she commanded him, just as she always did. All the way home, he felt her from afar, laughing, calling to him, the same way her presence turned heads in any crowd. Her call captured him, destroying his free will. He felt her will locked onto him now.

He probably drove too fast. He wouldn't know, because he lost track of time. All he knew was the screech of the tires as he finally wheeled into the garage beneath the apartment building in Barroca. His pounding footsteps echoed back at him as he raced up the stairs. His shoulder slammed against the door to the apartment he shared with Roz, but it did not yield.

Muttering to himself, he dug into his pockets one by one for the key. Where was the damned key? Just as he found it, Dona Silvia's door squeaked open.

"Oh, it's you," she said.

He grunted, fumbling with the key. "Whom did you expect?"

Dona Silvia shrugged. "I don't know. She's not here."

"What do you mean?" He punched the key into the lock as if it were the dona's fault his wife was apparently not home.

"You tell me. There is always much activity in there."

A chill worked its way down his spine. He twisted the key, pushed open the door, and called. "Roz?"

"She's gone, you see."

"What do you mean, 'gone'?" He'd always feared this day would come. Roz was like the butterfly, ephemerally flitting through his life. Something seized in his chest, and he couldn't breathe.

"A man was here," Dona Silvia said, "looking for her."

"A man?" Gilberto could barely spit out the words. "What did he look like?"

"A big man. Old enough to be her father, but he tried to look young with thick hair dyed a shiny black."

Klaus. The dona had just described Klaus. "What did he want?"

"Her, I suppose."

Gilberto swallowed hard, finding his voice. "But he didn't find her because she wasn't here then?"

"That's right. She'd just left."

"Where did she go?"

Dona Silvia harrumphed. "How would I know?"

"Did she have a suitcase?"

"Not today. That was yesterday. I thought it was Irmã's, since she planned to run away with her boyfriend, but I could be wrong."

"Do you think," Gilberto said, his voice quivering, "she was waiting for him? Somewhere? Maybe outside?"

"Maybe."

An electric charge shot through Gilberto as he plunged back down the stairs. He hoped to God he wasn't too late.

* * * * *

Roz swallowed her scream as she backed away from the body, its blood still wet. An image of that other dead man, the one she'd left behind in Denver, flashed through her mind. Except, that one hadn't had vultures attacking him. Nausea roiled through her, and she turned away to heave into the bushes. There was hardly anything in her stomach to come up. Trembling, she staggered backwards, crashing through weeds as the vultures taunted her with their sharp calls. At the street, she nearly lost her balance on its uneven surface. But she recovered, turned, and bolted up the hill towards her apartment building.

By the time she reached Silvia's door, she was panting. "Dead man," she managed to gasp to Silvia's scowling face, and she pointed behind her.

Silvia's eyes widened beneath her drooping hair rollers. "You didn't go with him? I thought you had."

"Did you hear me?" Roz raised her voice. "You have to call the police!"

Silvia pulled Roz into her apartment, shut and bolted the door behind her. "That's what I told him. He was just here."

"He's dead, do you understand me?"

"Okay," Silvia said, "I didn't know. Why don't you tell me what happened?"

Silvia guided Roz to the nearest couch, and little by little, Roz spit out the story. She didn't know the word for vultures, so she couldn't tell her neighbor about that. What mattered was the dead man.

Roz sagged onto the couch, while Silvia called the police.

The police.

Gilberto. Where in hell was he?

Roz wanted to give him a piece of her mind. He should be here with her. First Irmã had left her, and now Gilberto.

She sat up from her slump, listening to Silvia's voice speak into the receiver. Her neighbor rushed through the story Roz had told her, answered a few questions with a simple *sim* or *não*, and then hung up.

"They are coming," she said, and then padded away in her slippers towards her kitchen.

Every time Roz blinked, she saw a vulture standing protectively over the dead man. Pocks riddled the dead man's face, where the vultures had feasted. She tried to blink the nightmare away, but couldn't. Her stomach clenched, and her own skin felt clammy. She touched her cheeks, making sure that she felt no pockmarks. She took several deep breaths, but her heart rate continued to hammer. She looked at the door Silvia had bolted. She was a prisoner. Had never been anything else. Because that's what it meant to finally find safety. She'd had to give up her freedom. Her eyelids fluttered. She should thank Silvia and return across the hall to her own apartment. She should... And then Silvia returned with a tray.

She set it down on the table beside the telephone and handed Roz a demitasse cup. "Drink this," Silvia said.

Instead of the black liquid of Brazilian coffee, the contents of the cup were clear. "What is it?" Roz said.

"It's what you need. Go on, drink it."

Roz tipped the cup to her lips and sipped. It burned like fire. "I can't," she said with a cough and handed the cup back.

"You have to." Silvia pushed it back into her face.

Roz shook her head and leaned away from the cup. "I have to go now."

"You have to wait for the police," Silvia said. "They are coming."

Roz pushed herself up onto her feet. "Tell them I'll wait for them at my place. Meanwhile, I've bothered you enough. Thanks for your help."

Silvia shrugged and downed the contents of the demitasse in one swallow. Roz fumbled with the bolt on the door and let herself out.

\* \* \* \* \*

It didn't take Gilberto long before he arrived at the lime green storefront of Klaus's drugstore. He yanked open the door. "Roz?"

But all that answered him was the bell jangling from above. He sniffed the air. Instead of Roz's perfume, he only smelled mercurochrome. He hurried down the central aisle, trying to look casual as he studied the shelves of bottles, tins, and boxes. If Klaus had brought Roz here, then where was she? The curtain at the back of the room swished aside, and a gray-haired man in a white smock limped to the counter.

"May I help you?" Klaus's boss, the proprietor, said.

"I'm looking for my wife."

The proprietor sighed and spread his gnarled hands along the glass top of the display case. "We have many wives who come here for their needs."

"Klaus will know. Where is he? I need to speak with him."

"About your missing wife?"

Gilberto pulled out his badge. He'd hoped to God this wasn't police business. But he feared that Irmã's disappearance and now Roz's whereabouts were connected to the elusive abortionist, whom he *was* investigating. Was that why she'd gone away with Klaus? Because he was a middleman, who knew where she could go for an abortion. But that would mean she was pregnant again. The last time she'd wanted the baby.

Now it was too late for that, because she apparently wanted to run away again.

His mind spun with uncertainty. His guesses were nothing but a fabrication. He didn't know anything, except that he had to find Roz. He'd sworn that she would never become a victim, not as Catarina had been.

The proprietor must've decided to cooperate. "Klaus had to make a delivery to one of our customers. It had something to do with a woman. You know how that goes."

Gilberto felt his heart lurch in his chest. He glanced at his watch. "When will he return?"

"Who knows?" The proprietor shrugged. "Sometimes it takes him all day to return from the mines."

Gilberto's frown went deeper, piercing his soul. "The da Costa mines?"

"That's right," the proprietor said with a nod at Gilberto's badge. "Are you related?"

Gilberto turned on his heels without bothering to reply.

\* \* \* \* \*

When the knock finally sounded on her door, Roz called out, "Who is it?"

"Ubaldo Ramos. *Policía Civil.*"

She opened the door, and he strode inside without waiting for an invitation.

"Senhora da Costa," he said with a frown and a surreptitious glance around the apartment.

The way he shook his head suggested to her that it was her fault the man in the vacant area had died. Oh God, they suspected her of killing him.

"You found the dead man?" she said.

"Of course. They are taking him away now."

"Do you know who he is? I mean, was?"

"Probably someone from the *favela*."

"Do you know how he died? Was it from those terrible bites? It looked as if something ate his flesh." The vultures. She'd walked there, too, in that vacant area surrounding the ravine, with the vultures leering at her, even though Gilberto had asked her not to. She hadn't gone in very far, but it had happened a couple of times.

Ubaldo shrugged, as if her questions didn't matter. "Acid, probably. They will tell us in the morgue. But first, you will tell me exactly what happened."

Once again, she related the tale of her walk and her gruesome discovery, just as she'd told Silvia, and just as Silvia had reported over the phone.

Ubaldo nodded throughout. He seemed to absorb her information directly into his brain, rather than write down any notes on paper. She knew Gilberto kept lots of notes. She'd seen him flipping through his pocket-sized notebook and staring at the ceiling, thinking.

"Do you think the...birds did it?" She still didn't know the word in Portuguese for vultures.

Ubaldo smiled and glanced over at the open window where Jorge sat in his cage, his head leaning against the bars, as if the little lovebird was listening to them. "Is that your bird?" Ubaldo asked, instead of answering her. "Your husband has told me about it."

"What did he say?"

"He doesn't like it, having a bird inside, but whatever you want."

"Where is Gilberto now? Doesn't he work with you? Why isn't he here with you?" *With me.*

"He's away on another assignment. We don't always work together. Sometimes he works with that friend of yours."

"What friend?" Roz sucked in her breath. She didn't have any friends, at least not in the police department. Her only friend was Marilia. All her life she'd been used to never having friends.

"You know, the North American. Sam Clinton."

"He's not my friend. I mean, I've met him, but he's Gilberto's friend, not mine especially." There was always something odd about the questions Sam asked her. As if he probed too deeply. He was far too inquisitive.

"Oh," Ubaldo said. "Well, maybe I misunderstood. Because he was asking about you."

"Me?" Her heart rate accelerated. Had Sam been sent here to Brazil to track her down? Although, he'd already been here before she arrived. Was that true? Now she felt too confused to know anything for sure.

Ubaldo went on. "He was probably looking for Gilberto."

Then, she would be the reason why Sam had befriended Gilberto. She glanced around the apartment, searching, but she did not know what she searched for. A way out? Out, of her own apartment? If Sam had informed Gilberto about her, about some of those ugly truths from her past in Ohio, before Denver, then that could be the reason why Gilberto was staying away. Was he leaving her? Oh God! Then what would she do?

Ubaldo was still talking. "Sometimes we work alone, too.

Like that time when Gilberto went to Denver on another case, and he met you. If it had been me, instead..."

He let his words trail off, and for an instant, Roz wondered what would have happened to her if it had been Ubaldo whom she'd met in that pawnshop, scarcely more than a year ago, rather than Gilberto. She didn't think she'd be here today, if that had been the case.

"Did he ever find that baby who was kidnapped?" Roz said, filling in the awkward gap of silence that followed his suggestion of what might've been. "That's the reason why he was sent there. That's what he told me." She was babbling now.

"He told you that?"

She nodded.

"What else does he tell you?"

"Nothing," Roz said. "He doesn't tell me much about his work."

"You're not the only one." Ubaldo pulled a cigarette from his shirt pocket, thrust it between his lips, and then searched his trouser pocket, no doubt for a lighter. The cigarette bobbed in his mouth as he spoke. "He doesn't tell our bosses, either, some of the ideas he chases."

"But that baby was official business, wasn't it?" Or had he gone to Denver looking for *her*?

"Don't worry about that. When they get kidnapped to another country, they are quickly adopted, and then they disappear. There's nothing we can do. That case is over. The kid is okay, don't worry about it."

"But Gilberto doesn't stop, does he? Even if the case is over, he keeps working on it." A tingle of pride in her husband ran through her, overcoming her anxiety.

"Don't worry. I'll cover for him so that he doesn't get in trouble." Ubaldo found a lighter and flicked its flame to his cigarette. "You'd like that, wouldn't you?"

"What I'd like," Roz said, annoyed that he hadn't asked permission to smoke inside *her* home, "is for you to leave." He was done with his questions. Who did the man think she was? "And tell Gilberto when you see him that he needs to come home." It had been a silly argument over Irmã, and that was behind them. Now it was past time to make up.

"Ask his mother where he is," Ubaldo said, heading for the door. "She's the one who called him out to the estate. Whenever *Mãe* calls, he runs. Meanwhile, I'll let you know how grateful you should be when I keep Gilberto out of trouble." He slammed the door behind him.

She didn't want Gilberto to be in trouble, but she didn't want Ubaldo's interference any more than she wanted Anabela's. If Gilberto lost his job, they'd have to move into that apartment at the family estate, and then Roz would become a prisoner for sure.

She had to talk to him, had to make it up to him, had to persuade him to come home. But the buses didn't run that far out of town, where the family estate was. They did, however, go downtown to a taxi stand.

She grabbed her purse from the bench and left, slamming the door behind her.

# Chapter Twenty-Nine

**Clouds stacked up** into thunderheads, threatening to downpour at any moment. Gilberto kept one eye on the sky as he pulled up to the guardhouse entrance to the mine. He hoped his brief stop at the station before coming out here hadn't made him too late. He hoped he could get in, find Roz, and get out before the storm hit.

The dust cloud that had tailed his Fairlane along the mine's private road settled as he leaned out his window to greet the guard, one of his mother's hired gunmen. The guard waved him through, and Gilberto parked at a distance from the vehicles already there—only two other cars. The *garimpeiro* bus was gone, probably shuttling the miners back to Belo, although he hadn't passed it on the road out here just now. He had a bad feeling in his bones about Klaus. There was a growing number of coincidences that connected his former father-in-law to the house of Umbrotamba.

Klaus supplied the cultists' needs, and one of these two cars must belong to him. But why had he brought Roz here?

The hints of trouble at the mine, Gilberto realized, must've had to do with the cult. Perhaps the organizers of the cult had been operating from here, disrupting the mine and controlling their operatives with drugs, dona Mariana of the pink house and burnt candle for one. Someone was in charge, or else had allowed this to happen—either that temporary manager who'd come down from the States, or the golden-haired da Costa cousin, Jacinto, after his return from the diamond mines. Gilberto had no idea. He'd been blind on account of Roz.

And now, the cult had her, too. Klaus had brought her for the *cult*.

His heart racing, Gilberto climbed out of the car and closed the door with a soft snick. His gaze swept around the silent equipment, the empty pit, the dark opening of the tunnel. She could be anywhere. He patted his pocket, feeling the outline of the ring he'd picked up from the station. It was still there. Good. He might need it to buy her release.

No one was about. The miners had already left the pit, yet there were still several more hours of daylight left. Irritation tightened his muscles. No wonder the mine was losing money. The cult's encroachment here must've chased away the miners. Did *Mãe* know about it? The place was oddly silent without the clanking and humming of machinery.

A chill shuddered through Gilberto. If this was also the site where the abortionist worked, then that asshole had been under their noses all this time.

Jacinto would have known all about it. Ubaldo, too? Perhaps that's what the two of them had been discussing over drinks in the shadowy corner of the pub last winter.

Gilberto's irritation grew, pushing back his unease. He crossed the graveled area without any attempt to silence his crunching footsteps. A delivery would've been brought to the manager's hut, and that's where he marched now. A primal sense of urgency drove him. For now, he only had to collect Roz and get the hell out. Tomorrow he'd deal with the rest. He stomped up the three plank steps and pushed open the door without knocking.

She wasn't inside.

Larry, the big, shaggy man whom *Mãe* had hired as temporary manager through a friend of a friend, rose from his chair, bumping against the wooden table he used as a desk. The brim of his floppy hat slipped down over the curls of his unkempt hair, shadowing the glance he gave to his companion as Gilberto barged inside. Klaus's back was turned toward the door, but Gilberto recognized his shiny black head. Klaus had traded his white smock for a plaid shirt. He swiveled around in his seat opposite Larry and scowled at Gilberto, the usual greeting from his former father-in-law. Cloth bags the size of his fist, tied up with green string, sat on the table between them. They looked similar to the ones he'd photographed in the victims' homes. Similar to the ones he'd found among Roz's things.

"Ah," said Larry, "it's Mr. da Costa. The guard reported that you were here." One of his large hands waved toward the radio against the back wall. "Please, join us and have a seat. *Cafezinho*? Or something harder?"

"Where is she?" Gilberto said, not wasting a moment.

"Your mother was here earlier today," Larry said, "but she left hours ago."

Gilberto grunted, covering up his confusion. Had his devotion to Roz blinded him again? Glancing around, he saw no demitasse cups set out on the table. Instead, there was only the row of little pouches, like the one Klaus had used to measure out herbs to his customer, that woman with the goiter. Angela, Ieda, and now Roz. Klaus and Larry hadn't been having an innocent afternoon coffee. Rage coursed through Gilberto, heating his veins.

"We're done here anyway," Klaus said in English. It wasn't as good as his Portuguese, but it was adequate, and essential to use since Larry had never learned more than the basics of Portuguese. Klaus leaned over to retrieve a satchel by his feet, sitting on the floor. Irmã would've said that leaving a bag on the floor was a good way to lose one's fortune. "I was on my way out. You can have him."

Gilberto caught a glimpse of limp and dirty cruzeiro bills stuffed inside the satchel before Klaus hastily snapped it shut. Payment, he assumed, for the medicinal goods the druggist had apparently delivered. He wondered if Larry had paid him with his own money, or with the mine's. Gilberto stepped between Klaus and the door, blocking the exit, and nodded at the sacks on the table. "Not so fast. You didn't bring all that for the *garimpeiros*."

"It won't work," Larry said with a snort. "Spirits don't control my mine, and I'm telling you, we don't need to make any angry spirits happy."

"Does my mother know what's going on here?" Gilberto asked Larry.

A chuckle rumbled from Klaus, who answered for the general manager. "She knows everything. And she pays well for her information." He lifted his satchel and tried to move around Gilberto. "Did she send you out here," he said, switching to Portuguese, "to report back to her?"

Gilberto folded his arms across his chest and shifted slightly to maintain his blocking position. "I stopped doing as she wished long ago."

"I don't think so," Klaus said.

The air thickened, charged with electricity of the impending storm, both outside and in. Gilberto felt the hairs prickle the back of his neck as he faced Klaus.

"Well," said Larry with a long sigh that scattered the tension in the air. He swept the bags from the table into a box on the floor. "We're headed to the pub in town. Care to join us?"

Gilberto ignored the invitation and turned to Klaus. "Where's my wife?"

"How should I know?" Klaus's retort snapped back in Portuguese.

"You came to my apartment today, looking for Roz. You brought her here."

"You're wrong, as usual." A grin worked its way across Klaus's fat lips.

Gilberto stiffened inside. He couldn't deny that he'd made plenty of mistakes before. That would change. "You'll stay away from her, do you understand?"

"I have many patients," Klaus said. "They need me."

"Roz is not one of them."

"As you wish." Klaus made his words sound like a spit. "And now, if you'll excuse me, I'm late."

Thunder rumbled outside. Roz must be out there, somewhere on the grounds of the mine. Gilberto frowned, fighting a moment of uncertainty. None of this made sense. Their story didn't add up. "Why didn't you two just meet at the pub? It would've saved you the trouble of coming all the way out here."

"It isn't your business."

"My badge automatically makes it my business."

"Wait a minute," said Larry, waving his hands in a placating gesture. He must've understood bits of the Portuguese that kept working its way into their exchange. The bite in their words filled in the rest. "Let's not be hasty."

Gilberto snorted, turning back to Larry and back to English. "The matter of drugs is police business."

Larry's face flushed. "Who said anything about drugs? Is that what you think this is? Hell, this ain't that. Anyhow, your voodoo is legal here."

Some of it, sure, but nevertheless, the mine was his mother's problem. "All I care about is Roz," Gilberto said, turning to Klaus. "Are you supplying my wife with any of your drugs? Be honest, for once."

"Honest?" Klaus sputtered, and beads of sweat sprang to his brow. "You want honesty?" he said, switching back to Portuguese. "You, the one who took my Catarina away."

Gilberto winced and touched his pocket, feeling the outline of her ring. Yes, his ill-fated first marriage *had* taken Catarina away from her family's home, although the truth was, she couldn't wait to go. Klaus had always blamed Gilberto for being responsible for her death. And maybe he was right. Because of the ring he'd given Catarina. Her killers could've taken any pregnant woman, but they'd targeted *her* for her ring.

"She doesn't have anything to do with this," Larry said through gritted teeth.

*How would he know what we said?* Either Larry understood more Portuguese than he let on, or else he'd heard her name and had recognized it. Catarina, the name of the tragedy in the boss's family, that tragedy no one ever talked about, pretending it never existed. A coldness seeped through Gilberto, in spite of the steamy air. Catarina had everything to do with everything that was happening today. Because the stone from her ring had come from this mine, he'd bought it off the pawnbroker and then had kept it hidden, feeling guilty for that impulsive act. He hadn't thought back then that it might buy Roz's freedom now.

"Move aside," Klaus said, shoving past Gilberto. "We're finished here."

Gilberto stepped faster, blocking Klaus's exit. "What have you done with her?"

"My next customer? Nothing, yet. I'm late."

Pieces of understanding slowly took shape in Gilberto's mind. "You make house calls for your customers," he said.

"It's the best way to get their business."

"All right," Larry said, reminding Gilberto of his presence. Under the shadow of his hat's brim, his flush deepened to a dark crimson. "That's enough."

*Why is Larry so concerned about Klaus's business?* But Gilberto hadn't come here to speak to Larry. He turned back to Klaus. "How many house calls have you made for Roz?"

Klaus stood mute. That he failed to come back with a snappy retort filled Gilberto with a sinking feeling of dread. The silence confirmed his suspicions.

Roz had complained about the heavy-handed assistant at her last miscarriage, the one that had overcome her at *Mãe's* house. They'd been Klaus's hands. Klaus often came to the house to deliver supplies for Tonio. Klaus had been there for Roz, too.

Gilberto trembled, piecing his speculations together. The statuette that formed the Umbrotamba altar in Dona Mariana's house could've come from anywhere, but Klaus also happened to sell them in his drugstore. And then there was the woman with the goiter who was an initiate of the dona's and also a customer of Klaus's. And a friend of Angela's.

Gilberto didn't like coincidence.

Coincidence got people killed. Catarina's death had happened coincidentally after she'd visited a cult.

It wouldn't happen to Roz, too.

"What did you give her?" Gilberto's voice iced over. "What did it do to her?" She'd seemed so uncharacteristically loopy after the miscarriage. Had Klaus's drugs done that? He wanted to punch this man, and it took all of his willpower to restrain himself.

"Nothing," Klaus said. "There is no harm. She is a fighter."

"Stay away from her," Gilberto said. "You understand me?"

"You never did like it," Klaus said, "that the women you care about come to me when they need help."

"Not Catarina," Gilberto said, spreading his stance, taunting his former father-in-law.

"That's a lie." The satchel slipped from Klaus's fingers and fell to the floor with a thud.

Gilberto went on, seething. "She always hated you. Blamed you."

"No." Klaus sucked in air, and the collar on his shirt quivered. "No!"

"Just a minute," Larry said, stepping between the two of them. "There's no need for this."

"Yes there is," Gilberto said. "Get out of the way."

Klaus huffed up, looking as if he would explode. "You... you..."

"No, it's *you*," Gilberto said with icy calm. "You let her mother die when she got sick, and you wouldn't take her to the hospital. Where did you take her instead? Is that where you've taken Roz?"

Klaus let out his breath in a blast of hot air and found his voice. "Hospitals are useless in this country. Where I come from..."

"West Germany?" Gilberto said, not letting Klaus's thought fade. "Are you saying they have better hospitals there?"

Klaus reached for his satchel, but his fingers fumbled. The latch popped open, spilling cruzeiros onto the floor.

"Our hospitals aren't so bad," Gilberto said. "Why do you avoid them?"

Klaus didn't answer as he scrambled to pick up the loose bills.

Gilberto pressed harder. "You don't have any use for hospitals here, and especially not there, where you came from."

Finally, Klaus rose from the floor, thrust out his chest, and clicked his heels together.

The image of an old soldier's stance at attention emerged in Gilberto's mind. Understanding slipped into place. "From the day you arrived here in Brazil after the war, we always thought you were running from the Nazis, that you wanted a second chance at life."

Gilberto's heart raced, and he paused to gulp in a deep breath.

"But you were one of them," Gilberto said. "A soldier. A *Nazi*. Weren't you?" This man before him, Catarina's stepfather, represented the very evil that Gilberto hated more than anything in the world. No, he *was* the evil. Gilberto flexed his fingers, balled them into a fist, and flexed again.

Klaus still didn't answer.

"But you never changed," Gilberto said, his voice finally rising. "Did you? Answer me, dammit."

Klaus's eyes glazed over as if empty of soul.

Gilberto felt chilled to the bone. "What did you do? Torture them? And then you brought your skills of torture here to Brazil."

"I had some experience as a doctor for the prisoners, is that what you want to hear?"

"Shut up." Larry sprang closer, grabbing Klaus's arm.

Klaus shook off his grip. "Because in this catholic country—"

"Didn't you hear me good?" Larry said. "You don't have to tell him nothing."

He didn't have to, because Gilberto understood now. All this time, he hadn't wanted to believe it, because rightly or wrongly, Klaus was family, and that connection had prevented Gilberto from seeing the truth. Now he saw clearly. "It was *you*. You're the one who's been doing the abortions all along, aren't you? *You're* the asshole!"

Klaus froze, panic shining through his eyes like a cornered rat.

"It's all about money." Gilberto shuddered. Had Roz given him money, too?

"A man has to support his women," Klaus said, "which is something you never learned."

Gilberto was one against two of them, and he reached around to the back of his trouser's waistband and slipped out his gun. "You don't care about the women. All you care about is their money."

"You can put that down," Klaus said softly, a foggy glaze replacing his momentary panic.

Gilberto shook his head. "I'm going to shut down your dirty abortion business."

Klaus didn't have a clinic because he made house calls. Gilberto figured he'd done them anywhere, as long as the practice remained hidden. Behind the pharmacy, or maybe even here? He cast a peripheral glance at the shelves behind the table, but he saw no equipment. Then he remembered the back room of the Umbrotamba house of the cult. The stinky, rusted can had been a douche can. How convenient that Klaus had lived near that pink house.

Gilberto pressed harder. "You conspired with Dona Mariana. You used her house to perform your abortions."

"Girls in need go to her. And she has tools."

Gilberto flinched. The lack of a denial was the same as a confession.

"How much will it take to keep you quiet?" Klaus said.

"Are you offering me a bribe?"

"That's how you police work, isn't it?"

"Not this one."

Klaus went on in his monotone. "Maybe you want a percentage of the profits."

"Uh-uh." Larry's voice growled.

"What I want is your ass," Gilberto said, aiming the gun at the spot where Klaus should've had a heart.

"You can't shoot me," said Klaus. "I'm family to you."

The hell he couldn't. Gilberto's fingers steadied on the gun. Klaus had betrayed the family.

Klaus wheedled. "Because of Catarina."

"Don't say her name. You're not good enough to speak her name."

"Don't you understand?" Klaus said. "The gang owns everyone now. They made an example of Catarina to show me how powerful they are."

Gilberto startled, looking up from the target he'd mentally drawn on Klaus's chest. "What gang?" Gangs hadn't invaded Belo, at least not that he was aware of. The city was growing fast, but not so fast to draw gangs here. Klaus—the Nazi torturer, who'd as good as killed Gilberto's father, the first Francisco da Costa—was deluded. "You're saying it was some gang member who killed her? Not a cultist? And you knew about this all along?"

"I couldn't talk." Klaus's gaze flickered toward Larry. Then he lowered his voice, speaking rapidly. "Look what they did to Catarina. You want them to do that to the rest of the family?"

"I told you, didn't I?" Larry shouted, his voice booming along with thunder. "You should've listened to me. You talk too much."

"Did they help you find your victims?" Gilberto said to Klaus, ignoring Larry. "Or was it through your drugstore?"

"Both," Klaus said, his chest swelling again. "Some of their members made their girlfriends pregnant and brought them to me as clients. For a percentage, you understand. You know Picapau. He was one of them."

"Picapau!" Gilberto's voice croaked as he staggered back a step, struggling to comprehend the enormity of the filth before him. His fingers trembled, and the gun wavered, losing its target. "That kid is part of this gang?"

"Was." Klaus shrugged as if it didn't matter.

"Fatima Souza, the dead girl in the alley, was his girlfriend?"

"I don't bother with their names."

"How many girlfriends were there?"

"Several."

"Angela Cardaso? It was *you* that she met in the pub where she worked. Did she have one of Picapau's *figas*, too?" *And the most recent victim, Ieda.* This gang, whoever they were, wherever they'd come from, must have targeted street kids to do their dirty work.

Klaus gave him a weak, sick smile of smug knowledge. Larry, standing next to him, eyed the gun first and then glanced at Klaus.

"Why?" Gilberto asked. "Did Picapau help this gang establish some kind of black market? For drugs?"

"Not drugs. Abortions. A place like this is fertile for that." Klaus chuckled.

Gilberto felt his insides twist, hardening his heart to the evil before him.

"He knew too much," Klaus said.

His use of the past tense sent an alarm charging through Gilberto. "Where is he now?"

"You will join him there soon."

"What do you mean?"

"Larry and I will take you there. It's not far from where you live with your lovely, new woman."

The ravine in Barroca, Gilberto realized with a wave of dread washing over him. The forbidden place where he knew Roz walked, drawn there by a power greater than his warnings. "How...how do you know where he is?"

Klaus guffawed. "Because I followed him there, of course."

"When?" Gilberto struggled against the trembling that threatened his knees. "What did you do to him?"

"I didn't have any choice," Klaus said. "It was me or him. If I hadn't followed him after he was done drumming for the dona's ritual and taken care of him first, the gang would've killed me."

"You killed him?"

"Can I help it if he got in the way of my bottle of acid?" Klaus bent down, reaching for his satchel. "Now I'm just going to put this money away, and then we can work out a deal."

"Put your hands up," Gilberto said. "There's no deal with you."

"As you wish," Klaus said, rising again. He held a silver canister in his hands, and within the space of a heartbeat, he aimed it at Gilberto.

Burning liquid splattered him.

Howling and screaming, Gilberto dropped the gun.

The gun went off.

A commotion of arms and legs fell onto the gun at Gilberto's feet.

Acid. It ate holes in Gilberto's shirt. Drops chewed out blistering pockets along one arm, up the side of his throat, to his chin, and maybe farther. Acid seared him with the force of a furnace. His hands jerked up and clawed at his face.

"He knows too much," one of them said. It was Klaus, Gilberto thought, but he couldn't be sure. Pain hammered at his brain. His vision blurred.

"Because of you." Larry. "You couldn't stop blabbing. Got to take him out now, thanks to you."

Gilberto was going to die, he realized, and he didn't care. Anything to end the pain firing through his body like molten steel. Although...a vision of Roz flashed through his mind, and oh God, he wanted to live to hold her again. "Roz..." he whispered, his heart beating for Roz, always for Roz...

An evil chuckle filled the room, echoing around his head.

"She messed with the wrong people in Denver," Klaus said. "And now they're looking for revenge. Lucky for them, they already had a contact in place here—"

The crack of the gun... And then silence.

Gilberto smelled the tangy, metal smell of blood. His? He hadn't felt anything beyond the burning of his own flesh. How long would it take before the acid stopped chewing at him? Was this the way the women had felt, subjected to Klaus's brutal methods with acid to force out a fetus?

"That takes care of one problem," Larry said. "He shouldn't have talked so much."

"You?" Gilberto managed to whisper.

"These hills make a perfect place to lay low. But it doesn't mean I can't do a job for the boys back home once in a while, does it?"

"For them?" Larry...the contact...

"Boss thinks you and your woman are the ones who killed his son. I almost had her a couple times before. I won't miss again, not after I finish here."

Footsteps thudded outside, and the door burst open, slamming against the wall. In the flash of a single instant, Gilberto recognized the voice of the guard swearing. And then he knew no more as pain ripped through his flesh and blackness engulfed him.

# Sue STAR and Bill BEATTY

# Chapter Thirty

**Sitting in the backseat** of the taxi all the way out to the da Costa estate, Roz twisted the hem of her skirt around her fingers and tried to ignore the pain that squeezed the back of her head. These last few months in Brazil, she'd almost convinced herself that she was safe here. She'd outrun her past. But now, after seeing what the vultures had done to that poor man in the ravine, she realized she was wrong.

Anything could happen.

Even...perhaps... Had Gilberto finally left her?

The old paranoia that had followed her all the way here from Ohio had hit her again. It had been building all day and finally blossomed with full force during her conversation with Ubaldo.

Seeing the dead man had brought it all back to her. Acid had pocked his face, Ubaldo had implied. Not vultures.

The man in Ohio—Janie's and her rapist, the son of their own mother's boyfriend—had had a pocked face, too. Although his had been pocked with scars from acne. He'd said she couldn't hide from him, not in the cave, not anywhere. He would hunt her down to the ends of the earth if he had to. He'd said she belonged to him, that she could never leave him. He'd said it was her fault that her little sister had died in the cave. Did she want to die too?

No. Not only had she found another way out of the cave and fled but also she'd ended up aborting his baby. The backroom

323

clinic procedure must've damaged her internally, and that's why she hadn't been able to keep her wanted pregnancies alive any longer than a few months.

Tears streamed down her face as she shivered in the backseat of the taxi. She didn't deserve Gilberto. Why had he loved her so? For her, it had been lust at first, but now... It was love, not lust.

Just when she'd driven him away. That last fight over Irmã had been one fight too many.

She loved him in so many ways, more than just for his goodness, his tenderness, his... Devotion. He never gave up on a case, and he would never give up on her, either. She had to believe that.

But why had he been away so long?

His mother had called him, Ubaldo had said. Gilberto always ran to Anabela, despite his claims of independence, but now she understood it was because of his family loyalty that kept him answering his mother's calls. Roz loved him for that, too. She would convince him to come home with her. He must let her make it up to him.

Their disagreement over Irmã shouldn't have erupted into a fight. It was a silly thing. Maybe their fight had been the one foretold by the fallen knife, the fight that Irmã had tried to repair with her superstition. But all that was over now. It was time to go home.

She only hoped that Sam Clinton wouldn't spoil it for her. What did he want with her? If he was as tenacious a police officer as Gilberto, and if his case was tracking her on behalf of the man she'd accidentally killed in Denver, or possibly the pock-faced son of her mother's boyfriend in Ohio...

*Não.* She wiped the tears from her face and reminded herself that the Ohio rapist was Janie's killer. Her little sister's death in the cave hadn't been Linda's fault. Linda was Roz now, and Roz was Brazilian. *This* was her home. *This* was where she belonged.

But where would home be if Gilberto lost his job? Ubaldo had suggested something about trouble, and he promised to cover for Gilberto. In exchange for what? What did Ubaldo really want from her?

She supposed that with the family money, Gilberto didn't really need the income from his job. Would Anabela waive their rent until another job came along, something better next time?

The mine. His mother had always wanted him to take over the mine, and Roz bet he could do it. But would he love it? Would he be happy? Roz only wanted to make him happy.

By the time the taxi pulled up to the driveway into the estate, Roz realized that Anabela would get her way in the end. The guard at the gate recognized Roz and let them through. When the taxi stopped before the steps to the mansion, she flung money at the driver and told him to wait. She raced up the steps to the front door and pounded on it. The taxi drove away. Finally, the butler opened the door. He lifted his chin, expressing his disgust at her smudged makeup and sweat-stained blouse.

"Where is he?" Roz said, pushing past the stuffy man.

"*Senhora,*" he called after her, but she ran on, clattering down the marble hall.

She pushed through the French doors, out into the glare of sunset on the veranda where Anabela and the twins were sipping cocktails. They startled when she burst outside. The twins spilled their drinks and giggled, and Anabela's nugget eyes and flat mouth widened into three circles of surprise. In that single instant, Roz knew.

He wasn't here. Anabela had never called him. Ubaldo had made a mistake.

Anabela recovered quickly. Her face settled back into its flat lines, and she glanced past Roz's shoulder to speak calmly to the butler who'd followed her out. "Bring a *guaraná*, and tell the maid to set another place at the table."

"I thought Gilberto was here," Roz said as the butler quietly withdrew. Despite her anxiety, she felt a tiny spot of warmth grow inside. Anabela had remembered her taste for the Brazilian soda. So Roz had won after all. She really was a da Costa now.

"No," Anabela said. "I haven't seen him for many days. He stays too busy with that job."

Tonio's birds screeched in the distance.

"I know. But he needs his job, as much as I need him. I love him, and I'm going to stay and prove it to all of you."

"Love?" Lines pinched around Anabela's lips. "What do you know of love?"

"I know now. Love is when someone else matters more than the world, more even than you yourself matter."

Anabela harrumphed. "Did I not tell you?"

"Actually, no."

"You dare to disagree? After all that I've done for my family? Look around you, girl."

Roz surveyed this backside of the house, where staff moved silently and efficiently, keeping the domain running. It was a well-ordered house and surrounding property, filled with family members. Those who no longer lived here kept coming back. As Gilberto would.

"Do you not see physical proof of the love that I have poured into my family?" Anabela said.

Yes, Roz did. The birds screeched again, reminding her that Tonio could've been placed in an institution, but Anabela had chosen not to do that. She'd kept him near her, establishing a special care facility for her son here on the grounds of her estate. Maybe that was love, too.

"You," Anabela continued, "who would upset the balance of such love."

Had Roz done that? She hadn't meant to. She'd only tried to adapt to her new home. To belong here. And she had. Gilberto *would* come home to her. He would finish whatever task he was doing at his desk in the station, and then go home. All she had to do was wait for him. Tension drained from her, flowing layer by layer from her head and down through her spine, leaving her limp and tingly. She steadied herself against the back of a patio chair. Maybe he was already in the apartment, wondering where she was. He wouldn't know she'd come here, to his mother's house. She would use Anabela's telephone to call him.

The maid who brought her *guaraná* escorted her to the telephone inside the house and down one long corridor. Roz dialed the station first, and the person who answered said no, her husband wasn't there. He'd left some time ago, on his way home.

They must've missed each other, which seemed to be the story of their relationship. *No more.*

Roz dialed Silvia next, but the neighbor told her Gilberto wasn't home, either. Was she absolutely sure, Roz asked. Was it possible he'd slipped past Silvia, unknown? Could Silvia just try knocking on their door, anyway? Dread gnawed at Roz's insides while she waited for her neighbor to check and report back. Her temples tightened, and a throbbing pain returned to her head.

He wasn't there.

*Obrigada*, she said, her voice quaking as she thanked her neighbor and then hung up. Where was he?

Still, Roz felt certain, she had only to wait. He'd come here next, she decided. Perhaps he was on his way now. Slowly, she made her way back outside to the verandah, where she sipped her drink in the company of her new family. The four of them watched the storm clouds boiling up over the land and over her life. Tonio's birds screamed, reflecting the anguish in her heart. The escaped bird had returned home.

Here, this was home.

Gilberto still hadn't appeared when they sat down to dinner. Whatever the meal was, Roz didn't notice. Chewing, swallowing, she waited some more, listening to the rain pound on the roof, filling the water tanks. Her mother-in-law praised God for the fresh supply of water.

When the last of the plates were finally cleared away, the butler entered, announcing a visitor.

Sam Clinton stepped around the butler, tapping a cane along the marble floor as he shuffled into the dining room. His shoulders sagged as his gaze swept the table, connecting with Roz first. Anabela rose from her position at the head of the table and extended her hand to him.

Sam shook her hand, explaining that he had a touch of gout, but Anabela's face remained impassive, not understanding his mix of languages. Sam shrugged and turned away, moving closer to Roz's chair. "I figured you'd be here."

"You're looking for me?" Roz kicked back her chair, rising. "Where's Gilberto?"

"Don't worry," Sam said, "he's going to be okay. That's what I've come to tell you."

Something exploded inside Roz, and her voice rose to a shrill. "What do you mean?"

Anabela also stiffened when Gilberto's name was mentioned. She lurched after Sam, clutching his sleeve. "My son?" she said in Portuguese, apparently sensing, as Roz had, that something was wrong. "Where is my son?"

Sam pulled away. He turned back to Roz, peering intently into her eyes. "I'm sorry, I didn't mean to alarm you. I've got some news for you, and it's not all good. There was a fight, out at the da Costa mine. He got in the middle of something bigger than him and ended up getting shot. But don't worry, he's going to make it, they think. He's in surgery right now."

*Shot!* Roz gasped, her hand covering her mouth. He'd been shot in a *fight*! Irmã had predicted a fight. But whatever had happened now couldn't be that fight. Irmã had fixed it with a crossed knife. Something else must've happened.

"What aren't you telling me?" Roz had never trusted this man.

"I wanted to prepare you," Sam said. "It won't be easy. He may not want to see you at first."

"Of course he will."

"Give yourself some time. There's been more damage than just from a bullet."

"What is he saying?" Anabela cried in Portuguese. "What about my son? What's happened to him? Tell me the truth."

The twins dropped their forks clattering onto their plates

and stared wide-eyed at their mother.

"He was in a fight at the mine," Roz said, "but—"

"Noooo!" Anabela wailed, and her arms flailed first toward the ceiling and then wrapped around herself. "My son is dead!"

The twins sprang from their chairs to either side of Anabela, surrounding her in a huddle of tears.

Roz's breath caught, and her knees trembled. Then she steeled herself. "No, he didn't die. Sam said he's okay." She turned to Sam. "Why was he out there?"

"Looking for you," he said softly, apologetically.

A shudder wrenched through Roz, ripping her heart as she tried to process what Sam told her next about the fight at the mine. His words sounded jumbled to her. She couldn't make sense of them. She only registered that Gilberto hadn't left her. And something about his gun... It was okay, Sam said, but he didn't know. Was it possible? Roz felt as if her mind was slogging through quicksand. Gilberto...

Keening wails quivered the air from the opposite end of the dining table, and in the distance, the parrots screamed.

Gilberto...

Roz sagged, and strong arms caught her before she could collapse. Summoning her strength, she twisted out of Sam's grip and then stumbled towards the three women. "It's okay, *Mãe*," Roz said. "He got into a fight at the mine, but he's going to be okay. I know he will."

Anabela clutched her arm, squeezing with a force that made Roz stare into her mother-in-law's feverish eyes. "It's my fault. My son would not have gone out there if not for me. Because I went there earlier today. I had to make Larry understand that if the *garimpeiros* didn't come back to work, then Larry was finished. You understand? We argued, of course, and then my son went there, to settle my business. Larry must've shot him, but it was a bullet meant for me."

Roz didn't know, except that the presence of Gilberto's gun in their bedside drawer had always made her feel sick. She'd known all along that the gun could only hurt him. She felt as if the room was spinning around her. "Was it Larry," she said, turning to Sam, "who took Gilberto's gun and shot him with it?"

"We think so."

"We?"

"Ubaldo and I. Ubaldo was the first to arrive on the scene, just ahead of the ambulance. The mine's security guard was holding Larry, and there were two men down. Luckily, Gilberto was still breathing, and the ambulance took him away. It was too late for the other one. We don't know yet who he was. Ubaldo took Larry into custody, and then he called me in to have a little chat with Larry."

"Did you find out why he did it?"

A moment of silence passed as Sam tilted his head to one side, considering her. Or perhaps he was considering what to say. Even Anabela and the twins had stopped crying. Finally, he let out his breath and dug into his pocket.

"It had to do with this. We found it on him." Sam pulled his fist from his pocket and uncurled his fingers before her. In the palm of his hand lay something blue, a gemstone twinkling in the fading light. It was the ring. The one she'd found in Denver and was pawning when she met Gilberto. What was it doing *here*?

"For a very long time," Sam said, "your husband has been after the bad guys who stole this ring. Well, he finally caught them. It turns out they were into a lot more than just theft. They kidnapped babies and sold them across borders, and then they got into illegal abortions right here in Belo. Your husband stopped them. He's a hero."

Roz gasped and reached for Anabela, steadying herself. She'd known all along. Gilberto had been a hero since that night she'd met him in the pawnshop. Her gaze flickered to the ring in Sam's palm. He held it out to her, but she didn't want it. She only wanted Gilberto.

Sam laid the ring down beside Roz's place at the table. "You'll have to decide what to do with it, now that the danger is over."

"Danger?" Roz tightened, as the old fears threatened.

One of the twins darted over to pick up the ring. The twins could have it, as far as Roz was concerned. "You have no idea about me—"

"Yes, actually, I do. You were in more danger than you ever realized, but your husband knew. That's why he asked me to watch out for you."

"It was you? And Gilberto asked *you*...?"

Sam neither confirmed nor denied her question. "Now it's over," he said. "I came out here to take you to the hospital. I thought you'd want to be there."

Roz felt a wall of numbness fold around her, choking her as she tried to understand what had happened. The danger he mentioned...it must've come from a network out of Denver. All along, she'd thought that the man with the cane was tracking her, waiting for his opportunity to drag her back to Denver. But it had been Sam, and he'd been *protecting* her. On her husband's orders.

She was safe, now that Larry, who was part of that network, was locked away. From here on, all she had to do was make sure that Gilberto recovered.

Roz turned back to Anabela and patted her arm. "We have to go to him."

Anabela sucked in her breath and squared her shoulders. She squeezed Roz's hand. "You go, Rosalinda. He needs you. You have already proved your love twice, and you will prove it again. When my grandchild is on the way, Klaus will tell us what to give you in order to carry him safely to term. I will not lose another of my grandchildren."

Roz felt her heart glow. She kissed her mother-in-law before turning to Sam. "Will you take me to him now?"

Sam nodded. "The rest of the family can follow along later." Taking Roz by the arm, he steered her towards the door. "He's going to make it."

"I know," Roz said. "He has to. Because I love him."

She wasn't playing a role anymore, and she was done running. She would get him back. And maybe...just maybe... With love to guide her, all was not lost. This time she meant it.

\* \* \* \* \*

www.ingramcontent.com/pod-product-compliance
Lightning Source LLC
Chambersburg PA
CBHW051334250626
47155CB00007B/2588